I0599109

SUCCUBUS LIPS
SUCCUBUS SIRENS BOOK ONE

LINA JUBILEE

Crimson Fox
PUBLISHING

Succubus Lips by Lina Jubilee

© 2018 by Lina Jubilee. All rights reserved.

Published by Crimson Fox Publishing and Lina Jubilee.

Crimson Fox Publishing, Turner, OR

www.crimsonfoxpublishing.com

Cover by Ali Lawson Book Design.

ISBN: 978-1948661119

CHAPTER ONE

"COME ON. PLEASE." NASH PUT HIS HANDS TOGETHER AS IF worshipping at an altar erected in my honor.

"No," I said, swiping my fingers across my tablet to watch another video of an adorable ninja cat stalking its prey. In the background, I still had the Nelian tracking app running. I was keeping tabs on it. So far this evening, two false alarms—one Typical confusing a Natch for an otherworldly elven invader, the other a couple of kids messing around with smoke bombs in an alley. Like smoke had anything to do with a Nelian attack. "Aurora, angel," Nash said, drumming his fingers atop the back of a chair. "You're killing me."

Roulette snorted from where she sat in front of the triple sixty-inch monitors covering one wall of the room. She was ostensibly monitoring Renegade activity on top of current news reports, but I saw the DM tab in the corner where she kept sending cute and racy messages to her boyfriend, Darien, who was out on assignment along with Wade and Chastity.

"I doubt that," I said, swiping the screen again. "*Sweet cheeks.*"

Nash cleared his throat, which drew my attention to the flush spreading across his neck. *What?* It was an accurate enough nickname. More accurate than the one he used for me. He ran his fingertips through his close-cropped blond hair and growled. Damn, he had a sexy growl. "If we need to go out there, we won't necessarily have time to have sex first—"

"La la la," said Roulette, covering both ears with her hands. "I'm not hearing my best friends talk about bumping uglies." Like she was being much more discreet in her little chat that kept popping up on one of those huge screens, the vixen.

Nash crossed his arms and walked over to Roulette, nudging her shoulder with his elbow. The grin on his face could have melted glaciers. I shook my head to clear it of all dirty thoughts and put the tablet on the table, closing out the browser.

Roulette spun around in her swivel chair and laced her fingers together, smiling devilishly up at Nash and then me. "But when *are* you two getting together already?"

"Rou," I said, rubbing my temples with my fingers. "Don't—"

Nash jutted his chin out. "Aurora thinks I wouldn't be okay with her using her powers on anyone else if we were an item."

"You wouldn't," I said, pulling my overly long sleeves over my palms and slipping my thumbs through the corresponding holes. "Who would? But that's beside the point." My voice got quieter. "I can't be with anyone, not long term."

In the library, my bare ass against some dusty volume of Descartes, his thick hands cupping me from below. Him nibbling on my ear, my hands threaded through his wavy, dark brown locks.

2

Why, oh why, do my thoughts inevitably drift to that night...? I had to stop myself from dwelling on him too long.

"I often find myself having such thoughts about that night, too. Though I certainly make no point of dismissing them."

That was why. That was Zander's voice in my head—leader of the Renegades, traitor of the Veras team, all-around hunk but a little *too* aware of that. Having a bond with a selective telepath who wasn't exactly the most welcome face around Veras HQ—he hadn't set foot in it in over a year—made for some potentially awkward situations to say the least. He had to be thinking about me at the same time I was thinking about him for me to hear his voice in my head, but... Damn, if that man wasn't almost always thinking about me whenever he popped into my head. I scratched my scalp and focused on my breath. *In and out. In and out. Clear your mind. Don't think about the leader of the Renegades, don't think about the leader of the Renegades...*

"Come on," he told me through our telepathic bond. *"You can't resist me. I'm far too good-looking. Right? What was the title you gave me just now? 'All-around hunk'?"*

You forgot the "little too aware" bit, I sent back through the bond.

I pounded my fists against the table, causing Roulette to jump in place and Nash to stare at me questioningly. Like he knew I had just been communicating with Zander in my mind. Like he wasn't happy with it.

I wasn't exactly ecstatic with myself about it, either.

"Sheesh," said Roulette, "you don't have to take it that hard. I'm sorry. I shouldn't have teased you."

Chewing on a hangnail on my thumb, I shook my head. "It's fine." It was the least of my concerns.

Nash took the seat next to me and looked at me a

3

moment more before speaking. He was probably deciding whether or not to say something about Zander, to ask if I'd found out anything important when we'd had our little telepathic conversation.

Just that he wanted to jump my bones.

"*I do.*" I could hear Zander mentally laughing. "*Always, darlin'.*"

I slapped my face with both hands multiple times.

Nash ignored it. "You don't think that's a good idea, though?"

Wait, what? Time to focus on what was in front of me. What had Nash wanted again? Right. To have sex. Right now. As usual.

Roulette snickered. "Anything to get into Aurora's pants, right?" She grabbed her can of ginger ale from where it rested precariously on the computer console and tossed her head back to take a sip.

Nash's lips went thin. "I'm serious." He looked back and forth at Roulette and me. "And you two should have sex, too."

Roulette spit her drink out, spraying several feet in front of her.

I couldn't help it. I laughed.

"I'm not kidding," said Nash, not a trace of a smile on his face. "Every day. Like clockwork. Have sex with us all."

Roulette and I locked gazes. She broke it first, shaking her head and putting her can back beside the computer keyboard. "You sure you just don't want to watch, big boy? Me and Rora. Toss in Chastity, too?"

Nash was turning red again. "I wouldn't need to watch, no."

"How magnanimous of you," I said.

Shaking his head, Nash scoffed. "You're laughing at me. You're both laughing."

Roulette was indeed giggling, and I found myself stifling a snicker.

"Okay, look," said Nash in an excellent imitation of Wade, the man whose Natch powers meant his intelligence outstripped the rest of ours combined by miles, "hear me out. Aurora, what do your Natch powers do?"

I rolled my eyes and hugged my arms to my chest. "You *know* what my powers do."

"Humor me."

I looked to Roulette for help, pleading, but she just smiled and shook that voluminous dyed bright red hair that popped so vividly against her imperfection-free dark brown skin. She turned back to the screen and the DM window popped up again, and I could see her sending Darien kissy emojis.

I sighed. "Yes, professor. I boost Natch power."

"For how long?"

I chewed on the inside of my lip for a bit. "Anywhere from a few minutes to a whole day."

"And *how* do you boost Natch powers?"

"Roulette?" I asked.

She flung a hand up in the hair, her attention still riveted on the screen. "You're on your own with this one."

I met Nash's eyes. He just nodded at me, as if to convey he wasn't dropping this until we finished our charade.

"I kiss them," I admitted, my voice growing quiet.

Nash *tsked*. "That's good for a few minutes, Succubus Lips." That was my "official" code name in our files, though I would clobber anyone who dared call me that in person. I didn't have a cute code name like Roulette, birth name Sasha. I side-eyed Nash, and he gently threw both hands up in surrender. "My bad. Miss Haddix. Please continue. How does a Natch boost their power via your Natch ability for one full day?"

"They have..." I didn't know why this was embarrassing me so much. Everyone in Veras knew it. Everyone in Renegade knew it, for that matter.

Oh, fuck, don't think about Zander.

Huh. Quiet for once on the other end of the bond.

I exhaled deeply. "They have to have sex with me. Penetrate me."

Roulette whistled and started fanning herself. "Okay, I think I might visit the little girls' room." She pushed back from the console and mouthed a silent "sorry" my way. I shook my head and waved her away. Once she turned the corner, I said, "Which would be kind of hard for Roulette and Chastity, okay? Don't tease her."

"I wasn't teasing." Nash pivoted his chair toward me, his knee bouncing. "I'm serious. Wade thinks maybe the women could stick their hands—"

I cradled my face in my hand, shielding my eyes from the inanity of my supposed best friend. My temptingly gorgeous best friend. Who was it who had decided we should stay friends-with-benefits again? Right. Me. Foolish me. "Can we not do this?"

"We tested that theory," he said quietly. "You and me."

"And?" I said, my own knee now bouncing.

"It might not have worked that well," he admitted. "Probably boosted a few hours. But that's better than nothing, Aurora. The women could get a boost for a few hours and maybe boost again when it wears off and then the men can boost once a day—"

"Nash, are you hearing yourself?"

There must have been more than a hint of anger in my

6

voice because when I removed my hands from my face, he actually shrunk back.

"You all have your own powers," I said, rage beginning to boil in my blood, "and they're actually *useful*. They worked just fine before you ever met me and they'll continue to work just fine without me."

"But *with* your powers, we're so much stronger, Aurora, you have to admit—"

I raised a finger to warn him to let me finish. It might have been a middle one. "My Natch powers are *so* useless."

"No, they aren't!"

"Useless in the field. They're… They *can* be degrading. You don't know how it feels to have to—to feel like you have to…" I stopped.

Nash's face went serious. "Did it ever feel like you *had to* with me?"

I didn't answer.

"Aurora, angel, I never want you to feel that way with me."

I ignored the fact that he thought of me as an "angel" again and bit down on my lips. "That's not what I meant. I don't… I have fun with you, Nash, I do. But I'm *literally* performing under pressure. It just…" I sighed. "And now you're telling me to just drop trou and bend over and let the whole *team* go at me? On a 'preventative' basis *in case* we're called out on a mission?"

"You wouldn't be performing under pressure then," said Nash quietly. "It might make it less stressful—"

I let out an exasperated sigh. "Nash, Roulette and Darien have each other and they're faithful to one another —and Roulette is my best girlfriend. It would be super awkward to do more than give her a kissing boost." I paused to glare at Nash then, and sure enough, his eyes

7

had popped at the thought. Like he hadn't seen me swap spit with her on the field half a dozen times already. "Chastity may be bi, but that doesn't mean she wants to do *every* woman she can, for Chrissakes, and I'd feel awkward too. Wade has a Typical boyfriend and needs a boost to his intelligence and cloaking abilities about as much as the ocean needs a drink of water. How much *smarter* and *stealthier* can the smartest and stealthiest man we know get?" Wade had never even bothered to get a kiss from me, which I totally respected. It was bad enough feeling like the Veras team's resident whore as it was.

Nash opened his mouth, but I kept speaking. I hadn't finished the team roster. "And then there's Jayden..." My throat went dry when I said his name.

Our team leader. My first real, can't-stop-thinking-about-fucking-him crush. His gorgeous, tortured self had made my toes curl the second I'd met him six years ago. True, I'd only been eighteen, and at seven years my senior, he'd already been edging his way to thirty at the time, but even now, though I was twenty-four, he thought of me as a "kid." Thirty-one wasn't ancient by any means.

Zander had never had a problem with the age gap.

There was still nothing on his end of the bond. Hmm.

"And then there's Jayden," repeated Nash, crossing his arms and pouting. I'd never much talked about that crush of mine, but everyone had known. I might have been a little trip-over-my-own-feet, eagerly-help-him-with-bring-ing-in-the-groceries kind of obvious about it. For years.

"Jayden would never so much as touch me," I said. "Not even if the world would burn without my boost."

Someone cleared his throat from behind me and I spun in my chair to find the man himself in the doorway. He caught my eyes and immediately looked away, removing his circular glasses and grabbing a microfiber cloth from his front pocket in order to wipe the lenses. I wondered if he'd really found a spot or if he just welcomed the distraction.

My face felt hot at the idea of having been overheard.

I had *tried* not to bring up those days, tried to act much more professional around him. My puppy dog days had been ages ago. I'd thought I was over it.

Damn, though, did he have the "hot geek" look down to a tee. His sandy-blond hair looked windswept as he put his glasses back over his eyes. "Any activity?"

Of course. Just ignore the whole me-embarrassing-myself thing. That's what you always do.

Clearing my throat, I turned back to my tablet and tapped the screen back to life. "Nope. False alarms."

"And the Renegades?" asked Jayden, looking at the gigantic screens. Nash noticed Roulette's message box was still open, so like a child about to be caught by the teacher, he jumped up and took her place in front of the keyboard, quickly closing the screen with a wave of his hand over the sensor that controlled the cursor. "Noth—wait a minute."

The diminished message box had revealed a flurry of activity on the #Renegades hashtag. "They're downtown." Nash's Adam's apple bobbed as Jayden stomped across the room to get a closer look at the messages popping up at a faster and faster rate.

He spun around to face me. "Why was no one monitoring this?" He looked more than disappointed—he was angry.

Zander provoked that in him.

"Hello, darlin'," said Zander over the bond. *"I could have really used your boost today."*

I swallowed as Roulette appeared in the doorway. "I was on Renegade duty, sir." Her voice lacked its usual boisterousness. "Aurora had Nelian."

Jayden narrowed his eyes on Roulette, but not before sending a pained look to me. I was *always* on Renegade duty, at least as a backup. Considering Zander and I shared that bond. But, to be fair, so did Jayden. Jayden and I were the only ones I knew of who shared telepathic bonds with Zander.

"Is he giving you a hard time, darlin'?" asked Zander through the bond. *"Don't let him blame you. I had to force myself not to think about you so you wouldn't be able to tell I was up to something."*

I sighed. But just the fact that Zander *had* been so distant for a matter of several minutes should have been indication enough that something was up.

Jayden was already turning to Nash. "Send a message to Wade, Chastity, and Darien," he snapped, though not unkindly. He was in full command mode now. "Abandon current surveillance mission. This takes priority." He spun to face my friend. "Roulette, suit up. Nash, you have five minutes to get the van ready."

"Yes, sir," said Nash, springing to his feet. He caught my eyes and cocked his head toward the doorway, likely indicating for me to follow him, but I didn't move. He and Roulette vanished down the hallway, their fleet-footed steps echoing across the space of the former recreation club Jayden had acquired with his inheritance to turn into the undercover operations for the team known as Veras.

Not that "undercover" really worked when the leader of one of the teams opposing you used to live here and had co-led the team alongside his dearest childhood friend.

"You remind him he and I didn't see eye to eye on almost anything," said Zander through the bond. *"Not on when to use Natch abilities. Not on you. And not on what it's going to take to save the world from these cross-dimensional invaders."* I

10

could almost see the sly wink he was sure to be giving me just then. He must have been too busy for a projection. *"See you in a few."*

Jayden turned on his heel, almost as if in answer to the words he couldn't hear from Zander in my head. Perhaps Zander was sending him his own snide message.

"You stay here," was all he said before stepping out of the room.

CHAPTER TWO

"WHAT DO YOU MEAN, 'STAY HERE'?" I FELL INTO STEP quickly behind Jayden. He may have had Natch powers that allowed him to manipulate the soil of the earth, but unless he was going to pick up the handful of dirt in the potted plant in the hallway and send it flying at me, he had nothing to stop me with amidst all this concrete.

Though Wade and I had theories about what would happen if Jayden ever accepted my boost. He and Wade were the only ones who'd never once experienced what would happen if they kissed me on the lips.

Jayden not trying it out was the only one of the two that really bothered me.

"I don't think it warrants further explanation," he said, reaching the garage and the set of lockers out front. Nash and Roulette were already zipping up their sleek, form-fitting combat suits. You didn't *have* to wear them if you didn't want to—being caught off-guard didn't always allow us to—but Wade had formulated them to be extra durable against bullets, knives, and energy blasts. Unless any of the above hit us in the face, of course.

Nash's fingers rested at the base of his throat atop the

zipper as he stared at me. I gestured my head toward Jayden, who'd carefully tucked his glasses into his shirt pocket and was unbuttoning said shirt in front of his open locker.

"Sir, why isn't Aurora suiting up?" asked Nash.

Jayden methodically folded his button-down and placed it on a shelf in the locker. Damn, if his muscles had no business being on such a studious, all-business man. I stumbled and had to catch my breath, to remind myself to breathe.

Maybe I'm not so over him, after all.

"Get the van ready," he said, never once looking at Nash.

Nash shook his head and clasped his hands in apology to me before heading around the lockers to get things moving. Roulette slammed her locker door and then grabbed my hand, sending a nervous smile my way. I hesitated, thinking about giving her a quick peck for a boost, but it'd be over before she arrived downtown. Unless I came along. Which would be the whole point of me coming along.

I settled for squeezing her hand back, my hesitant smile the best luck I could offer unless Jayden saw sense. I watched her as she turned the corner, the drum of the garage door opening just before the van's engine whirred to life. Then I turned back to face Jayden.

Jayden in his tight, form-fitting briefs. His package practically burst out of the cotton, and it only got worse when he lifted first one thick, defined leg and then the other to slide into his combat suit.

His eyes are up there. His eyes are up there. I clenched my teeth and forced myself to stare up at his face, which didn't seem at all bothered by me catching more than a glimpse of this racy little show. But then again, we were all kind of on top of each other here and I was certain he'd gotten more than an eyeful of me when I'd been here changing before.

He'd gotten *quite* a good look at me the night he'd walked in on Zander and me making out in his office.

"*He was jealous,*" came Zander's voice over our bond. "*Don't believe him if he says otherwise.*"

I shook my head to shoo the pest away. I often wondered how much of my mind he got glimpses of whenever I thought about him, but it seemed to be, just as it was with me and his mind, that he only got the thoughts that I wanted him to hear—*and* the thoughts that involved him. Which is why I found my libido's too-frequent wanderings to that night more than a little annoying.

"*Thank you, darlin',*" said Zander. "*It drives me wild to know your libido can't stop focusing on me.*"

Jayden slamming the locker door shut jarred me out of the conversation in my head. "You're talking to him right now." It wasn't a question.

I didn't want to lie. "Nothing important."

Zander chimed in. I supposed we were both thinking about him, so he was going to be able to hear what was going on if so inclined. "*I don't know. I count one of the wildest nights of my life as pretty damn important. Even if it ended in blue balls.*"

I squeezed my hands into fists. "Nothing about whatever he's up to."

Silence on the other end of the bond. I supposed he actually *was* up to something and couldn't focus entirely on me.

"This is why I don't want you along," said Jayden. The movement of the van's tires echoed as Nash pulled it out onto the driveway, where it idled, waiting for the team leader.

14

The team leader who possibly looked even *more* heavenly in this skintight suit than he had virtually naked a minute before. Possibly because my fingers curled at the instinct to rip it off him.

"We don't need you with the Renegades," he said. "Go back and watch for Nelian activities. Contact Wade if something comes up."

It was hard to argue with the fact that *someone* needed to be monitoring for Nelian activity. "I can do that from the van," I pointed out. "I just need to grab my phone." Wade was *this* close to being able to use a computer program to detect the energy surge Nelian portals gave off whenever they appeared, but they apparently gave off different energy signatures each time, almost as if they knew they were being tracked. Until Wade cracked that puzzle, we had to resort to locals reporting strange activity. Because even in the midst of a horde of otherworldly elves strolling down Main Street, you could count on half a dozen people stopping to snap pics and post them on their social media profiles.

Human, Earthly Natches were old news. Nelian elves —*they* could get you lots of likes and reposts. Typicals— the non-powered humans—and Natches alike seemed in awe of them.

The fact that they all looked like super models with pointed ears, a variety of smooth skin tones, and long, silky, dark green hair probably helped. Even if they sent a car flying into the air right behind you two seconds after your camera's flash went off.

Nash laid on the horn of the van and Jayden stiffened. "I don't need you near the Renegades."

Translation: I don't want you near Zander.

"Because he's jealous, darlin'," said Zander in my head. *"Just like I told you."*

15

Zander may have once been Jayden's best friend, but he knew *nothing* about how the man felt about me. Jayden always acted like spending more than twenty seconds in my presence reminded him that I had a problem with b.o. I didn't, but sure enough, Jayden's nose went up in the air as his eyes wandered around the room and he turned to go. He paused. "Just stay in the briefing room."

Scoffing, I crossed my arms. "I'll be waiting for your call," I said. He was acting like fighting the Renegades was going to be a piece of cake. "Then I'll join you."

Zander hadn't just taken Kouta and Lila with him when he'd formed his own offshoot of Natch "talents." He'd teamed up with Torynt—a former enemy we used to keep in line whenever he went around bothering the Typicals with unnecessary displays of his powers. Like blowing wallets into the air and snatching the cash. Or sending women's skirts flying. Another cocky one, that guy.

Zander really was a bad guy now.

"I prefer to think of myself as a forward thinker who knows the old rules of the world were made for Typicals and don't apply to the next stage in Mother Nature's plan for humanity." A flash of something like irritation shot down our bond. *"Excuse me, darlin'. Your friends have arrived."* He went quiet.

"Go," I whispered aloud to Jayden. "The others are there."

Jayden left without another word, and I stood there not moving as the sound of the van's tires peeling down the driveway died down, as the garage door closed again, as the motion-sensing lights shut down. Just remembering.

"Wade, this is Aurora Haddix," said Mr. Roberts—or "Jayden," as he told me to call him. My eyes kept flicking up to him and my palms were going sweaty as they clutched the handle of my sole piece of luggage. So this was my new home.

My new life. My new "family."

And we lived in a former-community-center-turned-superhero-team-bunker? I didn't know what to call it. But now I knew the old rec center I'd frequented as a kid hadn't been abandoned, despite outward appearances. It was all high-tech in here.

Mom and Dad hadn't exactly been thrilled to discover —years later than most parents would have—that I was a Natch. Most people were cool enough with Natches, but there were some Typicals who saw them as a threat—an aberration. My parents had apparently secretly been in that camp, even if I hadn't noticed them say more than a word or two that qualified as prejudiced. Evidently, as long as no Natches crossed their paths, they'd been content to project the air of acceptance and civility. Tell them their daughter had had Natch powers all along and well, that was a different story.

So I'd only had time to pack one bag and rush out to the car that Mr. Roberts—Jayden—had had waiting for me.

He and Chastity had appeared in front of me at my summer job to offer up a display of their own powers and a convincing plan for what might be a better use of my next few years than the community college I'd been enrolled in for the fall.

Joining Veras. Fighting to make sure that other Natches didn't misuse their powers to break the law. The group wasn't officially sanctioned or anything. It was more like a volunteer effort to help where the city's laughably ill-equipped police force didn't dare to tread and for that, the government seemed to look the other way. Room and board and an allowance included—apparently Jayden was pretty good with investments. They'd found me posting anonymously about my suspicions concerning my powers on a "Am I a Natch? Strange Tales of Discovering Natch Abilities Way Past Infant and Toddler Years" forum. Apparently, not-so-anonymously since their friend Wade had been able to trace the IP address to my job at Dila's Soft Serve Ice Cream.

I still shivered at the memory of Jayden casually causing a clump of dirt to rise up from the patch of grass beside the outdoor picnic table where we'd had our discussion. Chastity's little sparkling light show in her palm had been cool, too, but the way Jayden had so casu-ally flicked his hand and caused the dirt to shape into a star in midair as he licked his ice cream cone had sent a fire between my legs. Talk about *power*. And he hadn't been cocky about it, either.

That had just been a day ago. Man, I'd moved fast. Trusting them. Trusting my whole future to these powers I'd never known I'd had. I shook my head now as the image of Jayden's display of Natch abilities kept flashing through my mind. *Don't crush on "teacher."* That would have been so gross in school, but dang, if he weren't the hottest "teacher" I'd ever laid eyes on. And he couldn't be *that* old.

"Ah, yes, the special lips?" said Wade. He was cute, too, an Asian-American with short, black hair and a ridicu-lously charming smile. He extended a hand out to me and I hesitated, wiping a palm on my thigh before shaking it. He cackled. "Glad to have you aboard."

"Well, we have to test it first." Jayden's lips pinched as Chastity filed into the room and took a seat at the big, round table. The room reminded me of Camelot, ready and waiting for King Arthur and his knights—except with giant screens covering one wall. There were news feeds and some kind of graph and 3D model on various spots throughout the grand span of interlocking monitors. "We don't know for sure that she's a Natch yet," Jayden added. He fidgeted with his hands, like he was nervous about something he couldn't bring himself to voice. Maybe he hadn't expected the first sit-down with my parents about the mere *possibility* of me having powers to devolve into a matter of me being kicked to the curb.

Gulping, I took an uneasy step toward the chair beside Chastity and sat down. At this point, I'd *better* be a Natch because even if I did turn out to be a Typical, I didn't think I could just tell that to Mom and Dad and smooth things over and move back in with them—I didn't think I'd *want* to, knowing they'd abandon their own flesh and blood if she turned out to have a special power since birth. Like I would have had any choice in the matter. Maybe if it turned out these people had been wrong, I could stay on as their unofficial Typical mascot.

"Well, that's what we hope to find out," said Wade, turning back to the screens and waving his hand over some kind of sensor to close out a few windows and bring up another one that seemed to be a collection of data. He spun around to face me, all business, just missing a clipboard in his hand. "When did you say you first noticed your potential Natch powers?"

My eyes flitted to Chastity beside me. She'd basically recited my forum post back to me, so I'd thought this was old news here, but she just nodded, a slight smile appearing on her ruby-red lips as she twirled one of the two long strands of her raven-black angled bob around her finger.

"Well, I... I kissed a boy," I said, suddenly embarrassed. My eyes wove around the room, my face growing hotter when I saw Jayden standing beside Wade, staring down at me. He didn't look judgmental or anything, it just —I was imagining talking about such things with my high school teachers and nope, this was *not* a conversation I relished having with authority figures.

Even ones as hot as Jayden.

"When was this?" asked Wade, typing something into the keyboard in front of the monitors and completely oblivious of my hesitation.

"About a month ago," I answered.

"You never kissed anyone before a month ago?" asked Chastity. "You're eighteen?"

I nodded, my mouth souring. "Er, yes, I'm eighteen. I did kiss others—a couple of times. But nothing happened then. He was... my first serious date." I didn't want to say what I hoped I was implying. He was the first boy I'd wanted to have sex with, too. Until he'd flipped out after our first kiss and scared the beejebus out of me, anyway.

I'd had to beat him off with a stick practically. My dad had called the police and it had gotten out that he was a Natch, and now the whole neighborhood was talking, and last I heard, his parents had shipped him out to the West Coast months before college started. They'd known he was a Natch, of course, but for some reason had instructed him to keep it all quiet. Didn't want the neighbors gossiping, I supposed.

"And what was different about this kiss?" asked Wade with the detachment of a scientific researcher.

"He was a Natch," I said.

"He knew he was a Natch?" asked Chastity.

"I guess *he* knew. But I didn't."

Jayden let an audible sigh escape his lips. Chastity seemed to notice me waiting for an explanation from the man, so she offered one. "He hates when Natches keep their abilities quiet. He understands why not *everyone* can just have accepting, rich parents and escape most of the prejudice and staring"—she glared at Jayden then—"but he still hates it."

"Natch is short for 'natural' for a reason," offered Jayden. "There's nothing wrong with what we are."

Someone scoffed from the corner of the room and I jumped in my seat to see a figure seated in the far shadows behind Jayden. I hadn't even noticed anyone else in here.

He leaned forward in his chair, his face coming into the light. *Wow.* He was hot. Like rugged, five-o'-clock-shadow, would-look-real-good-in-leather hot. What was it with this team of Natches? Did being a Natch automatically make you more beautiful?

I thought back to Tobias, the boy I'd kissed, and shrugged. He'd been okay. Cute, but not gorgeous like any of the specimens here. I supposed I'd mostly been caught up in the attention he'd paid me. He'd come by for ice cream most days in June, and by the end of the month, he'd asked me out. I'd fallen for it hook, line, and sinker, only snapping out of the effects of that little flirtation when I'd kissed him and he'd hit the ceiling. Literally. Floated and hit the ceiling.

"Sorry," said the man, gesturing toward me and leaning back in his chair, crossing an ankle over his knee. "Please continue embarrassing yourself. I'm finding this all very fascinating."

My face went hot and Jayden turned around to snap at him—the most emotion I'd seen in the man yet. "Zander, knock it off. She's just a kid."

An invisible fist punched me in the gut at that. This fascinating, stoic "teacher" of mine thought of me as a kid. There was no chance he'd ever... I cleared my throat. "Technically, I'm an adult..." I started. Jayden frowned at me, so I dropped it and sighed.

"So what happened when you kissed him?" asked Chastity, though she knew that from my post. They all did.

"He floated and hit the ceiling," I said. "Apparently, he'd been hiding the fact that he could fly and he said at the feel of my lips, something like a spark shot through him and he lost control. He *had* to fly, even if he usually had to tell himself when he wanted to. If it weren't for the ceiling..." I bit my lip. "He said he felt like he could fly higher than ever before—like he could have floated up into the clouds."

That Zander guy snorted. "That wouldn't have been very smart, considering the effects would likely wear off," he said. Jayden, Wade, and Chastity all glared at him. "What?" he asked, shrugging. "Aren't I right? Kid would have floated up to the clouds, then a few minutes later when it wore off, blam, right back to the ground." He smacked his palm against his fist for emphasis.

So they did all know this story from the post. They were just making me recite it to see me squirm. I clasped my hands together between my legs and squeezed, trying to calm my rapid heartbeat.

"If he could fly normally, I'd assume his Natch instincts would have kicked in and saved him from such a fate," said Jayden as he pushed his glasses up. "Even if the supposed effects of the kiss had made him think he could achieve higher heights than usual."

Supposed effects? Did he not believe me?

"Well," said Wade as he finished typing something into the documents on the screen, "I propose a series of tests. A full-body scan, some heart rate monitoring, a brain scan, an array of stimuli—"

Zander laughed, a hearty, growling sound that curled my toes. He stood, shaking his head and clasping Jayden on the shoulder. "If you make her Wade's lab rat, she'll never breathe non-sterilized air again."

Wade frowned at that but said nothing. A jolt of panic shot through me—had he planned on making me his guinea pig for days?

"I propose something far simpler," said Zander as he tucked both hands into his jean pockets and strolled over toward me. He towered over me, staring me down, a grin lifting the corner of his lips and something like amusement dancing in his eyes. "May I?"

"May you wha—?"

But before I could finish speaking, he'd bent over, his lips brushing mine.

"Zander!" Jayden shouted, but I didn't see what he or anyone else did in that moment.

A jolt flew through me—not at all like how it'd been when I'd kissed Tobias. Zander seemed to stagger back a bit, his lips leaving mine, and taking something strong and powerful with them. He righted himself and smiled at me.

"Wow. Well, why hello, darlin'."

I jumped. I'd just heard—there had been a *voice* in my head. And it hadn't been mine.

Zander removed one hand from his pocket and traced his lips with a finger, practically salivating as he looked down at me.

"That was me," said the voice in my mind. *"My Natch abilities include telepathy when I bond with someone. Though it's mostly projection."*

"Zander, I don't know where you get off thinking that's the *least* bit appropriate—" said Jayden as he grabbed hold of Zander's arm, but then Zander was behind me, running a strangely feathery-light hand through my hair, yet he was still in front of me, and I screamed, closing my eyes.

He chuckled.

"It's not funny," snapped Jayden.

Chastity *tsked* beside me. "He's not projecting behind you anymore, dear. You can open your eyes."

When I did, I saw Wade typing furiously, his focus on the screen. Jayden and Zander were arguing—or Jayden was lecturing Zander and Zander kept staring at me, a mischievous smile on his face—and I was lost. Utterly lost.

"You don't get it," said Zander, seemingly not at all bothered by Jayden's lecture. "I feel *amazing*." He put a hand up to Jayden's face, as if to hush him, and it worked. He turned and focused on the door. "I feel like I could project for miles. If you or someone else I bonded with were halfway around the world, I'd have no problem talking to you." He focused, closing his eyes. "Maybe I don't even have to be *bonded* with someone to talk to them—"

Chastity jumped beside me, shoving her chair back and standing on her feet. "What the fuck? Stay out of my head, Zander!"

Jayden looked puzzled. "You bonded with Chastity too…?"

Letting out a bellowing laugh, Zander clasped Jayden by his upper arms. "No, I'm happy to report for Chastity's own sanity that I doubt we're permanently bonded."

"Thank *god*," said Chastity, sitting back down. She squeezed her palms together and brought out a little light spark like she had at the ice cream place during her demonstration. It looked to be just a way to pass the time, a glaze of boredom falling over her eyes.

"And I can project—I can project so far! I think I can project to Hong Kong!" Zander was bouncing on his heels.

Jayden shook his head, aghast. "You can't project yourself more than a hundred miles or so, Zander, we've tried this—"

Zander closed his eyes and focused. Half a minute later, he grinned.

"What's so funny now?" asked Jayden.

Wade halted his furious typing. "People are posting to social media in Hong Kong," he said. "About the ghostly spectral man who appeared in front of The Peninsula Hotel for a few seconds and took off."

Jayden's jaw dropped and he took a step back, shaking his head. "No…"

"It's true!" said Zander. "Her lips really can—" Then he frowned. "It's gone."

"What?" asked Chastity, closing her hand and letting the lights vanish.

"The boost is gone," said Zander. He stared at me. "Must not last more than a few minutes, like with her and the flying kid." He took another step toward me. "So maybe you need to keep going at it for another pick-me-up…"

"Zander, *no*," said Jayden.

But Zander had already wrapped his arms around me, lifting me up from my seat and letting the chair knock over, his lips on mine.

I was too shocked to react. But damn, did my toes curl.

CHAPTER THREE

I SAT THERE ALONE AT THE BRIEFING ROOM TABLE, CHEWING on a hangnail on my index finger, staring blankly at the feeds I'd tossed up on the giant screens. My tablet still had the Nelian-spotting app running, but it was relatively quiet compared to all the #Renegades posts flitting past the screen.

The Renegades may have mostly only been locally active, but they were still renowned around the country— probably even the globe. Before the Nelians had appeared —also conveniently only in my town—they had been all the rage. The military had learned not to interfere too much with Renegade activity—unless they wanted a lot of destruction to follow, thanks to Renegade members Kouta and Torynt primarily—and so by the time the Nelians had appeared, our so-called armed forces had barely cared. Since the Nelian invasions had yet to spread to the rest of the world, it almost seemed like we'd been totally neglected, left to deal with it all on our own. The local police were slow to act, if at all, in our suburb. So that basically left us. "Why not let Natches battle other Natches and these superpowered aliens?" the mayor had proposed in a televised town hall one day. "They seem to have it under control."

Sure, sure.

They really did seem to leave all non-Typical crime up to us at this point. I often pondered why Jayden hadn't negotiated some kind of contract with the town considering, but I knew he valued privacy. Typicals were such cowards. It was a wonder so many still stayed in our city.

I supposed it helped that casualties throughout it all had miraculously totaled zero. So far.

On a slow, elf-free day, Renegade spottings were still likely to start a trend, though. They quickly devolved into debates for and against the rogue team's activities and whether or not Natches ought to be regulated with their own special set of laws.

Frankly, even if I were an anti-Natch Typical, I wouldn't have seen the point of special laws. Zander and company were quite capable of breaking the existing ones without additional restrictions.

Whoa! That fire guy just went sailing into a wall. Ouch #Renegades vs. the other guys.

I flinched. Veras was the "other guys." Fewer people remembered our name. Actually, maybe no one even knew it. It wasn't like we posted video speeches like Zander did.

But more importantly, "fire guy" had to be Nash. He'd wanted a boost and I'd turned him down. He was *hurt* because I'd turned him down. I hadn't even been against it. Nash was hot—I wasn't too much of his friend not to see that. It was just the kind of clinical way he'd asked—like I was nothing more than a tool—on top of how frequently he asked and the jumble that all these emotions

27

wound up causing in my brain that had made me hesitate.

And then there was the way my thoughts kept dwelling on Zander, even when I didn't want them to. I stared at the corner of the room where I'd initially seen him, remembering my first day here.

His kiss had driven me wild right from the start—even as my heart kept pounding every time I'd looked at Jayden. Then Nash had joined up a year later—hot, impulsive, and sometimes the sweetest guy you'd ever meet—and he'd been my age, so we'd kind of gravitated toward each other and toward Roulette and Darien as friends. Chastity and Wade were a few years older, but Jayden may as well have been an old man for the way he kept everyone at a distance. Everyone except Zander. They'd founded Veras together because they'd grown up attached at the hip.

I knew Zander's fallout with Jayden had been over more than just me—more than just that night—but it still stung that I had played any role in it. Zander seemed no worse for wear—which didn't exactly earn him sympathy points in my book—but Jayden was devastated over the loss of their friendship.

It might have been hard to tell since he typically kept his emotions in check, but I could tell. It came from years of observation.

Hmm. All these thoughts about Zander and silence. It seemed my friends were keeping him plenty occupied, too occupied for his thoughts to travel to me.

Fire guy's up! He's limping, though. #Renegades wreak havoc downtown.

Pounding a fist against my chair's armrest, I sighed and threw my arms atop the table, sliding down onto my chin and staring at the screens via the awkward way I'd positioned myself. At least Nash was okay—he usually was. Roulette was a healer half the time. That was the reason for her code name—every time she tried to use her power, you didn't know if she was going to blast out a white ray of healing energy or a searing red jolt of pain. She usually tested it on a garbage can or a rock to be sure. If it went flying, she was dealing out the hurt. If it just shimmered, she could shift her hand and focus it over an ally's injuries. With my kiss, she healed faster and hit harder, depending on the luck of the draw.

Nash got more firepower—literally—after my kiss and outright turned into Hephaestus on Earth after we had sex. No wonder he was so addicted to it.

Sparkling hot chick takes them out! #Renegades losing? The post accompanied a five-second video and I jumped up, scrambling over to the console to click *play*. Chastity was kicking ass, spinning in midair—she was a black belt in taekwondo in addition to having powers—and she temporarily blinded Lila, Kouta, and Torynt before drop-kicking all three with one blow.

Yes!

It looked like she'd knocked them out cold.

Relief spread throughout my body. Maybe Jayden had been right. Maybe I hadn't been necessary.

People seemed to be confused about the Renegades' objectives at the moment. Wade could have run a simulation on the computer and come up with any number of motives. The nearby bank had cash that would fund Zander's activities—that seemed to be one thing he really missed about us: leaving Jayden's fortune behind. Or maybe there'd been a Natch spotted nearby—a kid, most likely—and Zander wanted to get there before Jayden or Natch Social Services made a house call, try to get the kid's parents on his side. Or maybe he wanted to stop some young Natch from being bullied.

Whatever the reason, it all came down to theatrics. Zander relished the attention, the way word-of-mouth spread tales of his activities far better than the most expensive PR campaign. Not that he'd be able to find a PR firm eager to represent a group that thought being a Natch should be a requirement for any world leader going forward.

Fire guy's back in top form! read one comment. *Roulette must have gotten her healing powers to work.*

His name's Flayme! responded another post. *And he's sooooo hot. He can heat me up anytime.*

I couldn't argue with that. Nash didn't exactly care if anyone called him his code name around HQ, but in Veras we didn't typically leak our identities to the public.

I didn't think anyone knew about me, though, as "Succubus Lips" or not.

Zander could have changed that at any time, but he'd never crossed that line so far. He hadn't leaked our identities, hadn't told anyone where we lived—hadn't even paid us a visit at HQ. And that meant he'd made Lila and Kouta stay quiet, too—which had to have been something of a task. Even after the rift between him and Jayden, there was still an undercurrent of mutual respect. To a point. Perhaps only as much as there had ever been.

Another comment caught my eye. *Earth guy's throwing dirt around now. Yuck. Ohhhh, that's going to stain. So scary. What a dumb power.*

I scoffed. Like the average powerless Typical nerd online was in any position to be picky about powers.

Don't you think Zander's cute? #RenegadeBae

Zander didn't bother with code names. He never had.

"I don't see the need to hide who I am. I'm proud of my abili-

ties." There he was in my head again. I supposed that meant Jayden was holding back enough that Zander didn't need to work up a sweat.

"I could take him even at full power," Zander insisted.

Sure. Because telepathy and projection are so much more powerful than having chunks of earth hurled at you.

I could feel Zander's scowl through the bond, but I was quickly distracted by a beep from behind me.

"Shit," I said to no one at all. I jumped up and raced back to the table, quickly swiping at the screen.

Nelians spotted uptown—miles from my friends and foes alike. And this sighting seemed credible. "Double shit," I said, sighing.

I raced back to the console, typing in the code to bring up communications with Wade. "We've got a hot one," I said before he could even start speaking.

"Where?" he said, all business.

I scrolled through the information on the app and relayed it to him.

I could hear him hitting buttons. "We're about fifteen minutes—ah! Sorry. Ball of water went flying past my head." That would have been Kouta. "That's fifteen minutes if we can get these fuckers to call a truce for half a second."

Wade didn't often get aggravated. The Renegades must have been especially annoying today.

"I'll head there first," I said, shifting my weight and ready to run.

"Do you really think that's a good—oh, *come on*! Damn it, Lila—" He got cut off.

Shrugging, I jogged down the hall, then opened my locker and suited up. With the van and jeep gone, all we had was the Vespa. I was a little shaky on it, but it would have to do.

I *SUCKED* AT DRIVING THE VESPA. I'D HATED TO HAVE SEEN how I would have handled a real motorcycle. With my skintight battle suit, I got more than a few honks and catcalls as I slipped my way in and out through congested traffic. It was only when I got closer to the suspected spot of origin that men had things other than checking me out on their minds. Like abandoning cars and just running the hell away.

My comm on the suit had been beeping practically the whole way over, but I'd ignored it. The last thing I needed was distracted driving causing me to lose balance on this little death trap on two wheels. At least its small size allowed me to maneuver around abandoned vehicles. And overturned ones surrounded by giant green vines.

I skidded to a stop when a mom and her kid appeared out of nowhere in the middle of the road in front of me.

"Fuck!" I said under my breath, swerving the scooter sideways. At my speed, I lost traction on the road and went skidding into a wall. I wasn't sure how much time passed until I got my wits about me. There was some kind of rumbling down the block that shook the ground beneath me. I shifted, sliding my sore leg out from underneath the Vespa and flipping off the ignition in frustration. One of the rims was bent. A little buffing wasn't going to hide the extent of *those* dents.

"Damn it!" I said, pounding a fist on the soft seat. Even that stung slightly and I looked at my hand and saw the road burn on the palm. Wade really needed to add gloves to the suits—at least for those of us without hand-based powers who didn't need them free.

I unclasped the helmet and laughed sardonically when

I saw how scuffed that sucker had gotten, too. At least I'd had the sense to snap it on.

"Maybe you should wait for your Nurse Nightingale friend before you get up."

I whipped around to see Zander's shimmering form standing behind me.

Scoffing, I chucked the helmet at the scooter and pulled my legs together, wincing. Nothing seemed broken. I probably had Wade's durable battle suit to thank. I put my forehead down atop my knees, clutching my thighs to my chest. "I wasn't thinking about you."

He chuckled. "I know. I've been trying to reach you. So have your friends." He always called them that. 'My' friends. Like he hadn't once fought alongside them all. My comm was still going off, so that explained that. "I don't need you to be thinking of me to project to you," he said, this time more quietly.

"How did you know where to find me?"

"Wade relayed your message to Jayden and we managed to… agree to a truce."

I lifted my head and stared up at him. His devious smile said more than he did—I imagined it hadn't been a simple matter of everyone just knocking it off and shaking hands.

"You really love fucking things up, don't you?" I said. There was a hint of anger there. It might have been the crash, the nearby destruction—the people still screaming and running past us, no one bothering to glance over and notice one of us was ten percent see-through. Or it could have just been that anger that had bubbled through me since the moment he'd walked out, vowing to do exactly what he'd done: build his own team of Renegades, approach problems as he saw them through a more aggressive, lawless path.

33

It could easily have been all of the above.

"*This* isn't my fault."

"It is," I said, finally standing and stumbling, slapping my sore hand against a nearby wall to catch myself. Zander moved to catch me, but his touch was like a feather —there, but not substantive, even when his fingers wrapped around my arm. That was what it was like to be touched by his projected form—a tease, a taste of what could be.

But what could never be again.

He frowned and dropped his hand, almost as if he couldn't bear the thought of this teasing touch, either. "We both want the Nelians gone," he said. "Both Veras and the Renegades."

Turning, I started limping toward where all the chaos was emanating from, letting out a slight scoff. I leaned against the wall as I moved, my leg too sore to support me.

"You can't go there alone," he said, his breezy projected form closing in behind me. "Your friends are on their way —my team is heading around the other side for backup."

I spun on my heel, wincing as the pain shot up my leg. "You recognize the Nelians are the real threat, but you go around doing stupid things, fighting people who once saw you as a friend—"

"We were busting up an anti-Natch meeting," he said, his lips thin. His eyes glazed over for a second and I recognized it as him probably focusing more on the people actually in front of him in whatever vehicle he was in on his way to the scene. "A meeting full of hateful Typicals."

"And you thought, what, busting up the meeting with a flashy, dangerous display of Natch powers would make them embrace us all of a sudden?" Shaking my head, I leaned back against the wall. I shuddered as a woman screamed and darted past me. Every second I was wasting here was a second that put another person in danger. Not that I was sure what I could do on my own, but I could at least *try*. I could at least direct an evacuation.

"You sound like Jayden," said Zander, his voice growing quiet once more.

Of course I did. I'd chosen to stay with him, hadn't I?

Looking into his spectral dark eyes, I felt that pang of regret. I would have felt just as sick losing Jayden—losing Nash and Roulette and everyone else, too—if I'd chosen to walk out on them with Zander. Worse because I'd have lost more people I loved. But that didn't change the fact that I missed him. My libido missed him. I missed the way he'd driven me wild.

Besides, it had been an easy choice, even if a painful one. I agreed with Jayden—violence was the last resort, not the answer.

Zander's projection took a step forward and his hand went to my cheek. It felt like a butterfly kiss and my head rolled instinctively into it, wishing there was something more solid there, more real.

"I miss you," said Zander, his voice cracking. "I miss Jayden, too. I wish you both could see—"

Shaking my head, I pulled away from his ephemeral touch. "I wish *you* could understand."

"Darlin', I *tried* his way. For years."

I opened my mouth and shut it at the sound of another boom from behind us. This wasn't the time for discussion. And it wouldn't matter anyway. I started to turn away again—

And Zander's ghostly hands gently turned my face back to his, his lips pressing against mine. My mind went numb at the feeling of the tease of his kiss, my eyelids closing and my brain flashing through images of us hooking up in Jayden's office—but this kiss was a taunt.

Pulling back, I ran my tongue over my lips, aching for the feel of more. "You can't get a boost from your projection kissing me," I said, my voice raspy, my breath shallow.

"I know," he said, running his ghost thumb over my cheek in a circle. "But it might be the closest taste I have of you as long as you're stuck hiding in Jayden's shadow."

Grimacing, I clenched my hands into fists—half out of annoyance, half to stop myself from running those hands through his spidery ghostly hair—and turned. No more distractions.

"Aurora, please, wait for—"

But with another resounding crash, Zander disappeared. Whatever had happened, he was more focused on what was in front of his real body, his real self. The real self I would never touch again. Not without hurting Jayden, betraying my friends.

Just as well. I had work to do. I kept limping, each step getting easier as the soreness evolved to numbness. When I reached a café with a shattered storefront window pierced by a half-dead giant vine and smoke wafting out of it, I knew I was truly there. I was the only one here. And somehow, it was going to have to be up to me until the cavalry arrived.

I could do this. I *had* to do this. I had to prove I was more than a pit stop in a van to boost my teammates' powers.

The ground shook beneath my feet and another giant, green vine popped up from beneath the asphalt, sending chunks of concrete tumbling down the trunk of the monstrous growth. So far, most Nelians we encountered had been shown to have this same, singular power—but what a massively dangerous power it was.

I stumbled back, leaning against the wall as the vine

soared right in front of me and struck into the apartment building above. I threw my hands up over my head, cursing myself for leaving my helmet behind.

Someone must have been looking out for me, though, because the worst I experienced was a couple of fist-sized rocks bumping against me before I felt myself being tugged inside through the café's broken storefront, small arms wrapping tightly around my waist.

The building rumbled above us as the giant vine retreated back to whatever Nelian elf had sprung it from their hands. Whoever it was pulled me to their chest, laying their head over mine and sheltering me from any extra dust and debris. It was only once the noise had relatively died down that I realized the softness beneath my cheek indicated a curvy, if lithe, woman.

The tension in her hands eased and I stepped back. "Thank—"

Before I could get out the second word, though, I got a good look.

It was a Nelian elf.

CHAPTER FOUR

"Who...?" I started to say.

"Run," said the elf woman. "Get out of here." She shoved at me then with such force, I wondered if she intended to hurt me. Despite the fact that she'd just saved me.

Wincing from the soreness in my leg as I regained my balance, I stared at her. She was beautiful—as were all these pointy-eared elves from this other world—and she had more distinctive curves than many of the other women I'd seen of her kind. Her pale peach complexion was probably even more flawless, her long, long hair a dark, rich shade of green. She studied me as I regarded her and her lips curled into a frown.

"Who are you?" she asked. "You don't seem like a typical human."

"I'm not a Typical," I said. "I'm a Natch."

She nodded, biting her lip. "One of those humans born with powers."

"Yeah," I said. Then I scrunched my eyebrows together. "Hey, I asked first—who are you and why did you save me?" I gestured behind us. "Especially considering your kind is currently shredding up part of my city?"

She took a step back. "We're restoring it," she said. "To its natural beauty."

Yeah, these Nelians seemed to have something against concrete and bricks and mortar—Wade and even the news cycles had figured out that much. I shook my head. "People *live* here. And you're an invader. It's not up to you whether or not this building gets to exist."

Her eyes narrowed. "It's not up to your people to change what the planet creates and offers to suit your selfish needs."

"So that's what it's all about, huh? Just lending Mother Nature a hand?"

She flinched as another vine whipped past the shattered storefront window across the block and down the street, and I had to grip on to the cashier counter to stay on my own two feet in the rush of wind as it passed. The vine seemed to have gotten kind of stuck partway, ceasing suddenly.

She grit her teeth. "If that means saving this planet, then yes."

"Then why attack one city in small pockets?" I demanded to know. "Why not just stay and whip your little branches around all over the world?" They were notorious for staying no more than an hour at a time, sometimes leaving their huge vines sticking half in and half out of a building and just clearing out after the damage. They'd bizarrely never attacked anywhere outside of our little city. They hated metropolitan areas? There were so many bigger, more populated cities around the world. But nope, they stuck with ours.

She didn't seem bothered by my seething rage. "You say you're a… powered human?"

"A Natch," I said, crossing my arms and ignoring the jolt of soreness from my hand.

"And you don't...?" She gestured to herself and the area around where she was standing. "You don't notice anything?"

My eyes practically rolled out of my head. "What? I *notice* your people tearing through uptown. I *notice* you strangely saving my life." Biting my lip, I let the savagery of my tone drop somewhat. It was true that so far no one had been killed in one of their attacks. Injured—definitely attempted murder—but miraculously, everyone had gotten out and survived when the Nelians had gone on their little rampages. Was it really this sole elf woman saving people one by one?

"Your powers," she said, ignoring my rant. "You aren't using your powers."

Snorting, I wasn't about to explain *why* that was. Instead, I changed track. "You aren't using *yours*. Instead, you're saving the people you've been sent to attack."

Her lips curled into a frown. "Try using them. Try attacking me."

I clenched my hands into fists. "No. I don't just use powers on command—" I let out a scream as another giant vine went soaring past, this time seemingly generated from someone just outside the café, but it stopped. Cut short before it could barely begin.

In the quiet that sucked up the air as the vine began to flop to the asphalt, its originator presumably letting it go, a voice echoed down the street—a deep and intoxicating voice that made my heart skip a beat.

"Alanna! Alanna!"

An elf kicked open the café door, sending the already-wobbly thing nearly off its hinges. "I *told* you to stay behind." Like the elf woman, there was a touch of

40

foreignness to the way he spoke, though it was no Earthly accent. My eyes were instantly drawn to him, and my breath hitched as I took note of how tall and lithe he was. His muscles were well-defined, which was startlingly obvious even through the tight earth-tone leather-like material that clung to his form. From their medieval-ish attire to their pointed ears, these other-worldly beings were truly high fantasy elves brought to life. During one of their first visits, they'd called them-selves elves from Nelia. Then they'd smashed up several buildings with their giant plants without giving humanity more than a second to register what they'd said. "Who brought you here?!" he snapped, oblivious to my apparent drooling.

"Brother," said the elf woman who'd rescued me—Alanna, I supposed. "My king." She put a fist over her breast and kneeled to the ground, ignoring the dust and debris coating the floor.

King? Shit.

Anger flushed his smooth, tawny face—darker than his sister's—as he strode in with his fists clenched, heading directly our way. He halted suddenly, puzzlement painting over the rage. "What's this human doing with you?"

"She's a powered one," said Alanna from her submis-sive position on the floor. "A… Natch." She curled her lips exaggeratedly around the latter word, like it left a distaste in her mouth.

The elf king stared at me and extended an outstretched hand slightly in my direction, his brown eyes narrowed and trained on me like a dog sizing up its opponent.

Yeah, I'm not going to attack you since my only "weapons" are more like energy drinks.

Biting my lip, I tried to seem intimidating even so. But it was hard when face-to-face with his beauty, which

41

didn't seem marred by the twitch of a snarl on his face, but rather enhanced by it.

My libido growled inside me, rushing from my groin all the way out to my fingertips, rumbling louder and louder inside me with every second of our standoff.

Damn, me, you need to get your mind out of the gutter at the most inopportune times.

"Oh!" cried out Alanna, her hand going to her lips as her gaze fluttered between the elf man and me. "Is that even possible...?"

"Quiet," growled the elf king. He was breathing hard as he stared at me, his chest visibly moving up and down. Lowering his hand to his side, he cocked his head. "You're not attacking."

Clearing my throat, I looked from him to his apparent sister. "I'm waiting for backup." True enough.

"Alarik," said Alanna, rising to her feet. "We should go." She looked at me. "I know you and she... But we need to go."

"We need not fear these beings, even the powered ones. They're too small in number." He laughed, and damn, if that laugh wasn't the kind that would have been more at home on a beach at twilight, his arms wrapped around a woman, her toes curled into the sand. I slapped my face with my road-burned hand and winced, taking in a sharp breath of air. Both elves stared at me then, Alarik's expression purely curious.

He took a step toward me, his hand extended again, and I jumped, my fists raised up like we were about to engage in some boxing, my knees bent and limber and ready to attack. Assuming I could get so much as a single blow in before he shot me through the wall with a vine straight out of *Jack and the Beanstalk*. All that work

42

attacking punching bags on a semi-daily basis wasn't going to save me now. *Fuck.*

Doing serious damage to my readiness for a fight, his hand instead went to my cheek as a slight grin emerged on his lips. His fingertips felt odd—soft and a touch rubbery at the same time, like a yoga mat that smelled of musk and flowers and everything guaranteed to make my panties flood with moisture. Damn it if that weren't the case—but the suit had been designed to absorb moisture. Perspiration, naturally. Not… what was making my knees shake.

"You're quite beautiful for one of your people," said this seductive elven king. His fingers danced lightly up the side of my face and he took a piece of my sweat-stained dark hair and brushed it off my forehead. Fuck me, I was *letting* him do this. I *craved* his touch. And I didn't just mean on my face.

"Alarik—" started Alanna, but then the street outside roared, a mighty gust of wind I first attributed to the movement of another vine, but as my head turned—the loss of Alarik's touch on my skin with the movement painfully evident—I saw it was a funnel of wind. Torynt—had to be. Though it strangely kind of sputtered out halfway. But in any case, that meant Zander and his Renegades at least had arrived, their goals always aligning with ours when it came to driving out these otherworldly invaders.

The elf king's jaw clenched, his hand still hesitatingly hovering beside me. He nodded toward Alanna. "*You* need to get out of here. Now. Ask Normak to… He's outside. He'll knock you unconscious."

Wait, what?

"Leave you? With her? You can't honestly mean to act on what's between you right now?" she asked. "Xerxes thinks I can be useful when these Natches show up—"

"Now!" barked Alarik. He gestured toward the open door and gaping window and Alanna stood, looking from me to her brother and back again, then nodded and made her way outside. Alarik practically bounced on his heels, his fists clenched at his sides as he watched her go. What did she mean, *what's between you*? I'd never met the asshole.

He turned to me. "Your *backup* has arrived. And yet you hesitate?"

I stared at him, a single eyebrow raised. "You haven't attacked me."

He opened his mouth—his lips sensuously curved into an 'o'—and then he clamped his mouth shut for a bit before uttering, "I can't."

"You *can't*?"

My gaze darted from him to the street. The tip of a huge vine curled around the corner, but an ice ball went soaring past and froze it in place. Tension left my shoulders. Darien, a.k.a. Ice-Blast. My friends had arrived as well.

He sized me up and down. "I'm not sure I'd want to attack you, either. A defenseless girl, all alone."

"I'm hardly a *girl*," I said, grinding my teeth. A flash of Jayden always dismissing me as some twenty-four-year-old "kid" tore through my mind.

"I'll say," said the king, his eyes roving up and down and sticking somewhere around my butt. He laughed. "Too much fire and fury for you not to have seen your share of battles."

"My king," said a voice from near the doorway, nearly causing me to shoot out of my skin. "Alanna is… That is, the princess won't allow me to put her in a condition to retreat." Another pale elven man. His hair mussed, his expression panicked. "She's trying to reach these powered humans."

"*Roots and sediment*," Alarik answered, clearly cussing in his own kind's way. The other elf's eyes went wide. Alarik waved dismissively at him. "Why did she have to come?" He sighed. "How many of our own has Alanna infected?"

"Half, my liege," said the soldier. His gaze finally rested on me, and he looked me up and down, clearly perplexed. "And so far, she hasn't gotten close enough to any of the powered humans to try—"

"Damn it!" said Alarik, as loud as could be. "I *told* Xerxes to keep her behind—"

"He thinks—" started the elf.

"I don't *care* what he thinks." His gaze finally fell on me, though he still spoke to his soldier. "How long before the portal closes?"

"Four turns, sir," said the elf.

Alarik grinned deviously. "Then give them our full might and fury. Half can still fight, so half will have to provide cover. And *someone needs to knock out the princess*! I don't care if you have to fight her to do it."

"But, Your Majesty—"

"Go!" barked the king. The elf did, scrambling, shouting out as he ran down the street.

Alarik and I stood there in silence a moment longer and then he grabbed me by the elbow. "Come."

"What?" I tugged my arm free. "Are you joking? No!"

He stared down at me as if I were an idiot. "Are you going to attack me?"

Grinding my teeth, I attempted to dig my heels into the floor. I supposed that was answer enough.

"You can't, either," he said, crossing his arms and

squeezing his chin between a thumb and forefinger, as if studying me. "You were affected by Alanna as well."

"What are you *talking* about?"

"You can't use your powers."

I growled in frustration. "My powers aren't exactly... of the offensive variety, okay? Satisfied?"

If he'd wanted to kill me, he could have done it half a dozen ways by now. And his sister *had* saved me, so maybe...

He lowered his hand from his face. "So you don't actually *know* if you can use them?"

"I, uh..." Shaking my head, something hit me. "Are you *incapable* of using your powers around your sister? Why?"

That was it. It looked as if I'd slapped him. His eyes went wide, but then they narrowed and he grabbed my elbow again. "You're coming with me." He tugged and I stumbled, my sore leg not allowing me any leeway to fight.

"Stop!" I said. Was he about to use me as a hostage? "Let me go!"

Damn, if my heart weren't beating wildly enough to jump out of my chest. Fright mixed with adrenaline mixed with that stupid, unruly libido of mine that tried to scream that I kind of *wanted* this asshole to grab me and yank me and take me away.

Fuck, you are stupid, me.

"We can test whatever your abilities are in Nelia," he said.

I laughed. "Good luck with that." Then panic overwhelmed me again. He was taking me to his kingdom?

We reached the doorway and he yanked me after him, causing me to stumble just in time to avoid a fireball soaring overhead.

"Aurora!" called Nash.

I whipped around to find him running at us from down the block.

Alarik sneered as he looked from me to Nash and back again. A few blocks away, the ground rumbled as the dirt the vines had unearthed went soaring into the air. Jayden had to have been there.

"This isn't over," hissed the king. The anger twisting his face relaxed as he looked me in the eyes and smiled. "*Aurora*. What a lovely name for a lovely human."

Before I could do more than stare slack-jawed at him, he dropped my elbow and retreated the opposite way, running at speeds only Olympic champions could hope to match among we human mortals.

"Aurora!" said Nash again as he arrived beside me. He took me into his arms and squeezed, kissing the top of my head. "Why did you go and do a stupid thing like that?" he whispered.

A wave of defensiveness rolled through me despite the voice of reason in my head. I pushed away. "A stupid thing like try to *help* people? Yeah, how could I?"

Nash opened his mouth, but we both flinched as a giant vine soared overhead a couple of blocks over, extending far above the roof of the tallest building. Debris went scattering and Nash took my hand in his, dragging me back to that infernal shattered café. He grimaced as he looked around. "I liked this place. Had good espresso."

Rolling my eyes, I dragged him farther inside so we could breathe easier near the back. There was a corner outfitted with sectional couches and a small coffee table that looked barely touched from all the chaos.

"We were all worried about you," Nash began. "Even... Zander." He bit his lip on the word. "He said he was trying to get in touch with you, but it was spotty and you were ignoring Wade's comms—"

I took his face between both hands and kissed him. Closing my eyes, I felt the fire I associated with this Flayme man shoot from my lips all the way down to the soles of my feet.

He pulled away slightly, grinning as he rested a hand on my forearm. "Thanks." Fire practically raged within his eyes—not in an angry way, but in the way a dying ember is suddenly given new life with the strike of a match.

His smile fell and he turned his gaze to my road-burned hand, pulling it away from my face. "You're hurt. We need Rou—"

I grabbed hold of his face tightly again and kissed him a second time.

Chortling, he pulled away. "I didn't need a second boost from those Succubus Lips so soon," he said. "Let me get out there and use my powered-up fire for a few minutes." He stared at his hand then, flexing it—and then frowning. He cocked his head. "It feels... I don't know. But I'll test it out and then I'll come back for a pick-me-up."

Dropping my hands from his stubble, I reached for the zipper at my collar. "Let's do the full boost."

Nash had the audacity to blush. After all his talk... "Now?" He looked around at the half-tattered café. "Here?"

As if in answer, I finished unzipping my suit, my fingers lingering in front of my pelvis where the zipper ended. "Turn into a god of fire and get out there," I said. "Blast those otherworldly menaces away."

Nash didn't have to be told twice. His hands raced for his own zipper and it was down before I could blink, one arm and then the other peeling out of the suit, which hung like a banana peel off his back. My eyes flitted to his crotch, where the slightest wisps of blond hair poked out from where the zipper ended. I reached forward, diving in, grabbing hold of his thick member.

"Whoa," he said, though he was not disappointed. "I don't even know if I need a warm-up, angel. You can *always* get me revved and ready—"

I kissed him again and peeled the rest of his suit down his legs, grabbing his cock firmly but gently and running my fingers up and down.

"*Angel,*" he breathed, removing his lips from mine and running both hands through my hair. It drove me wild when he did that.

I quickened my pace, stroking up and down, relishing the quick, pert firmness that yielded to my touch, but not giving him an inch as I kept up with the movements.

"*Angel!*" he groaned. "I can't—you work so damn fast."

Like we had time for lollygagging in the midst of a battle.

His shaking hands gripped the gap in my suit, clutching to either side of it and ripping the material off my shoulders with gusto enough to make my knees wobble. The adrenaline surging through my body as he came at me with all intent of *devouring* me made the soreness in my hand and leg fade into the background.

"Those tits," he said—ever the charmer. His lips went to a nipple and I dropped my grip on his cock, my hands riding up his six-pack, up to his pecs, and around his shoulders. He pinched the nipple lightly between his teeth and I cried out.

Pulling back, he started peeling the rest of the suit off my torso. "On the couch," he said. I obeyed, helping him take first one and then the other sleeve off so the suit just clung around my hips. His arms gripping me tightly, my back hit the cushion, and I was already arching, my groin begging to meet his lips.

He tugged hard on the suit, exposing my ass to the cushion below.

"Beautiful," he said, as if speaking a forbidden word. "Beautiful…" he repeated, his lips touching my navel and moving slowly downward.

"We don't…" I said, meaning to tell him we didn't have time to make this pleasurable, but I had to bite down on my lips—hard—as his mouth moved to my clit, his tongue poking out to run circles around the key to my pleasure.

"Take me," I wheezed through heavy breaths. "Just… Take me…"

"Angel," he said, coming up for air.

"*Please!*" I begged. To get him that power boost fast. To drive away the Nelians. But in that moment, mostly because I needed him inside me—now.

He leaned back up and readjusted himself, slapping his hands on either side of me on the couch—one hand on the back of it, the other mere centimeters from my waist. He locked eyes with me as he slid inside, the moisture that had been there all day—with thoughts of too many damn sexy men in front of me, including that forsaken Nelian king—gliding it in like it was the perfect fit. I groaned. "More," I whispered.

He obliged, pulling the tip back and rushing back in, over and over, each thrust causing my groans to bubble over more. "More," I said again.

I waited for my power to kick it all up a notch, to lead us both to levels of ecstasy we as mere mortals had no business experiencing. Right before we should have gotten there—just as his seed went pumping through me—we heard a voice from the doorway.

"Flayme! Succubus!"

Jayden.

Reality set in and I gasped as Nash fully removed himself. My limbs were shaking, my crotch turned to jelly.

"Getting a boost, sir," said Nash, all business as he slipped his arms back through his suit and zipped up.

I turned to see Jayden grimacing, then, catching my eyes, pointedly staring at the ceiling. "I can see that. Glad you're okay, Aurora. We'll talk… We'll talk later." He nodded over his shoulder. "We need you, Flayme. The elves are pulling back into a circle around their portal, and with a little more firepower we can push them through—"

"Roger!" said Nash.

I sat up and slipped my arms through my suit. I ached everywhere, but the moment of passion still carried my hot blood throughout my body, easing the pain.

Nash snapped his fingers to make a ball of flame appear just as I zipped up.

"Hmm," he said. He shook his palm to let it go, then snapped his fingers again.

"What is it?" I asked, the thin lines of his face sending dread to my stomach.

"Nothing, just…" He looked at me. "I don't think that did anything to boost me."

Dread turned to nausea as the cold, hard truth of what Alarik and Alanna had been saying hit me.

That elf princess had stolen my powers from me.

CHAPTER FIVE

WADE REAFFIXED THE ELECTRODE ABOVE MY BREAST, apologizing as he tugged on it and caused a welt to appear on my skin. "Sorry about that. Just one more test."

Roulette pinched her lips from where she was sitting beside me. "If you're saying it works, it works. I don't know how much more testing you need to do."

For about five minutes of this test, Wade's power-studying program indicated that I had indeed become as powerless as the average Typical. But he hadn't had a chance to run much data before it had all of a sudden surged back, apparently hitting all the same data markers it always did whenever Wade felt like strapping me up to his machine and making me his guinea pig. He'd mumbled something about a "temporary occurrence," which made sense—around an hour had passed between when Alanna and Alarik had left my side and when I'd finally gotten home and strapped in to Doctor Frankenstein's machines. Roulette had ridden with Wade, Jayden, and me to go back in the jeep, while Nash, Darien, and Chastity had stayed onsite trying to see what they could do to work with rescue personnel and minimize the damage done to uptown. Jayden had kept me explicitly out of view of the Renegades before they'd left following the Nelian elves' retreat into their portal located in the middle of an auto store. But I'd exchanged a glance with Zander as I'd made my way to the jeep, wondering if he was trying to reach me through the bond because I wasn't hearing anything, even when I thought only of him as I walked by.

Roulette had summoned her healing powers just before we'd gotten inside the vehicle and I was right as rain, except for the shock of losing my Natch powers. And even that had worn off, according to Wade's data, so I was absolutely giddy now.

"Your abilities may have returned, but I want to run a few more tests to be sure there are no other residual—"

I tugged on the electrode Wade had just affixed. "Good enough for me." I knew that by lying down on this table, I'd been signing up for tests and scans and data for the rest of the night. I'd been willing when we'd needed to get my powers back. Now, not so much.

"But I haven't finished—"

I ripped off the last electrode and jumped down, exchanging a grin with Roulette.

"She's good," said Roulette. She looped an arm through mine. "If Nash were here, he'd recommend some *practical* testing…"

My face flushed. "That was how we figured out it *wasn't* working."

Her lips looked ready to reach to her ears. "I figured it had to have been something like that."

We stopped in the hall as we passed the briefing room and I looked inside for Jayden. He was likely in his office. "Now that things have died down, I need to share what I found out about the elf who did this to me and... their king."

Roulette frowned. "Should it wait for the others?"

"They'll have to know, too," I said, "but I should let Jayden know ASAP. In case it comes in handy."

She shook her head. "They've never appeared more than once in the same day." Her comm beeped and she clicked it on, the worried look on her face melting. "Hey, babe. What's up?"

"Nothing," came Darien's voice. "Just checking in..."

With Wade still fiddling with and frowning at his machines and Roulette receiving the away team's update, I decided to lump them in with the whole team's debriefing whenever everyone else arrived home. Until then, I would run what I'd found out by the team leader. It made sense in every practical, military-style strategy. Never mind that my heart about jumped into my throat as my feet carried me down the hall to Jayden's office-slash-bedroom.

My knuckles hovered over the door for a full minute before I knocked.

"Come in," said Jayden curtly from inside his office.

I opened the door and peeked inside. Jayden was hunched over his desk, peering over a laptop and comparing whatever he'd found on the screen to a folder packed to the brim with papers. He didn't look up. "What is it?"

My eyes wandered over to his bed in the corner—double-sized, no frills, taking up as little space in the cramped office packed with shelves and filing cabinets as possible—and I willed myself not to think about how Zander and I had once maneuvered ourselves there right as Jayden had walked in on us.

"Too late," said Zander over our bond.

Damn it. I took a deep breath and squeezed my hands

54

together in front of my abdomen, counting the seconds it took me to exhale and shutting my eyes.

"That hard for you, huh?"

I opened my eyes to find Jayden looking up at me, what could only be called a soft, pitiful smile working its way onto his face. He removed his glasses and put them down on the desk in front of him, pinching his temples with one hand. "To not think of *him* every time you're in here?"

I hated when he knew what was going on in my head. "I honestly try not to."

"I know," said Jayden, releasing his face and sighing. He grabbed his glasses and slid them back on. "He was just in my head telling me..." He drifted off. "Talking about you."

When we had so many other things going on? I wished he would use these bonds he shared with Jayden and me to do something useful. Like communicate about Nelian elven movements. Or broker a lasting peace that didn't involve the Renegades busting down walls and breaking out prisoners every other day.

"They're innocent Natch prisoners, I'll have you know," said Zander over the bond. I didn't need to be able to see him to picture the grin on his face that came next. *"And it's never a waste to think about you. Darlin', do you have any idea how easy it would be for the Renegades to win if we counted you among us?"*

I bristled at the implication that it was all about my powers for him. But what else would it be, honestly? Why did I lie to myself or even *care* whether or not there was something more?

But I did care. My heart sunk like I'd had the wind knocked out of me and I focused so hard on the bird's nest on a branch beyond Jayden's office window, I didn't even register whatever nonsense Zander was saying to try to get me riled up. He simply ceased to inhabit any corner of my mind.

Jayden cleared his throat. "You wanted to see me?" His squeaky office chair snapped me back to the moment.

"Do you remember the noises that thing was making when I carried your succulent, bare ass over to that—"

Shut up.

Clearing my throat, I dug a thumb nail into my palm to focus on the discomfort. "Wade says my powers are back. Back in top form."

Jayden threaded his fingers together and laid his elbows on the desk atop the paperwork. A cursory glance told me they consisted of information about Nelian elves. "Wade gave you the all-clear to leave his laboratory," said Jayden. His tone clearly indicated he wasn't convinced.

"He didn't so much *let* me as he's been saying my powers have returned for an hour now and I'd had enough of it."

Jayden leaned his lips forward to touch the index fingers at the top of his steeple. "So the effects wore off... after how long? About an hour."

"Based on my account and the time it took to travel back to HQ, Wade estimates it to be anywhere from seventy to a hundred and ten minutes. The effects of this elf's power, I mean."

Jayden dropped his hands off the desk and leaned back, clutching his squeaky chair's armrests. You'd think with all his money, he'd get that replaced or at least fixed at some point. There were cracks in the vinyl from years in the sun, too. "You're sure it was this woman elf?" he asked. "All right. Tell me everything."

I didn't miss that he hadn't indicated a feeling either way—relief or regret, even, *anything*—that my powers were back. His chair swiveled slightly and he stared off out the window. The mama bird was balancing a slithery earthworm between her beak, her ugly-cute little wet-looking babies all stretching their heads up to snatch it.

"Her name was Alanna," I said. Jayden snapped out of whatever he was daydreaming about and swiveled round to face his computer, immediately starting to type. This was part of why I hadn't told him all the details on the car ride home. That, and he'd been the driver and he'd looked distracted enough already, his thoughts clearly weighing on him as Chastity and Darien had exchanged ideas for clean-up with him over their comms. "She was a princess."

Jayden frowned, his fingers hesitating over the keyboard. "Another elf called her a princess?"

"Yes. And she bowed to another elf—a man—and called him her king and her brother. A third elf referred to that man as 'Your Majesty' as well."

"You're certain she didn't mean 'brother' in a 'brother-hood' way?"

I supposed I hadn't thought of that. They did look a bit different, despite the shared green hair. I felt suddenly stupid as I took a corner of the desk between my fingers. "Maybe. But… I don't know. My gut told me from how they interacted that they were really siblings." Not that I'd know since I was an only child.

Jayden's lips went thin as he stared up at me and I real-ized as my eyes traveled down that the top of my battle suit was still unzipped. My cleavage spilled out, the open zipper forming two curving lines that just barely stopped beyond my areola. His gaze got stuck there, a slight twitch to his jaw indicating he hadn't failed to notice and I had to bite my lip to keep from smiling. I made no move to zip up.

His irises flew upward and made another wild, quick

movement when they rested on my bottom lip between my teeth.

Note to self: Biting lips drives Jayden wild.

He coughed and focused pointedly on the screen. "Tell me about this king, then."

I did, giving him the name, explaining how he'd happened upon us—giving Alanna credit for saving me and adding my theory that maybe the elves really *did* try not to hurt anyone—and told him as much as I could think of. Alarik and Alanna alike being overly curious about my powers and whether or not I could still use them—which I'd only figured out later on had to have been because they'd thought I might have lost them. And how Alarik himself and perhaps half the battalion had lost their ability to produce those vines, I presumed because of proximity to Alanna.

I left out all hints of Alarik's rather overt interest in me for reasons beyond my powers. At least, I *thought* I wasn't imagining that. I did tell him Alarik had grabbed me by the arm with the seeming intent of taking me somewhere —probably back to his home on the other side of those portals.

"Why?" asked Jayden, leaning back in his chair. He grabbed a pen off the desk and put the cap between his lips, spinning the writing utensil slowly between his upper and bottom teeth. Jayden did sometimes have an oral fixation like that.

I wondered if his oral fixation translated to oral talents in other spheres.

If he had a sexual partner *anywhere*, he was damn good at keeping that little secret. I knew for a fact he hadn't slept with anyone in Veras, and he really was almost never elsewhere without a member of his team beside him.

I wondered how he kept his urges in check for that

long—it'd been *years*. I'd have collapsed from desire onto my bed, my hands running up and down between my thighs as thoughts of Jayden's tongue in their place overwhelmed me.

I'd done that more than a few times, even *with* regular doses of Nash inside me. And fucking Nash was no chore, believe me.

"Aurora?" called Jayden. I snapped back to the moment, clutching the corner of the table harder, and I realized I'd been standing on my toes and biting my lips again, thinking about pleasuring myself to the new memories I had of him changing this morning.

I blew out a breath. "I don't know. To see if my powers were indeed gone? They seemed unsure whether or not this princess' nullification power would work on a human. On a Natch."

A flash of panic drove across Jayden's face. "But they didn't know *what* your particular powers were," he said. "They just happened upon a Natch and would have taken whoever it was for their experimentation, correct?"

I nodded, though I couldn't say for sure that the second part was true. Maybe their evil king was a huge flirt and would have touched any woman that way. Would have looked at any woman as if he wanted to possess her, as if he wholeheartedly desired her.

Shivering again, I moved around the table to get a better look at what Jayden had entered into his computer.

Coughing, Jayden moved his head slightly so my breasts wouldn't flush up against his head. It hadn't been my intention, but damn if I weren't disappointed he'd noticed and made efforts to keep the contact from occurring.

"Is this accurate?" he asked, his eyes so focused on the

screen, they didn't even blink. "Anything else to add? Anything at all. Any detail could prove important."

I opened my mouth, about to tell him about Alarik's flirtations, but I didn't want that hanging between us. There was already Nash and... He-Who-Shall-Not-Be-Thought-Of-By-Name between us. There was already his stubborn desire to remain my "mentor," as if he'd raised me himself instead of meeting me at eighteen. Besides, the king couldn't have meant much by it. He'd just been trying to catch me off-guard. I nodded. "Looks good."

Jayden's eyes rested a moment on my cleavage before he shoved his chair back from the desk and stood, closing the laptop screen with such speed, I practically had to jump back to get out of his way. "I'll discuss this with Wade and he can add his theories to his algorithm. When the team arrives home, we'll have a quick debriefing and update them. There's still the matter of Zander and the Renegades' activity today to go over, too." He winced after he said that, his best-friend-turned-enemy probably messing with his mind at the sound of his name.

Did he really have nothing better to do than sit there and think about me and Jayden, hoping to catch one of us thinking a stray thought about him?

"You'd be surprised how often that works," said Zander over the bond. *"The both of you—you can't get me out of your head. I'm flattered, but it can be exhausting."*

I sent daggers over the bond, hoping he'd take a hint.

Jayden was already brushing past me, nodding his excuses, the laptop tucked under his arm.

He stopped halfway to the door. "Aurora, when was your last period?"

That was like a splash of cold water to the face. "What?"

He spun on his heel and pushed the bridge of his

glasses up his nose. "Your last period. Fertility increases at the midway point of the cycle—"

"I *know*. I'm not a prepubescent girl who's yet to have a health class." I wrapped my arms around myself, both intentionally and unintentionally causing my breasts to jut out more. "You know I can't have a baby. Wade told me as much—it's been proven time and time again." Wincing, I bit my lip again, cursing myself for reminding him I'd had plenty of unprotected sex with Nash—neither of us slept with anyone else, despite the open relationship—and had never even had a close call. "Wade said the energy there— inside me, in my uterus or wherever it's strongest—it can't sustain a fertilized egg. That it just vaporizes whatever sperm are in there." I felt a little sick, like I was talking about this kind of stuff with my dad.

Damn it, don't think of him as your dad—that's what he wants you to do. That's why he won't fuck you.

"I know, but..." He tapped the laptop under his other arm, his eyes flitting toward me and then quickly over my shoulder to the bird's nest outside. "You didn't have your powers when you had sex with Nash today."

Oh, god, did this feel weird talking to him about it. It didn't feel weird to talk to Wade or Roulette about it—he was a detached scientist and she was one of my best friends. But I did *not* want to talk to Jayden about fucking Nash, even if Jayden had walked in on us today, even if that was far from the first time.

My mouth opened and a strangled noise came out as my palm went instinctively to my abdomen. *Impossible.* "I, uh—I just finished it," I said, clearing my throat. "So I should be the least fertile in the cycle."

He nodded. "I recommend getting Plan B anyway," he said. "Just to be sure. You and Roulette can have a few hours or..."

I nodded, chewing the inside of my cheek.

He fiddled with the bridge of his glasses again. "Unless you *want* to have a child right now... with Nash..." His voice went quiet.

I shook my head, but it was slow, detached, like I was observing someone else doing it. I'd long ago accepted I wasn't having a child—it hadn't even bothered me because I'd no interest in being a mother when I believed wholeheartedly in giving my all to the team. But I'd so long ago written it off as not happening, that it felt strange —scary—to think otherwise.

Though not only frightening. A little... a little wondrous, too.

"But my powers are back," I said. "Wouldn't they neutralize whatever's potentially going on?" I gestured to my abdomen.

"Maybe," said Jayden. "It's something to run by Wade. But just to be sure." He nodded. I nodded. Damn it, if things weren't awkward. He left the office then, his footsteps echoing down the hallway.

After a moment, I went to follow him, but my hand lingered on the door, my gaze darting to the bookshelf where Zander had first dug his hands into my pants.

"Want to reenact that, darlin'?" Zander's projected form appeared at my side and I startled, then I laughed— only there wasn't any humor in that laugh. Only weariness.

I shut Jayden's office door closed in front of me. He'd be occupied with Wade for long enough for me to deal with this. I just hoped he didn't run back because he forgot something before I had a chance to dismiss this ghostly vision.

"Better lock it this time," he said. "That was our mistake the last time you and I were caught alone in here."

He visibly winced. "I may not agree with everything Jayden does and thinks, but I do agree it wasn't exactly cool of me to attempt to fuck his crush among his most private possessions."

I shoved a finger against the lock, not to take his advice, but to give me a warning if Jayden decided to pop back in before I had a chance to get a handle on the situation.

"I'm not his crush," I said, folding my arms across my chest.

"Keep telling yourself that. You make a great pair. Always denying yourself when it comes to one another." Zander's spectral eyes darted to that very exposed cleavage I'd forgotten about and this time, the heat hit my face almost immediately and I grabbed hold of the zipper to drag it up.

Zander's feather-light projected hand laid on top of mine halfway up. "Don't," he said. "I like it." He grinned like a wolf about to devour his prey. "Always thought Wade's suits could use a bit more flair."

Since his spectral hand had probably a tenth of the weight of his real one, he couldn't stop me from slowly, seductively slowly, zipping it all the way up. I grinned maliciously.

"Tease," he said, his ghost hand going again to my cheek.

I took a step back quickly, putting some distance between us. Not that he couldn't project right beside me again, but he kept a respectful distance. "You never project into Veras HQ," I said, frowning. He couldn't hurt me like this, but I had to know what tricks he had up his sleeve.

He shrugged. "Out of respect for a dear friend," he said. "Besides, no need to spy on you all. You're utterly predictable."

I kept backing up, stopping when the back of my knees clunked up against Jayden's bed. My gaze darted to it, the feeling of Zander's hands up my shirt, under my bra, sending fire down to my groin.

Zander did appear beside me—though he'd probably just had the projection walk. I'd been *that* distracted. "It was shit of me to do to Jayden, but you had to admit, kind of wild." He leaned closer to my ear, whispering, though there was no sense of his breath. "Naughty. I almost wanted us to get caught—but only after we'd been able to complete the deed."

"What the fuck are you doing?" said Jayden then, when he'd walked in on us.

One of Zander's hands was under my shirt, wrapped up around my back and around to cup the side of a breast. The other was clutching one of my ass cheeks, still at that moment sliding down into my wetness.

Jayden stormed into the room and grabbed Zander by both shoulders, tugging on him. "Get off her!"

Zander's grip in both places went loose, sliding out from beneath the baggy sweater and yoga pants that had moments before been halfway down my legs. "All right, all right. Calm down!" He looked from me to Jayden again. Jayden was seething, his hands clutched into fists at his sides. I was in shock, my groin burning with hot, steamy desire, my brain screaming at me that I'd fucked up.

I'd really fucked up. Jayden was my crush, not Zander. Zander was fucking gorgeous and so confident and he knew what he wanted and didn't hesitate to take it, which drove me wild...

Fucking damn it. Which one did I want? And was I throwing Nash out after all the times we'd fucked both for power boosts and for fun?

"She's a child!" screamed Jayden.

64

That got me angry. I jumped to my feet. "What the hell are you talking about? I'm twenty-three!"

Jayden looked as if I'd slapped him. "I just—I mean, we're your teachers. We've known you since you were a child."

Zander laughed. "She was eighteen. And I've never thought of her that way." His eyes traveled up and down Jayden as he put his hands on his hips to add to his cocky swagger. "A woman this fuckably hot—who fucking boosts your power when you make love to her—and you keep telling yourself she's a kid? Grow up, Jayden." He looked me over, his eyes roving from top to bottom. "I've settled for kisses for fucking years out of respect for your wishes, Jayden, but no more. Not if she's willing."

Damn, if I weren't willing... I had to breathe deep to shove away the desire to jump him right then, even in front of Jayden.

He whirled on Jayden. "I'm going to see what her powers can do for me after I've been inside her. And you don't have the right to stop us."

Jayden's face fell, his eyes darting up to Zander and to me. "You said you'd... You said you understood."

"God damn it, Jayden, fuck her if she'll have you"—he turned to me then and gave me a sly wink—"and she will certainly have you, or don't. But don't tell other people what to do. You don't say anything about Flayme fucking her."

Jayden's lips trembled. "He's her age. He joined us two years ago, he hasn't known her since she was a—"

"If you say 'kid' one more time..." Zander threw a finger in Jayden's face.

I felt sick then—nauseous. Embarrassed, surprised, and annoyingly ready to fuck them both in the middle of a heated argument. I excused myself and brushed past them to the hall-way, holding back the hot tears.

Zander had left that night.

Projection-Zander sighed and ran a hand through his dark hair, moving beside me and sitting down atop the bed. I wondered if projections even needed to sit atop beds and if he was lying on one right now wherever he was, focusing on sending his false form to be with me.

"It wasn't just because of you that I left," he said, and he'd probably been reading my mind. "It was the last straw. I'd hoped you'd come with me, but I wanted to get set up first." He gave me a onceover, the magnetic pull of his eyes compelling me to sit beside him. "But I should have known you wouldn't leave him." He stared off toward the window. The mamma bird had left now, the little babies struggling to be heard, but there was no reply.

"Nash, too," I said, eager to reassert myself into this complicated mess. Nash and I made sense. What we had was special. Casual but passionate. It worked. Even if he... He was a *little* more into me than he ought to be if I had these thoughts about other men.

Zander chuckled. "You're just not content to have one man, are you?" His ghostly finger ran across my cheek and under my chin, gently guiding my face to his. I didn't have to obey—his projected fingers were so weak—but I did, the jelly between my legs doing more of the forcing than his finger's movements. "But I understand that, darlin'. I do. With a power like yours, it would be selfish not to share it, to share you... And I don't want you to give up anything your little heart desires. I don't want to hurt you."

Scoffing, I pulled my chin away. "You think starting a rebel group that works directly against Veras wouldn't hurt me?"

He shook his head. "No politics right now, darlin'." He looked back at the bed and patted it. "What do you say?"

I guffawed. Then my face fell. "You're serious."

"We never finished what we started," he said. "And damn, you don't know *how* long I fucking waited for that."

"It won't work on your projection," I said. "The kisses don't work. There's no reason to think that *sex* would. Besides..."

A faltering smile quirked his lips. "You probably wouldn't be satisfied with a ghost of my dick inside you?"

I giggled a little. I couldn't help myself.

"Why don't I watch?" he said. "Put on a show, darlin', and let me help you." His hand grabbed hold of the zipper at my throat.

"You honestly don't care that you won't get a boost?" I asked.

He shook his head and leaned in, his feathery spectral lips dotting lightly across my cheek, my neck. He tugged on the zipper and moved his lips down along the space between my breasts.

I stood, unzipping the suit the rest of the way and removing my arms from it, standing to pull one leg and then the other out of it.

Fuck me, I thought.

"Thatta girl," he said, grinning.

I brushed past him, his chilly form making my legs quake, and lay down on the bed. Closing my eyes, I inhaled the scent of Jayden, pictured him changing at the lockers, remembered his eyes darting at my breasts and my lips, his breath hot on my cleavage as I'd leaned over him.

"Whatever you're doing, it's working," said Zander, his voice low. "Keep it up, darlin'."

I realized my hands had already found their way to my groin. A feathery-light touch between my outer folds made me shake, stretching my foot out to tighten the muscles in my legs and catch hold of the sensation. My eyelids shot open and I saw the ghostly form of Zander going down on me, my brain overwhelmed with the thought of this hunk fucking me, too.

I squeezed my arms tighter on either side of my breasts as I rubbed up and down my sex.

The spectral Zander looked up, biting his lip. "Oh, fuck," he said, gazing up at my chest. "I wish I could fucking taste you. Darlin', I'm *imagining* how you taste and it's driving me insane—"

"Keep going," I breathed. He complied, his head going down again. "Keep going." And for the next few minutes, I forgot about everything—Plan B, devilishly handsome kidnapping elves, Jayden and Zander's fight, Nash's zeal-ousness—and just brought myself to ecstasy, my roguish enemy guiding me along the way.

CHAPTER SIX

"Morning after" pills had their "best by" date right in the title. So after the day—and night—I'd had, the morning after would do. I'd made my way to my own room, flushed with shame of what I'd done in Jayden's bed, and asked Zander not to follow.

I needed some time alone with my thoughts, even if those thoughts contained him far too often. For once, he'd agreed to go a night without making smarmy comments every time my mind drifted to him.

"The least I could do after the beautiful peep show," his projection had offered. If a smack on his spectral shoulder had had any impact, I would have done it to punish him for making light of it.

It hadn't felt light. If anything, it had felt so close to having him in the room near me. I wondered if I would ever have to masturbate alone from now on—what, after experiencing his feather-light assistance in the activity, would be the point?

I felt a wry chuckle cross the bond and I blinked, realizing with a start that just because he'd promised to keep quiet for a bit didn't mean he wasn't "listening" over the bond.

After splashing my face with cold water, I brushed my teeth, my bleary eyes staring back at me in the mirror. My dark brown hair was wild, messy, like a dozen hands had just woven through it.

"*Really?*" came Zander's voice in my head. "*You want a harem of six men now?*"

I pictured daggers. Shooting from my eyes.

"*Right,*" he said over the bond. "*Sorry. Busy day today anyway.*"

Sighing, I hung my toothbrush back on the rack I shared with Roulette and Chastity and spit in the sink. A busy day for the Renegades didn't spell anything but bad news.

I ran my hairbrush through the knotted strands. Apparently, even spectral hands could get it all tangled up.

The old recreation center was smaller than one might think when serving an entire community—I supposed that was why they'd rebuilt across town and sold this property. I shared a fairly large dorm room with Chastity and Roulette, and Nash, Darien, and Wade were in the room beside ours. Wade spent more than half his evenings at a condo downtown with his boyfriend, though, so Darien and Roulette often shacked up together, with Nash getting the short end of the stick and sleeping on the couch in the living room beside the kitchen. Or sometimes Chastity slept there if Nash and I were similarly occupied—then there were the nights Chastity stayed out "with friends." I had no reason to doubt this team had anything but really healthy amounts of sexual activity—everyone except Jayden, that was.

And he would sadly *never* take me up on my offer to fix that.

Wade had a theory he'd once voiced to the group at large—minus Jayden—that our mentor was asexual, in which case he might not be interested in anyone, let alone me. But there were different degrees of asexuality… Like demi-ace. That might explain why Zander had been so insistent Jayden had a crush on me.

I shook my head and finished running my brush through my hair. I had enough going on. And I had enough sexual partners to choose from. I walked back into the room and swapped my pajama sweats for tight jeans and an off-the-shoulder white sweater. No need to look like a scrub just because I felt like one.

Giggles echoed from the hallway as a door opened and shut. I'd recognize that laugh anywhere.

"Rou," I said, meeting her and Darien outside the dorm room door. Both were dressed already—or maybe that was what they'd slept in after changing out of their battle suits following last night's briefing. They looked stunning as usual either way. "I need to go to town," I said. "Come with?"

Her lips pinched as she exchanged a look with her boyfriend. He ran a palm over his scruffy cheek. Tattoos across his fingers spelled out "Lita"—not a former girl-friend, but in honor of his beloved *abuelita*, his deceased grandma who'd lived with his family growing up. She'd been the most supportive member of his family when it came to his Natch powers. "I can wait," he said.

So I'd be messing up a brunch date? No. Heaven knew we all needed more of those.

"Never mind," I said. "Actually, maybe you can help me anyway—" I met Darien's eyes as I grabbed Roulette by the elbow, widening my peepers and hoping he took a hint. "I'll go grab some coffee," he said, giving us some space.

"Thank you," I said. He was a total sweetheart. A little part of me was jealous of Roulette for snagging him, but I was jealous that he got to monopolize my amazing friend, too. They were such a great match.

Roulette's gaze wandered up and down, clearly enjoying watching him go.

I dropped her elbow and leaned closer to whisper. "Do you have any Plan B?"

That got her attention. "Uh, why? Is Chastity asking?"

She might have been the better person to ask, actually, since I didn't think she was on regular birth control like Roulette, but she seemed to have spent the night out with friends.

"No. For me. I, uh—" I opened my mouth to speak, but it went dry. A yawn from behind me almost made me jump out of my skin and I turned to find Nash shirtless, his bare feet sticking out from beneath his flannel pants and padding across the hard floor. "Morning, ladies," he said as he scratched his abdomen. The dark blond fuzz around his belly button leading down to what I knew to be a thick and satisfying member sent butterflies roaring through my stomach.

"Morning," said Roulette. Her lips soured and she jutted her head toward him, arching her eyebrows as if to say, *"Does he know?"*

I tried to shake my head as subtly as possible. Nash still seemed to pick up on it, though, because he kept walking, but his pace slowed and he hovered near the entrance to the men's dorm room, staring at me as he slowly opened the door.

Rolling my eyes, I cupped my hands around my mouth and whispered in Roulette's ear. "Just in case. Jayden thought, well, when I lost my powers yesterday, I might have been able to fertilize eggs normally—"

72

"What?!" Roulette pulled back and shouted.

I hissed at her to keep quiet and she covered her mouth with her hands, muttering, "Sorry" as Nash padded back over to us.

"What's going on?" he asked. It seemed painfully obvious he was trying to keep things casual, but his Adam's apple bobbed as he crossed his arms stiffly against his sculpted chest.

Roulette bit her lip and turned to me. "I don't have any, so yeah, let's go." She laid a gentle hand on my forearm. "I'll get some coffee and we can go."

She pushed between Nash and me to head down the hallway. I turned over my shoulder. "Darien can come with us," I said. "I just need a lift downtown. I can take the bus back since the Vespa is…" I left the rest unsaid. I knew the clean-up team had grabbed it and tossed it in the back of the van, but it would need a lot of work before it was roadworthy again and Wade was far too occupied to bother with it.

Nash pointed his chin in her direction. "Why are you third wheeling on their date? If you need to go somewhere, I can take you in the van if they've got the jeep."

"And leave Wade and Jayden and Chastity if she shows up without a vehicle? No." I shook my head. "It's not that important."

The space between his brows furrowed, and the concerned look made him even sexier, if that were possible. "If it's not that important, what's with all the secrecy?"

"I just… I just don't want everyone to know."

"Just Roulette."

"Yeah… And Jayden, I guess."

That had been the wrong thing to say. He tried not to look hurt, but the way his shoulders slumped gave it away. "Oh," he said, his voice cracking.

"I probably have to tell Wade, too," I said, sighing, "and Roulette will likely tell Darien." *Damn it.* "It's just... Jayden suggested I get some Plan B."

Nash shook his head multiple times. "What is a Plan B?"

Ugh, men. Sometimes they're just too ignorant about things that could lead to eighteen years of child support. "The morning after pill?" I tried.

Realization flooded his features, which relaxed as his jaw gaped open. "For *you*?"

"Yeah..." My throat went dry. "Just as a precaution."

"But you don't *need* birth control," he said. "You can't —" His mouth clamped shut. "Yesterday. When it turned out you'd lost your powers. You and I..."

"Yeah," I said again.

"Then it would be mine," he said, swallowing.

"It *could* not exist. It most likely doesn't exist. Even if I were a Typical, it wouldn't be formed this early on. That's why there are 'morning after' pills to begin with." Suddenly hot, I let out a deep breath and fanned my face with my hands.

Nash took my hands in his, his eyes searching my expression—for what, I didn't know. "But you... you always thought it wasn't going to happen." His voice went quieter. "What if... What if this is your one chance?"

Swallowing, I gasped at the flush that spread out from my core. "Even if I wanted this, there's no guarantee now that I have my powers back that my uterus would be a hospitable environment for an egg—"

"*If* you wanted it?"

Were we really about to have this conversation? "Nash, would you seriously be ready to be a dad right now? With everything we have going on in our lives? What kind of environment would Veras be for a child?"

"We wouldn't have to stay," he said, a tiny muscle on his jaw twitching as he closed his mouth. "We may be Natches, but there are countless of our kind out there, living normal lives."

"No," I said, pulling my hands away and clenching my sweaty palms at my side. My blood ran cold. "I don't— Nash, I don't want to go. I don't want to be a mom. Not now—maybe not ever. I don't know. I'm not even thinking about that right now. And if I ever *did*, I'd be fine with adoption. If I ever got to a point in my life when I want to pack up and retire, walk away from our friends—"

"We wouldn't be *walking* away," he said. "We'd be moving on with our lives. We'd still be in touch, maybe even be on standby if things got really bad, but we could get away from this city, away from the danger caused by these crazy plant elves—"

"There's no running away from this danger, Nash." Shaking my head, I took a step back. "We could run off to the middle of nowhere, but that doesn't mean that the elves would never extend beyond the city's borders. That doesn't mean I could just cook meals and clean house and not worry about my friends on the frontline."

He threw his hands up. "Who said anything about making you into Suzy Homemaker?" Scoffing, he shook his head. "I know you have no interest in marrying me. I wasn't asking that."

"No, you were just asking me to run off with you and raise a child together. What a big difference." I didn't mean to let the sarcasm be so biting in my voice, but it came out anyway.

"And lord knows no one can ask you to give up even the *slightest* chance you might shack up with our team leader someday," snapped Nash.

Of course, Jayden chose that moment to open his office

door—but since he was still some distance down the hall, I doubted he'd heard us. Even so, he was headed our way and I didn't want to continue this conversation within earshot. I didn't even want him to pick up on the roaring tension between Nash and me.

"Fuck you, Nash," I said, though it hurt me to say it. I turned on my heel, yanking my hand away even as Nash grabbed it, his voice going softer.

"Angel, I'm sorry. I shouldn't have—"

But I pulled harder, heading to the kitchen without a word.

THOUGH I'D PROMISED ROULETTE AND DARIEN I'D BE OUT OF their hair the moment we parked, Roulette insisted on coming into the drug store with me. Darien waited in the jeep out front, chatting with some friends from back home on Skype.

"Did you tell him what we're here for?" I asked in a hushed whisper as we got in line for the pharmacy.

"No, but he's not stupid," she said. She picked up a box of pain relievers that touted "strong enough to work on Natch pain" and raised an eyebrow. Wade had warned us away from any products claiming to work on Natches in particular. Our body chemistries were basically human and our powers added and took away different things in our DNA. There was no way to manufacture something for all of us. And since we were only about twenty percent of the population—so far—I wondered why any company even thought it profitable to tweak their products to attempt to appeal to us in particular. Especially since it probably turned away more Typicals than it gained in new Natch customers. "I assume he figures we're not all cloak and dagger about running to the store for tampons," she murmured. "Plus, with us all learning about the power-sucking princess…"

The man in front of us glanced over his shoulder, a scowl dragging down his lips, and I elbowed Roulette to get her attention.

"What?" she said, putting the box of pain reliever back on the shelf. "Do you have a problem with powers, *sir*?"

Wincing, I cradled my forehead.

The man muttered something unintelligible and faced forward.

"That's what I thought," spat Roulette.

"Rou," I said quietly, "let's just get what we need without brawling with half the county—"

If she had a retort, though, I didn't hear it over the rumble outside. The bottles and boxes on the shelves on either side of us shook and scattered to the floor.

"Oh, *shit*!" I did hear her scream that.

The man in front of us covered his head with his arm and ducked, cursing.

When the rumble went quiet, the lights overhead flickering, the murmurs and gasping from everywhere in the building settled into my bones.

"Damn you fucking Natches," began the man in front of us, sitting upright and dropping his hands. His shiny forehead glistened and he jostled his glasses as he went to wipe the sweat away.

"It's the Nelians!" cried a woman from the front of the store. "A giant vine just passed by—everyone, evacuate!"

A child began bawling and Roulette's head snapped toward the sound, her hand extended. The man who'd been blaming Natches narrowed his eyes and shoved her aside, scrambling to his feet to head for the exit.

"Asshole!" shouted Roulette. I helped an elderly

woman stand, my leg muscles straining with the effort, and Roulette scurried toward the crying sound.

"Aurora!" she shouted, waving me over a few aisles down. The pharmacists and techs bulldozed past the old woman and me, though one stopped to help me support her. "Go," he said, noticing my friend waving me down.

I nodded and left her to him, skidding past packages of adult diapers to join Roulette. The kid at her feet—a boy probably no older than eight or so—had a bone sticking out of his arm, an overturned shelf next to him perhaps the culprit of the disaster.

"Fuck," I said, looking for a parent anywhere. All I found were streaks of the kid's blood.

Roulette was already pointing her hand at the ground. "Let's do this," she shouted amidst the chaos. The ground continued to shake as there was another rumble.

"God damn it," I swore. "Why the hell are they launching an attack two days in a row?"

Nelians downtown today, I sent to Zander through the bond, quickly picturing his head over my groin and hoping he was thinking about me. *I'm at a pharmacy. I don't know where they are, but we're definitely feeling the effects here.*

"Shit," he said back. *"On our way."*

I focused on the here and now. Roulette let out a gasp as her hand blasted a hole in the floor. "Dammit," she said, closing her hand and turning it off. "Again!" Same problem. She swore harder as the boy's cries grew louder. Finally, her hand shot out a white light and nothing shattered. "Yes!" she shouted, pivoting back toward the child. He flinched, maybe thinking she was about to send a hole through him, but she directed it at his arm. Slowly, the bone started moving and the boy let out a bloodcurdling scream.

"I know, baby," said Roulette. "It'll hurt, but then I'll fix it. Rora—"

She didn't have to ask. I took her face between my hands and shifted it toward me, planting a five-second kiss on her lips.

Her hand glowed brighter and I let go. The healing went really fast then, the kid screaming as his bones locked into place, his sinews mended and his skin connected. Finally, he gasped, the tears stopping.

"Fuck yeah!" said Roulette, jumping up and closing her palm, shutting off the light.

I grabbed her by the arm. "Let's get him out of here," I said, just as a shrieking woman ran toward us, almost losing her balance in the blood.

"Henry!" She took him in her arms.

That took care of that.

"Mom, these girls saved me—" started the boy, but his mom was totally ignoring him, dragging him to his feet by the elbow and making their way to the front of the store.

For a moment, I wondered if he'd bother to tell her we'd practically made out to do it, too.

"Come on," said Roulette. On instinct, she lifted her wrist to her mouth, but without her battle suit on, she was missing her comm.

"Babe!" shouted Darien from the doorway. We hurried to meet him, Roulette falling into his arms and flinching as a giant vine soared past the window. "*Shit!*" he cried as Veras' jeep tumbled over with the movement.

"We're not headed home until this is over anyway," said Roulette, her brows scrunched together, her face resolute.

"I called it in," said Darien, tugging on her to leave the store. "Chastity is closest, and the others are on their way."

We hit the street then, the rumble of the vines moving

downtown louder and more perilous beneath our feet—as were the echoes of the screams as people ran away.

The fact that no one had yet died in one of these attacks was a miracle. Benevolent elf princess or not, they got no credit for that in my book.

"There!" shouted Roulette, pointing down the street to a spot several blocks away. An elf stood at the corner, her arms wide, vines growing outward from them.

"The fucker," said Darien, dropping his hands from Roulette's waist. He started sprinting, shooting ice at the vine along the way.

"Boost me," said Roulette, turning toward me. I did, quickly pecking her on the lips before we started running and she aimed her open palm at the vine, her shoulder slamming into a retreating man and both completely ignoring the encounter. "Damn it!" she said when the vine started blossoming flowers instead of getting blown to bits. The luck of the draw had been a healing blast, not a destructive one. Apparently, her healing powers even worked on flora, and with my boost, those flowers were curling outward fast.

Very fast.

We both dodged as a bright purple blossom jutted out our way, Roulette tumbling and skidding on her butt.

I glanced down the street, but Darien was blocks ahead, caught in a battle with the elf woman. His ice had at least stopped her from growing the vines further.

Roulette's healing blast certainly hadn't, though.

"Fuck, fuck, fuck!" said Roulette, flicking her hand open again. This time the light burned through the blossom practically about to absorb us, shredding it to pieces that curled into ashes. "*Yeah!*" she shouted, clearly enjoying this.

I rushed up to her and grabbed her under both elbows,

grunting as I lifted her to a standing position even as her hand kept blasting a hole through the blossom clear into the vine. She pivoted, taking that destructive power down the length of the plant, eating away at it and stopping just short of blasting through to the buildings and retreating pedestrians on the other side.

Then all of a sudden, the light emanating from her hand went out, the destruction of the vine halted.

"What's wrong?" I asked. Even if her boost from my lips had died out, she still should have been able to dole out *some* destructive power.

"I... I don't know." She flexed her fingers and shook her hand again. Nothing.

My blood ran cold. I dropped my hands from her, looking around, searching—

The elf princess Alanna peeked out from around the corner of an alleyway behind us.

"Hello," she said quietly, and I heard her despite the chaos unfolding nearby.

Roulette looked gobsmacked. "This is the power-sucking princess you were talking about?"

Alanna stepped forward, removing the hood of her cloak from her head. "You know I'm a princess?"

"I told her," I said. "Remember me? Yesterday? Coffee shop?"

A cry rang out from the north and Roulette and I both looked to see Darien staring at his hands, the elf woman he'd been battling doing the same—neither using their powers. The elf recovered first, though, and spun, kicking Darien in the gut.

"Babe!" shouted Roulette, but before she could so much as take two steps, Alanna rushed in front of her, crouching down in one fluid movement, her cloak billowing to the side. She extended a fist straight into

Roulette's stomach and Rou collapsed, spewing bile from her throat and gasping in pain.

"Rou!" I scrambled to her side like a fool and Alanna did a spin kick similar to that of her elven comrade and I just narrowly missed it, falling backward and slamming the back of my head on the sidewalk.

"Uh, shit!" I said, rolling over and feeling dizzy.

As I rolled, I blinked and Darien on the sidewalk down the block came into focus, the elf woman straddling him.

Fucknuts, I thought. *Help!* I pictured Zander, but I didn't know if he could hear me in the nullifying princess' vicinity. I didn't know whether or not his powers could reach through.

A spark of light resounded overhead, and I blinked. Chastity. Down the block in the other direction.

But the light cut out as she tried to aim it down, Alanna somehow protecting herself with her nullification powers in a sphere-like shape over her head.

"Chastity!" I groaned, my voice too quiet as I sat back up. I put a hand to the back of my head and pulled it away to find it dotted with a little blood. I dragged myself over to Roulette. "Chastity is here," I whispered.

"Stay down," said Alanna, reaching for small knives she kept in sheaths on her belt. "If you don't want to get hurt anymore, stay put."

She walked around to the other side of us, putting herself between us and the approaching Chastity, her knives at the ready for close combat. She didn't seem afraid of Chastity's light powers at all—nor, I supposed, should she have been. Chastity kept blasting it straight at her, only to find it fizzling out partway. My teammate hesitated at the end of the block.

She'd probably figured out that if she took another step, she'd lose her ability to produce her power at all for around an hour. But she was a hand-to-hand combat master. *Come on, Chastity*, I thought.

"Darien," said Roulette, her voice cracking.

I whipped around, ignoring the way my head pounded at the movement. Multiple elves were picking up a slumped-over Darien, dragging him away.

"What the—?" Then I remembered. Alarik had wanted to take *me* just yesterday. And a depowered Darien might serve just as well for whatever they'd had in mind.

Roulette struggled to her feet and Alanna spun around. "Stay *put*."

Chastity roared, running toward us and spinning to kick Alanna, but Alanna spun right back, her leg flying over my head and narrowly missing Roulette's back. Rou stumbled forward and a man darted out from beneath the remnants of the giant vine beside us, righting her.

"Alanna, I asked you to stick to the north," he barked, his voice low and sultry.

I did a double take. Alarik. Of course.

Ignoring him, Alanna cried out as her knife soared over Chastity's head. My stomach plummeted in relief as my teammate bent down and stuck her leg out in an attempt to swipe the princess off her feet.

Roulette seemed woozy and she tried to push Alarik away, but his grip on her shoulders tightened as his gaze roved beyond his sister in combat to me on the sidewalk.

"*Aurora*," he said, both curious and seductive.

Fuck me. I had to squeeze my thighs together to tame the blood flow headed for my apex and focus on anything but his beautiful eyes.

"Let her go," I snapped, stumbling up to my feet.

A boom echoed from somewhere far down the street and a spout of water soaring above the building rooftops let me know Kouta was down there—most likely with Zander in tow.

Silence on the bond. If he was thinking about me, his powers weren't reaching me.

"Curses," said Alarik, looking over his shoulder. "Alanna, that's enough. We've got one of them already." He looked down at Roulette in his arms and then at me. "Let's take at least these two if you can't secure that one."

Chastity roared then, jutting her leg upward in a kick. I really owed it to my teammates to get better at the type of fighting even Typicals could do since I had little to offer otherwise.

But Alanna jumped back, turning her dodge into a feint and spinning back around, kicking Chastity in the side, sending her tumbling, and knocking her out cold.

"Chastity!" I screamed, stumbling toward her. But Alanna flicked her knives back into her sheaths and grabbed me by both arms. She was stronger than me, and no matter how I struggled, I couldn't get free. Two other elves appeared from beneath the remainder of the vine, ducking to get around the mess of it Roulette had made. "Your Majesty," said one. He stopped, looking at a petal from a blossom that had grown from Roulette's unintended healing trick. The petal alone was as big as his head. He picked it up. "How…?"

Alanna pinched her lips. "It was the one you have, brother. I saw before I got too close. She made it grow in one moment, then destroyed it the next."

Roulette groaned and used what appeared to be the last of her strength to try to get out of Alarik's grip, but it was no use. He studied her. "Take it with us," he said, nodding toward the elf with the petal. "Help Alanna—"

A blast of wind skirted down the street, dissipating as it seemed to hit that invisible, block-long sphere around

Alanna. Torynt. Alanna spun us both around, and sure enough, Torynt, Lila, Kouta, and Zander alike paraded down the street straight at us at a slow gait. The entire team of Renegades.

"We have to go," growled Alarik. His lips turned down as he looked at his sister. "Too many of us are infected to fight."

"I can nullify them too," she said, and I used her momentary distraction to try breaking free again. No dice. She just gripped harder. She laughed. "We know it works, brother. The evidence is all around us."

"These are enough," he snapped. "We retreat!"

I could see Zander stop a couple of blocks over, extending a hand out beside him to order his team to cease its movements. They watched him and he focused, staring straight down the street at me. Probably trying to reach me through our bond or project—but neither was taking.

One of the elves came over to take me from Alanna as the other went to assist Alarik with Rou. "Be careful with that one," he said over his shoulder toward us. "I don't want her left behind—"

A thunderous noise shook the skies overhead.

Zander was pointing up and Torynt and Kouta were both shooting their elemental powers up in an arch, high, high above us—above where Alanna's nullification powers could apparently access.

That's my boy, I thought. I wanted to holler and pump my fist.

"What is that…?" asked Alarik as the other elf took a weakened, slouching Roulette from him. His features morphed into clear distaste.

"It can't hurt us," started Alanna, but the tsunami spun, hitting the water tower atop an apartment building.

It creaked. "Roots and sediment," she breathed. Both she and the elf beside her looked up. "Run!" she screamed.

Yanking away, I bolted in the direction opposite where they were dragging Roulette, cursing myself for letting her go, but rushing to Chastity's prone body, hoping against hope she was okay.

"Chas!" I started. The elves had already begun running in the opposite direction.

"Leave her!" Alanna's voice cried.

"*No!*" said Alarik, but whatever else he said, I couldn't hear as the water silo let out a final groan and tipped, water sloshing.

I couldn't be distracted, though. I put shaking fingers along Chastity's neck. A pulse. I slipped my arm around her, trying to drag her down the road. I had to somehow get on my feet and flip her over my shoulder—

"Aurora! Move!" snapped Zander from beside me. His ghostly projection had broken through. Alanna must have been out of range—must not have ever passed close enough to him to take his powers away entirely.

"I can't!" I screamed. "Chastity—"

Lila popped into existence beside us, flesh-and-blood Lila. She could teleport to any place she could see.

"Get them—now!" screamed projection-Zander.

She wrapped one arm around my shoulder and slid the other between the concrete and Chastity's back. Water started pouring from the skies, rushing over my face like a waterfall, and in a blink, we were gone.

I was panting even when we landed down the block, clear of the impact. The sound of the water tower falling to the asphalt resonated in my ears, the debris floating into the air already surging our way.

"Again," snapped Lila, hugging us both closer. We

appeared at the end of another block, much farther from the impact.

Soaked to the bone, I breathed in and out, so close to hyperventilating.

"Relax," said Lila, annoyance coloring her tone. "We're clear." She let us both go and I cradled Chastity. Damn it, we needed Roulette. And *she* needed us.

A van squealed around the corner, trapped behind a barricade of cars abandoned by their drivers when this whole thing had started.

"Veras!" I said, a mixture of elation and relief surging within me.

Lila stood, frowning.

Projection-Zander appeared beside us. "Lila," he said.

She growled. "I know, boss." She shook her head, rolling her eyes. Then she placed her hands on my shoulders and we blinked out of existence again.

CHAPTER SEVEN

I DIDN'T HAVE MUCH TO FIGHT BACK WITH, EVEN WHEN AT A hundred percent. Dizzy from my head wound and overwhelmed with everything we'd just been through, I didn't stand a chance of fighting back. A couple of teleportations down the road, past that disaster site again, and I was right beside Kouta, Torynt, and Zander—*real* Zander. Flesh-and-blood Zander I hadn't been this close to in a year.

"They're gone," he said to Lila, completely ignoring me. If I'd had the energy, I would have snapped at him for that.

She nodded and shoved me forward against Kouta, who caught me in his muscular arms.

"Hey," snapped Zander. "Be gentle with our guest!"

"Sorry, boss," she said, smacking her lips and tapping her toes.

"Your *guest*?!" I began, my heart pounding. "Zander, if you think I'm coming with you—"

"Put her in the back seat," he said, and Kouta dragged me toward a Dodge Charger I knew they'd taken to crime scenes. Inconspicuous, they weren't.

Torynt opened the back door and Kouta shoved me toward it. I stuck my legs out to press against the door and the area above the wheel well, trying to stop him from shoving me inside.

"Now that's not nice," said Zander, grabbing hold of my leg and pulling it down. He frowned. "See? You got scuff marks on the car."

Spitting at the vehicle, I sneered at him. "Fuck your car."

The lascivious grin on Zander's face might have meant that had turned him on.

"You know it did, darlin'," he said over the bond.

My legs went weak.

Kouta used the distraction to shove me inside, pushing me over to sit beside me. Before I could scramble out the other door, Torynt got in on that side and squished me, Zander taking the driver's seat and Lila the passenger's.

The wayward leader readjusted the rearview mirror to look at us and then pressed the button to start up the ignition. "Buckle up," he instructed.

Huffing, I crossed my arms as everyone else obeyed.

"I mean it, darlin'," he said.

Kouta and Torynt exchanged a look and between them they buckled my belt across my abdomen.

"All right," said Zander. He shifted the car into reverse, rested an arm around Lila's seat, and strained his neck to look behind him. I opened my mouth to say something, but his eyes were focused above me as he stepped on it, the Dodge Charger's tires squealing backward as we reached outrageous speeds.

THEY DIDN'T EVEN *TRY* TO CONCEAL THE RENEGADES' BASE OF operations from me. Then again, by the state of the place, they weren't the type to stay in one hideout long.

"There's a shower at the end of the upstairs hallway," said Zander, throwing a pastel pink bath towel at me. "Though the master bedroom has a bigger one—and a Jacuzzi tub."

Lila parked her butt on a giant sectional couch, kicking off her shoes and resting her sock-covered feet atop a coffee table cluttered with stacks of outdoors-themed magazines and a TV remote. She grabbed one of the magazines and flipped through it, her face never once twitching or revealing any sort of actual interest in the activity.

"Where are we?" I asked. Kouta literally bumped into me as he padded down the hallway into a kitchen. Torynt—a guy we used to *stop* from causing havoc before Zander had gone all offshoot on us—bounded up the stairs two at a time.

I was sore, filthy, and worried beyond measure. But I had to laugh in disbelief at our surroundings. A McMansion in the midst of a quaint little suburb.

"Did I not mention we're a fan of Airbnb?" asked Zander. "Never stay in one place for too long with a team of Natches on our tail, right?"

"And you can afford this?" I shook my head. "You know what? Never mind. I really don't care." I shoved the towel back at his chest. "And you can shove your shower. My friends were kidnapped, injured—my team has to be wondering what's going on. I'm leaving."

Zander moved to stand between me and the front door. "You're not our prisoner."

"*Good*," I said, laying a hand on his chest and trying to shove him aside. "I got confused for a minute there," I snapped dryly.

"What are you going to do?" he asked. "Walk home?"

"If I must." I patted my pocket for the phone that I'd apparently lost who-knew-where during that battle. A throaty exhale escaped my lips.

"You were going to call a Lyft, weren't you?"

"Or a friend," I snapped. "To check in with them and see how Chastity is and if they know anything about Roulette and Darien—"

Zander's eyes glazed over then and his muscles stiffened as his brow narrowed. He was focusing on his telepathic bond—with Jayden, presumably. He chuckled. "Oh, boy, is *he* worried about you," he said. "I told him I had you, that you weren't taken along with the other two by those elves." He went quiet again. "He assured me Chastity will make a full recovery, even without Roulette to rely on, and—" He cut himself short.

I gave him my best "spit it out" look.

The corner of his mouth twerked upward. "He wants you home, darlin'," he said. "But I thought that went without saying."

Glancing around where we were standing, my heart thundered in my chest at the thought of being "home" in this cozy abode with a man like Zander—

A crash in the kitchen was followed by Kouta cursing and then shouting, "It's okay. Just dropped the frying pan." Though neither Zander nor Lila had flinched.

Kouta had never been fleet of foot. Nash used to joke that it was because Kouta's watery powers made his hands slippery. That wasn't true as far as I knew. Then again, how *would* I know? I'd done the kiss boosts with Kouta but had never gone further.

What was it about Nash that had made me choose him to go all the way with? Besides the fact that he was defi-

91

nitely willing and he was hot and he so often made me smile?

Okay, that explained everything.

"So, were you going...?" Zander stepped aside, though his muscles were tense, and I wondered if I actually brushed past him if he would reach out to pull me back.

It was quiet in my head despite thinking about him—and from the way his eyes roved over the length of my body, he was clearly thinking about me.

"It's quiet in there," he said, lightly tapping the top of my head.

I blew out a breath. "Actually, I'm thinking about you right now—I think I'm still affected by Alanna's powers."

He frowned. "Alanna? That elf woman who had like a bubble of negation around her?"

"You caught on quick to that," I said. "Nice thinking with the water tower. Other than putting Chastity and Roulette and me in danger."

Running a hand through his hair, he winced. "I wouldn't have let any of you get hurt. Any more than you already were."

Tsking, I filled him in on what we'd discovered about Alanna and her powers—even about Alarik. Well, minus all the come-hither vibes the elf had been throwing my way.

The enemy of my enemy was my friend and also my friend turned enemy and all that.

"You didn't tell me any of that last night," he said huskily.

Dammit. The vessels in my cheeks were about to burst. Had that really only been a night ago?

He shrugged and dangled the frilly towel back at me. "But we were otherwise occupied, I know."

Kouta let out a "hoo-yah!" as something sizzled from the kitchen and the fire alarm started beeping.

"S'okay!" he shouted. "Just forgot to switch on the fan."

Chuckling, Zander shook his head. "He's a klutz, but he's a good cook. Stay for dinner? Then I'll give you a lift back myself… if that's what you choose. It'll give you time to get your powers back and boost your energy."

Chewing on my bottom lip, I snatched the towel from him. Knowing Chastity was okay was a relief, but Roulette and Darien…

"You can't find your friends in the next hour," he said quietly. "Not if the elves took them."

"Wade…"

"Is probably trying to figure out their portals, right?" He nudged me with his elbow. "And unless he lets you kiss or fuck him—which, stick in the mud that he is, I don't picture him having evolved his position on—there's not much you can do to help him. Besides, you can't even do that right now."

I took a deep breath and let it out, feeling all the exhaustion flooding out my body with it. I grabbed the towel from Zander and shuffled silently up the stairs, trying to ignore the smarmy look he shot me as I passed him.

WHEN I STEPPED OUT OF THE SHOWER, A NEW SET OF CLOTHES was waiting for me, which I had to assume had come from Lila, either on Zander's orders or on the very off-chance she felt like being obliging herself. My own outfit was dirtied and ripped beyond repair, but I might have preferred it to the way Lila's navy-blue leggings and workout tank top clung to me like a second skin. Lila was taller than me—lither. And though the leggings stretched to accommodate my round ass and thicker thighs, my rack was half-spilling out of the front of the tank. It didn't help that they had socks, but no bra or panties for me. I supposed I wouldn't have fit in hers.

Zander could hardly take his eyes off the bulge at the top of the tank top all dinner—even Torynt and Kouta threw a look or two my way. Lila spared one glance and rolled her eyes, focusing instead on cradling a glass of red wine and sipping from it.

Kouta had put together a three-course meal culminating in maple-glazed chicken that left my full and satisfied stomach jealous that he'd ever left us and stuck us with Rice-A-Roni and Hungry-Man meals. As if having his cooking skills on the team was more important than him not committing crimes.

"I'm stuffed," I said, patting my belly. My fullness was soon forgotten when a shot of fire raged upward from my groin when I caught sight of Zander slowly and methodically licking cake off the tongs of his fork, his tongue moving in circles in echo of the feather way his projected self had done to my nether regions the night before. I shivered.

"Oh, you're back in my head," he said over the bond. *"Welcome home, darlin'."*

I bolted to my feet and started stacking my empty plates. "It was great, Kouta," I said, a wary smile flitting across my lips.

Torynt stood, letting out a belch and scratching his scalp through his disheveled sandy-blond hair. "I got it," he said, taking the plates from me. "My turn to clean, Sweet Lips."

"It's Succubus Lips," corrected Zander. "I picked the name for her."

My lips puckered.

Torynt snickered as he retreated to the kitchen and I clenched my suddenly-empty hands at my side. "Okay, well, it's been real, but I think my powers are back by now, so I'm going to get going…"

Snorting, Lila pushed back from the table and danced her fingers over Kouta's shoulders, her wine glass still in her other hand. "And here I thought we wouldn't be the only ones filling these hallways with moans and groans tonight." She took another sip of wine. "Meet me upstairs?" she said huskily in Kouta's ear.

He didn't have to be asked twice. Pushing his chair back and grabbing the wine glass from her hand, he set the glass down and embraced her, putting his lips to hers.

She giggled and slid her hand through his, dragging him toward the hallway and up the stairs.

Zander's eyebrows arched as he put down his fork and wiped his fingers. "You have to excuse them," he said. "They get rather worked up after a battle."

Grunting, I nodded. It had been no surprise to me that they'd gone off with Zander as a pair. They'd been an item since their time with Veras.

As promised, the sound of Lila's moans pierced through the air even from this distance, the only other sound the running of the faucet water from the kitchen and the clink of dishes being loaded into the dishwasher.

"You're welcome to stay," said Zander, pushing his chair back and standing. His smile grew mischievous. "Kouta doesn't usually last that long from all auditory evidence," he added. "Shouldn't be long now before they grow quiet."

Lila's voice grew louder and she called out her lover's name.

The skin on my palms grew clammy as I pictured the way I'd had to bite my tongue last night to keep from calling out myself.

"Yes, but would you have called my name or Jayden's?" asked Zander, clearly having been in my head but voicing his response out loud. He tried to keep his tone playful, but his voice cracked at his former best friend's name.

Torynt came back in from the kitchen, whistling. We didn't speak as he picked up more of the plates, plunking utensils in glasses and pinching them together with a finger in each. He tittered as his eyes darted from me to Zander and back. "So have you, like, asked her yet?"

Zander shot him a withering look and Torynt shrugged his shoulders, as if to say "my bad," and retreated back to the kitchen.

Lila let out one final, satisfied roar.

"Ask me what?" I demanded in the near-silence afterward—Torynt's soft whistle and clanking notwithstanding.

Zander's fingers moved over his mouth, drawing attention to the five-o'-clock shadow that looked *amazing* on him. "We've never done a full boost, you and I. Just kisses."

"And?" I asked, putting my all into clearing my mind of all desires to follow through with that.

No dice. He chuckled, making my heart race.

"Just a kiss makes me able to hear thoughts from people I haven't bonded with," he said, ignoring the silent, wordless exchange between us. "And I can project clear across the world. What could I do with your full boost?"

"What do you mean?" I asked, but a thought struck

96

me. "You could… project across worlds? Like to this Nelia place the elves say they come from?"

He gripped the back of the chair beside me. "Maybe," he said. "It's just a theory."

My hand went shaky at his proximity. "And you could try speaking with Roulette or Darien?" I asked. "People you've never bonded with, across another dimension?"

"I could try," he said, swallowing visibly. "Then maybe have Wade run tests on my mind while I'm talking to them or projecting there—see if he can find some way to breach the connection in physical space."

Some of that went right over my head, but I got the gist of it. "Wade can never figure out when they'll appear next," I said, thinking aloud. "He says the portals are too volatile, always changing…" I spun to face Zander. "You'd call a truce for this?"

He let go of the chair and gestured at himself with both hands. "Hey, I'm always willing to have a truce with my fellow Natches. It's *you* guys who're the aggressors."

I rolled my eyes and bit back a comment.

"But I don't see the point in giving them false hope," he said.

"What do you mean?"

"I don't want to drop you off and float the idea past Wade and Jayden—I sure as hell don't want to float it past Jayden. He'll shoot it down before we even try. Because he tries to hang his misbegotten principles on my shoulders."

"So you're saying—"

Before I could so much as blink, Zander had put both his arms on either side of me and stepped forward, guiding me backward until I was flush against the dining room wall. One hand rested above my head against the flowery wallpaper, the other traced a line around the edges of my too-small tank top, resting at the line where

97

my breasts pressed together. "I say we should see if it works before I take you back to Veras HQ." His voice practically rumbled, his breath tickling the top of my head. My knees were weakening, threatening to take me sliding all the way down to the floor.

"Oh, okay, gotcha. Sorry about that." Torynt's voice broke through the moment and he started whistling again as his footsteps carried him away.

My head turned on instinct to get a glance at the disturbance, but Zander's fingers jumped from my breast to my chin, directing my face back to his.

Our eyes locked, and for once, despite thinking about him and how much I needed to jump him, my mind was utterly silent.

His lips pressed against mine—soft at first, then hungrier, more demanding.

I leaned up, knocking his hand off my chin so I could grab the back of his head between my fingers. He felt so *solid*, so real, the softness of his hair such a shock after being used to the spectral fraction of his touch.

It'd been too long.

I kept gasping for air too quickly, the moments our lips pressed together, his tongue exploring my mouth, not lasting long enough.

He pulled back, the smile on his face like a kid in a candy store. "The kisses definitely work again," he said, his eyes fiery. "I feel like I could go for a stroll along the French Riviera."

"Not without me, you're not," I said, pulling his head back for another kiss. "I've always wanted to go to Europe. Your projected form isn't getting there before me."

Chuckling, he pulled away from the wall and took my hand in his. I nodded, and though I expected him to lead me to a bedroom by the hand like Lila had with

Kouta minutes earlier, he instead tugged me to him, bending to slip an arm under my knees and the other behind my back, cradling me like a bride on her wedding day.

It made my insides melt. "You're *not* going to carry me up a flight of stairs safely—"

But we were off, him bounding up the stairs practically two at a time, seemingly effortlessly. I supposed he still worked out like a bodybuilder—his muscles were testament enough to that.

We arrived at a door at the end of the hall and I thought he'd put me down, but he kicked it down, causing me to both gasp and giggle.

"You're going to damage this house," I said as he carried me over the threshold. "And it's not yours."

"Thank you for the warning, Miss Building Inspector." He kicked the door closed behind us, louder than he'd opened it, as if in purposeful defiance of my chastising.

I grinned. "I'm not the one paying."

He carried me across the room and tossed me playfully atop the king-sized bed's duvet. I bounced and laughed, though I cut myself short when a pang of guilt shot through me at the thought of Roulette and Darien out there, suffering.

"What's wrong?" asked Zander, his hands frozen at the clasp of his pants.

"Rou," I said. "I can't—I shouldn't enjoy this when she and Darien are out there—"

Zander leaned over me and placed a gentle finger over my lips. "This is to help them," he said. "I won't lie and say I didn't want it otherwise, but this seriously could help."

"Doesn't mean I should *enjoy* it," I said quietly.

He put his other hand down beside me and nibbled on

my ear. "Don't be like that," he whispered as he pulled away.

My groin grew wetter, my body revving up with a shot of ecstasy moving up and outward, and I closed my eyes, letting him spread kisses along the side of my neck, my clavicle, down to my cleavage.

He paused and I heard rustling, the presence of his body leaving mine.

My eyes shot open, feeling his absence even before I knew what was going on. He wasn't standing in front of me getting ready. He was walking away.

My hand reached out for him, grasping the air.

His lips curled up into a cocky smile as he glanced over his shoulder, his bare feet—he must have taken his socks off while my eyes had been closed—slapping into the bathroom. "Hang tight, darlin'. I have an idea."

He vanished behind the open door leading to the bathroom and I jolted up on the bed. Then the sound of running water filled the air.

"Hang tight," he called out, his voice resounding. "Let's take a bath."

Screw the bath, I tried sending over the bond. *I want you inside me.*

Laughter echoed over the mental bond between us.

A few minutes passed and, sure he wasn't coming back, I sauntered over to the bathroom, cupping a hand around the edge of the door. I bit my lip as my stomach went weightless at the sight of a bare-naked Zander in front of me, his sculpted ass looking as fine as something chiseled out of marble.

He spun around, smirking. "You came early."

Running my free hand down my thigh, I tried not to go with the pun and tell him I was in danger of just that. His penis hung flaccidly—thick, long, and in need of my lips around it—and at that thought, his face colored and it started getting stiff.

"*Okay*," he said, breathing out hard and turning to flip off the faucet. He dipped a hand in the water and shook it out, nodding. "It's ready."

I walked in and started peeling off the tank top.

"Uh-uh," he said, meeting me halfway. His hand shot out to cover mine. "You just relax. Let me do everything."

"Even undress me…?"

"*Especially* undress you."

A flutter soared through my chest and I let my hands go limp. The sweet smell of lavender hung in the steamy air.

Zander lifted me by the waist and placed me on the edge of the Jacuzzi tub, droplets of water from the bath soaking through the thin layer between the ceramic and my ass. He grabbed my tank top from the bottom, slowly rolling it up, his knuckles grazing pointedly along my skin, lingering at my abdomen, at the sides of my breasts.

"Lift your arms," he said—commanding, leaving no room for objections.

I obeyed. He tore the shirt up over my head, ruffling my hair with the movement. He tossed it on the floor behind him and kissed me once more, cradling my face. "Beautiful," he breathed as my powers kicked in and made my toes tingle. His hands roved down my chest and his palms pawed at my breasts, squeezing with want—need—just short of causing me pain.

I cried out and his fingers loosened just slightly, but his cock went stiffer and he peppered kisses along my jaw, bending down to reach the top of my breasts.

I started slipping, gripping on to his back to steady myself, but it only worked so much.

My butt dipped into the warm, soothing water, despite

my pants still being on. I laughed, holding on to him for dear life.

"It's okay," he growled. "It's a pretty deep tub."

He moved his hands to my back and gently lay me down in the water, my rear end sinking until it settled on a seat inside the tub.

He tugged on my leg and brought my foot up to his mouth, gripping the toe of my sock between his teeth.

I couldn't stop giggling, but then he ripped it off, moving his hand down my leg, reaching up my calf and to my thigh.

I gasped as his other hand moved in massaging motions over the arch of my foot.

A mewl escaped from my throat.

"That's it," he said. "Relax. Come for me."

He released my leg and grabbed the other one, repeating the whole maneuver with the other sock.

Nash and I rarely spent this much time on foreplay. Time was always of the essence—and thinking about Roulette, it was now, too.

Zander growled. "*Me*," he said. "Right now, you're mine. I want thoughts of me flooding your mind until you're about ready to burst."

Then he tugged on the pant leg, causing me to jump up and send my other leg floating upward in the water. He took advantage and grabbed the pant leg on that one, too, pulling the sopping pants off in one, long motion.

A smile worked its way onto my lips as he tossed the pants on the bathroom floor.

"No," he barked, putting one of his legs and then the other into the tub. "I want you quaking too much to even think about laughing." He crossed the short distance and wrapped his arms around me, pulling me to him. The warm water lapping at my thighs might have soothed some of the soreness, but it did little to relax the raging blood collecting at my apex. I stood on tiptoes in the water and moved my lips toward his.

He pulled back and put a finger between our lips.

"I do the work today," he said. "Just surrender to me."

I felt my knees going weak, but he held me tighter with one arm, his lips trailing down my neck as his hand moved lower. A finger ran between my labia, rubbing up and down, circling my clitoris.

A squeak escaped my lips.

"*Come,*" he whispered in my ear. His finger moved down and pushed up inside me, finding little resistance as it opened the entryway.

I moaned again and started to stumble, but he squeezed me tighter against him.

"Beg me," he whispered.

"What…?" I breathed.

"Beg, darlin'," he said. "Beg and you shall receive." A second finger pried my pussy wider and went inside.

I screamed happily. "Please," I said, my breaths growing shallow. "*Please.*" All I could think about was my intense need to have him inside me.

"Yes, ma'am," he said, removing his fingers. Slapping his hands on either side of my waist, he twirled me around in the water. "That's my girl," he said into my ear as he smashed my ass against his thighs. With a little bit of maneuvering, he—hard as a rock—slipped between my labia and inside my welcoming pussy.

I moaned, the sound permeating the steam and echoing throughout the bathroom. He kissed the top of my shoulder and for a moment, we both shuddered as my powers went to work, flowing from inside me and into him. He let out a gasp as the power flowed between us.

"Fuck, yes, darlin'!" he said, pulling out slightly.

"No," I moaned. "More, more!"

He obliged, plowing back in, causing me to stumble. His hand shot up around the front of me and caught me by the breast. "As much as you want, darlin'." He gyrated, pulling slightly out, and went back in again. Again and again, squeezing my breast, splashing the water over the side of the tub.

He shot his seed inside me and I trembled, screaming, "Zander!"

He chortled. "I made you say my name," he said. He pulled out, the suction from the movement causing my jelly legs to quiver. He wrapped his arms around my shoulders and started swaying. "I'll always share you because I know you're meant for more than just me. You're too important to Natchkind. But when you're with me, you're mine. Got it?"

Nodding my head numbly, I relished the feeling of his body against mine for a moment more. The room went quiet, the only sound the fizzing popping of the bubbles.

Then his arms tensed. "I found them!" he said. "I spoke to them through the powered-up bond."

I whipped around to face him, caught up in the impossibility of the moment.

"I know where they are," he said. "I can *feel* that other dimension. Darlin', I think we can save them!"

CHAPTER EIGHT

"YOU HAVE A LOT OF NERVE SHOWING YOUR FACE HERE," SPAT Nash as he reached forward to grab me by the wrist and tug me to his side.

Zander regarded him with amusement and shoved past him into the old community center. His Dodge Charger waited outside, his team back at their temporary headquarters, on standby for a message from Zander if need be. Not that he'd bonded with any of them the way he'd bonded with Jayden and me, but with my day-long super boost in him, it'd be child's play for him to send a message to any one of them, whether or not they were actively thinking about him at the moment. He'd figured it'd be perceived as less *threatening* if we came alone—though since two of the other Renegades had once lived here as well, it wasn't even a matter of secrecy.

"Nash, you knew they were coming. Just let it go." Jayden approached from the end of the hallway, rubbing his temples. He took his glasses out of his front pocket and affixed them to his face, his gaze flicking from smug Zander to the place where Nash gripped me on the arm. A jaw muscle twitched as his lips went thin.

Zander tucked his thumbs into a pair of non-existent suspenders running up his chest, walking down the hallway as if he owned the place. "I take it Wade's laboratory is still where it's always been?"

Jayden sighed and sent me a look—pleading, perhaps, or forlorn—and turned to follow his former best friend. "He's waiting for you. He's got some of his tracking programs up and running."

"Don't take too long to join us, darlin'," said Zander over his shoulder.

Though he could have easily said that in my head.

Nash closed the front door, never once letting go of my wrist. Then he smashed me against him, resting his chin atop my head. "I was so worried about you," he murmured.

I didn't know what to say. It hadn't been my idea to go with the Renegades, but I'd stayed long after I'd—probably—been able to go. And then I'd… Well…

Even though I'd always made a point of us keeping this relationship wide open, it was also the first time I'd actually had sex with someone besides Nash. Not for lack of trying with Jayden or an openness to try with someone else on the team if it really became necessary. And then there was that almost-day with Zander almost two years back. But still… This made it real. My open relationship.

And I knew that Nash never took advantage of that. He was an open book, and he wouldn't have been able to hide another occasional sex partner even if he'd wanted to.

Was it wrong that I didn't feel guilty—that I wanted them both more than ever? That I still wanted Jayden, despite all the lies I told myself? That on occasion an image of that bastard elf king staring me down even popped into my head?

Damn, if my disgusted parents could see me now. They

hadn't even waited to find out *what* exactly the full depths of my powers were and they'd already been turned off.

Nash swayed us back and forth and I reached out to embrace him as well. "I'm sorry about Rou," he said. "And Darien. I wish I'd been with you—"

I brought us to a stop. "This has nothing to do with you having been there or not. It just happened." I pulled away, my gaze darting to the toned calves jutting out of his workout shorts. "I don't want to live my life thinking elves could pop out at any minute—"

"Though they honestly could," said Nash, his hands falling to my elbows. "I think today proves that." I winced as he bumped a bruise and a sour note appeared on his face as he examined my arm. "Let's get some ice on that," he said, sliding his hand in mine and guiding me to the kitchen. Murmuring voices echoed from Wade's lab down the hall.

Chastity was on the nearby living room's couch, a bandage on her head, zoning out in front of the TV.

"Chastity!" I said, breaking off from Nash's grip. He puttered into the kitchen behind me as I sat down beside her. "You're awake?"

"Just barely," she said, covering her ear as I slid in next to her on the couch. "Take the energy down a notch, will you?" She glared at me out of one eye, taking in that too-small tank top and another set of leggings Zander had wrangled from Lila's room. He said she'd muttered something about me owing her for all this laundry I was making, but that just reminded me that I needed to get to my own room ASAP and put on some clothes that didn't threaten to pop my boobs out with every movement. And I *needed* some underwear or my every curve and dimple was going to stay on display to everyone.

"I'm just glad you're okay," I said, taking Chastity's

hand in mine. She grimaced but nodded. "Sorry I—I couldn't stop them."

Nash came back and handed me an ice pack wrapped in a dish towel.

I took it from him and looked from him to her and back as he slid in on the couch on the other side of me. It made for a tight squeeze. "Both of you," I said. "Stop blaming yourselves. You did what you could as soon as you could. I don't want us stuck at home, huddled in the corner just waiting for a call to go out and fight. We're Natches, but we're people, too. We can have lives. Besides, last time, Chastity, you were *on* a call when another call came in."

"Yeah, a call to stop your bad boy *boyfriend* from breaking the law," snapped Nash.

Chastity's non-puffy eyebrow jutted upward. She grabbed the remote and switched off the TV. "You know, I think I'm going to get some rest. Just call me if something happens." She gave my hand a squeeze before she went. "Thank Lila for getting us out of there if you see her," she said. "I know it was her, even if I was unconscious."

Nodding, I bit my lip and watched her return to the hallway.

"I always thought she had a thing for Lila," said Nash. "Though Lila was only ever crazy about Kouta." He put an arm atop the back of the couch and around my shoulder as I jostled the ice pack against my biggest bruise. "She was always less puppy dog about it than you were with Jayden."

"You act like you were here from the start," I said. "I was long over my puppy dog days by the time you walked into Veras."

"So you *say*," he replied. His eyes traveled up and down my body, affixing on my breasts. At his proximity, my nipples had hardened and threatened to burst through the tight fabric. The fingers on his free hand traveled up under the tank top to take a breast into his palm. His hand was hot against my icy skin and I shivered.

He leaned into my ear. "I'd say you need to put on more clothes because it's cold in here," he breathed. "But I can think of a more pleasant way of warming you up." His hand moved up from under my tank top out the top, tracing his calloused skin across mine. He stopped then, his eyes focused on the side of my head, and pulled away, removing his hand from under my shirt. He sighed and clasped his hands together between his legs as he leaned forward, his thighs spread. "You have teeth marks on your ear," he said.

Instinctively, I went to feel, the slight indentation of Zander's love mark still there. Zander must have been focusing on Roulette and that other world, though, because he didn't burst into my brain with some sexy observation.

Nash tapped the bottoms of his palms together and turned to face me, a faltering smile on his face. "I know this thing between you and me, it's not the same thing for you that it is for me."

I grabbed him by the chin, shifting his face toward mine. "That's not true," I said.

He chewed on his bottom lip, his eyes darting down. "No, it is, Aurora. And I told myself I'm okay with that. I will be okay with that. I *have* to be okay with that." Our eyes met. "Because I love you. And loving you means accepting that other people need to be on the receiving end of your powers." He sighed and pivoted himself to fully face me, taking my hand in his. "You think I don't care about Veras' mission of keeping the peace, but I do. Just because I offered to run off with you doesn't mean I don't get that."

"Nash—"

"No, let me finish. Please." His fingers traced lazy circles over my palm. "I've prepared myself for Jayden to get over whatever's holding him back and to finally make love to you—"

I opened my mouth to object, but he sent me a withering glare that got me to clamp my mouth shut.

"And I knew that when that happened, your heart would really be in it. In a different way than it is with Roulette or Chastity or Darien or anyone else you kiss or might consider doing more with if the situation called for it." He guided my hand to his thigh, resting it mere inches from the bulge threatening to pop out from his shorts. "I didn't care," he said huskily. "As long as you still cared about me—as long as I had you to myself when I had you —I didn't care."

I swallowed then, shifting toward him, ready to rip those pants off and slide that thick, juicy member I knew so well down my throat.

He chuckled then and put a hand to my chin, tilting it upward, his other hand still keeping my palm dangerously close to his crotch. "But *him*, angel? He betrayed us."

Gasping to try to tame the tingle in my too-tight leggings, I leaned back. "You know."

He rolled his eyes, letting my hand loose so I could cradle the ice pack again. "Jayden told us you were both on your way, that Zander had boosted his powers beyond what he'd done before—the boss was none too pleased to report that, by the way—and there was no mystery *how*."

Muttering to myself, I played with the dish towel covering my ice pack, the nippy cold sending jolts down my body and helping to cool the fire between my legs. "Can I speak now?" I asked.

"Yeah," he said quietly.

"Nash, you don't know how much you mean to me. Not just your friendship, which is, like, one of my biggest sources of comfort, but the sex we have…" I cocked my head. "It drives me wild." I faced him again. "You're hot and amazing and I love you so much that I wish you weren't in love with me."

He scoffed, though his cheeks darkened. "That doesn't even make sense."

"No, it does," I admitted. "Because I know—I don't know why I'm this way, but I know. I can't love only one person. And that's not fair to you."

"Did I ever say I didn't think this was fair?" he said, shaking his head. "Angel, I just told you I *accept* that I'll share you—"

"But only if you approve of my partners," I added.

His Adam's apple bobbed. "So you love him too?" he asked quietly. "Zander?"

I gnashed my lips tightly between my teeth and nodded. "Not enough to run off and leave you or Jayden behind to join his cause because I won't compromise who I am or what I believe for any man, but… yes."

Nash laughed. "You just admitted you love Jayden, too."

Gasping, I squeezed my ice pack. "I love him from afar," I said. "I've accepted that. I've tried not to be bothered by that. I mean, how greedy can I be?" I tried to smile.

Nash let out a breath and rolled his eyes. But then he snapped back to attention. "And Mr. Traitor Bad Boy, he can *share* you?"

Nodding, I gripped Nash's hand with my cold fingers. He winced, my flame boy up against ice. "He does. I won't say he doesn't wish I would join his team, but he won't force me to stay with him and he knows I have others in my heart. He accepts that."

"How magnanimous of him," muttered Nash. He took a deep breath and scratched the golden stubble on his chin. "If you'll stay with us—in Veras," he started, "I'll accept your love for him. But only if he doesn't take advantage of it and start using your boost to commit his crimes."

"He wouldn't," I said assuredly. "He understands how that would hurt me. Besides, there are ways we can be together that don't involve my actual boost—"

"Oh-kay," said Nash, removing his hand from mine and rubbing it behind his neck. "Maybe it's best I didn't think about that right now." He must have seen something like disappointment on my face because he slid forward really quickly and pushed his lips against mine. The small surge of power danced between us. "That doesn't mean I don't love you, angel," he whispered. "Or that I won't share."

I leaned back, ready for him to take me despite the high probability that any number of people could walk in on us out here in the living room at any second.

But as he shifted into position, hovering over me, his warm hand sliding down the front of my pants, sending a shudder up my spine, a huge rumble shook the ground and thundered clear across the air.

"Shit!" called someone—Wade, I thought—from down the hall.

Nash's hand popped out of my pants and he jumped to his feet, a fireball already forming on the tips of his fingers. "What is it?" he shouted.

I got to my feet behind him, letting the ice pack fall to the floor and tugging on his elbow. "Wade's lab," I said. "Let's go."

We did, running into a groggy Chastity in the hall. "What's going on?" she asked.

"We don't know," I answered—and then there was another rumble and I had to grab on to Nash's arm to anchor myself. When it subsided, Jayden popped out of the door to Wade's lab. "It's the Nelians!" he shouted. "They opened a portal right outside our front door."

We all exchanged a look. "How?" I asked as we drew closer to our team leader. "I thought they could only do that once a day at most." Then again, that was just a theory. We had no idea how they opened these rifts, really.

Jayden swallowed and looked over his shoulder to Wade, who was furiously typing on his computer as Zander looked aghast.

"They caught him talking to Roulette and Darien in his projected form," said Jayden. "He might have tried talking to the elf king himself—"

My eyes widened. "Why?"

Zander snapped back to the moment. "To see if I could get him to reveal anything," he barked. "And I did—they figured out Roulette's healing powers can boost their plants, make them grow more vigorously." His eyes narrowed. "But then they realized it wasn't working *quite* as well as it did downtown today and they scared her somehow into revealing the role of your kissing boost." His eyes met mine. "They want you, darlin'. Her healing powers strengthened their plant life. But they need you to make it even stronger." He swallowed visibly. "And that elf king has a real unhealthy obsession with you."

This from Zander? I blinked. I didn't know if I wanted to find out what Zander had read in Alarik's mind.

CHAPTER NINE

I kissed both Nash and Chastity just before they launched themselves out the front door, taking approximately no time to gape at the giant vine weaving down the street and around the old, rusty swing set that had been there from the community center's active days. I did take note that the vines seemed determined to leave the big oak tree in our front lawn alone, twisting and turning around either side of it and leaving it untouched.

A hand on the small of my back made me scream, but I turned to find Jayden, his eyes focused on the battle that had begun between fire, light, and vine-wielding elves. "Is the princess with them?"

My eyes darted about. There were only four elves in sight—including Alarik. He stood next to another elf who tightly gripped a form in front of him—Darien!

"No," I answered. "Not that I see. But look!" I pointed to our comrade.

Jayden's lips went tight and he tugged me to his side. Confused, my mind went to inappropriate places, considering what was unfolding around us, but I felt Wade's stealthy presence pass us by and I realized even he was getting in on the action, probably aiming to sneak up and take Darien back before Alarik could notice.

My hands rested on Jayden's chest. "He'll need help," I whispered. "A distraction."

Zander padded up behind us. "They're on their way," he said, referring no doubt to his own team. "Twenty minutes at most."

We didn't have twenty minutes, though.

I grabbed either side of Jayden's face. If both Nash and Zander were right—and Zander visited Jayden's brain, for Pete's sake—Jayden needed to get over this distance he put between us and just deal with it. "Let me boost you," I whispered.

His mouth opened slightly, his eyes so wide behind his glasses, but then they softened, and his mouth went thin. He nodded.

I put my lips to his and it wasn't just the transfer of my power to him that sent sparks flying through my entire body. It was a long overdue *need* to feel his lips on mine, feel the weight of his hands on the small of my back as they moved down in massaging circles to cup my butt cheeks.

"Okay, Romeo," said Zander. "I know that's long overdue, but it's not exactly the time…"

Jayden pulled back, startled, stumbling. He nodded at me and then launched himself forward, ripping the largest chunk of earth I'd ever seen him grip out from beneath the swing set, sending the old rusty thing tumbling against the nearest vine.

"Damn," said Zander. "He should have done that sooner."

I chewed the inside of my cheek and watched Jayden join up with Chastity, the two of them forcing an elf backward.

"Stop!" yelled Alarik, a dagger held above his head. "If you want your friend unharmed, *stop*. All of you—I want to talk."

Everyone did. Even Nash just crouched before his still opponent, his hand on fire, ready to strike.

"Thank you," said Alarik, lowering his dagger.

Zander growled from behind me. "I should project through his chest," he muttered. "Confuse him, maybe. Make him think he's been stabbed?"

"Wait," I said, resting a hand on Zander's arm. Alarik stared pointedly across the lawn straight at me.

Darien struggled to get free of his captor—his arms were tied behind him with thin vines—but to no avail. The princess must have taken his powers before they'd left their dimension.

Alarik directed his dagger at Zander and me as he took several steps toward us. My teammates bounced in place, seeming to ask each other whether or not to strike, but I shook my head as the elf dragging Darien fell in line behind his king.

"You were the ghost in my kingdom," snapped Alarik. "The one in my head."

Zander scoffed. "And not a pleasant place to be." He grabbed hold of me possessively. "She's for Natches, you creep. Not pointy-eared dicks."

Alarik scowled and I blinked, not really appreciating being talked about like a piece of meat, but also feeling kind of exhilarated at the idea of Zander being so possessive of me just then.

"We're here to trade," said Alarik, jutting his chin upward. "Your ice Natch for the Succubus Lips." His gaze fell on me, and I might have started sweating from the actual smoldering I could feel from the intensity.

Distraction, I reminded myself. *Distraction.*

"Free him first," I said, as slowly as I could.

"Aurora, no," said Zander, but I just tapped his bulging muscle, willing him to listen to me.

Zander, Wade's there, I said through the bond. *Waiting for the chance to strike and get Darien free.*

I felt a grunt across our bond—he clearly wasn't happy with the plan, but he was willing to play along.

Wade's powers didn't always come in handy in a battle, but they would in this case.

"And what's to stop you from retreating the moment I hand him over?" asked Alarik. He pointed the tip of his dagger at Darien's cheek and Darien spit at him, cursing in Spanish.

Letting go of Zander, I took a few steps forward, reaching for Alarik. "I want to see Roulette," I said, and I knew in that moment that that was true, and that I was really going with him. "Give him back, please, and take me to her."

"Aurora!" said Jayden from behind Alarik at the same time Nash broke the truce and threw his fireball straight at the king. Alarik flicked his free hand behind him and sent a vine blasting in Nash's direction, knocking him off his feet.

"No!" I screamed, just as an invisible force latched itself to the elf holding Darien and Darien stumbled forward. *Wade.*

But Wade was quickly knocked out, visible and on the ground. Alarik sheathed his dagger as both of the other elves broke into battle once more. Then he gripped my wrist. "Then come," he snapped.

I let myself be tugged along, tumbling forward.

Zander's projected form appeared in front of us and Alarik hesitated, then cocked his head and pushed forward, the spectral version of Zander offering too little resistance. "I'm sorry," I said to him, turning to look behind me at the real Zander plowing ahead, though he could do little with hand-to-hand combat in this situation. *I need to get Rou back,* I sent to him over the bond.

The elf king took me across the street to where his portal shimmered. Gasping, I took in the sight of a lush, green forest bathed in sparkling moonlight on the other side of the portal.

"Brace yourself," said Alarik. Before I could react, he let go of my arm and bent down to fling me over his shoulder, resting a hand tightly on the center of my ass as my torso slumped over his back like a sack of potatoes.

THE THREE OTHER ELVES STEPPED IN BEHIND US AND ALARIK turned around, potentially nodding to two Nelians who stood on either side of the portal here in this lush forest world, their arms extended outward, their faces scrunched tight as they focused. I assumed he nodded because I couldn't see him from my vantage point draped over his shoulder. Without straining my neck, all I could see were dirt pathways, bountiful shrubbery, and Alarik's tight, tight ass. Elven attire seemed to leave little to the imagination.

A sound like a generator overloading and popping broke out as the elves holding the dimension open—apparently—lowered their arms and the portal snapped together, dissipating into nothingness. "Your Majesty," said one as they both kneeled. The battle-worn elves who had followed him to our front yard followed suit. "We await your orders," said another.

"Scout ahead," said Alarik, his muscles suddenly growing tense beneath my abdomen. "And check behind us as well. And *be cautious*," he added, almost as an afterthought. "We should be far enough from Alanna out here, but…"

Someone was clearly paranoid.

The elves peeled off in all directions, leaving this supposed king and me in the middle of the path. He stood there nonchalantly, as if he didn't carry a *human woman* on his shoulder.

"Can I be put down now?" I asked, my voice a little muffled on the leather-like material of his jerkin. "It's not like I have anywhere to run."

Instead of replying, Alarik hesitated, then bent down, lowering my feet to the ground and shifting my body so I slid to standing. I stumbled, and his hands went tighter around my back to steady me.

A little squeal escaped my lips, more from the surprise of the feel of the dirt beneath my feet—it was softer than any dry dirt had business being—than anything. But even to my ears, the little sound seemed dirty.

The slight smile that quirked his lips revved something up in me that had *no* business getting going right now. None.

Fuck, though, this asshole was gorgeous.

I shoved at his chest, as much to snap myself out of it as to paint him a clearer picture of where things stood. "You can let go now," I snapped.

He did, but slowly, dropping one hand from my back and moving the other up to lightly take a strand of my hair in his grip. "Like starlight," he said, running his thumb over it in gentle motions.

I stepped back, tugging at the hair to get it out of his grip. "My hair?" I asked, incredulous. It was dark, but it wasn't as dark as night. And it didn't have any bright spots in it. Unless I'd missed some gray hairs coming in early...

He shook his head just slightly. "All of you. Bright like a spot of succor in endless darkness."

I pet the hair he'd fondled absentmindedly. So he was a poet as well as physical perfection. Nice to know.

"Maybe I should call you black hole, then," I said. "Since you destroy everything around you." It wasn't the cleverest retort, but I was no Wade.

And my patience was wearing thin.

He found it amusing. "As I said, a bright spot."

If he liked his women to sass him, sure. Exhaling, I crossed my arms. "Where's Roulette?"

Alarik tensed like a jittery bird and held a finger to his lips as he looked this way and that.

I wanted to snap at him that he could take that finger and shove it, but his anxiety soon transferred to me as a rustle shifted the trees beside us, a chill of cold air blasting my way. I ran my hands up and down my exposed arms, shivering.

A voice cried out from ahead and Alarik withdrew his dagger from his sheath, reaching a hand around my front to stand between me and the cause of mayhem.

A bloodcurdling scream sent more shivers down my spine. "What was—?"

The elf king hissed at me—not rudely but with a twinge of desperation. His eyes narrowed as he scanned our surroundings.

Out of the frying pan and right into the fire, apparently.

What did Alarik have to fear here in his own world? He barely had to fear the Natches in mine. The elves never stayed long, but they certainly wreaked enough havoc that it hardly seemed to matter that they'd retreated. Entire sections of our city had been made uninhabitable by their vine growths.

"Your Majesty!" cried a lean and tall elf as she ran up behind us. Damn, she'd made me jump. She'd been too quiet. "Was that Cassius?"

He nodded. "Gather the others," he said, his eyes not moving from the spot in front of us where the commotion had started. "Take my consort to the haven."

She grabbed my arm.

I blinked. Me? His *consort*? "Excuse me?"

But they just spoke over my head.

"Hurry," he breathed, but she barely got me a step away when the ground began to shake and the bushes before us parted.

A giant, mouth-breathing pig-like thing burst through, its tusks covered in blood.

"Run!" hissed Alarik, and he extended his hand toward the creature, sending a twisted, speeding vine out from his palm.

As the elf woman dove, shielding me and dragging me to the side, two other voices rang out as more elves returned to our position. They seemed to be shouting out a battle cry with far more fury than anything I'd seen them utter on Earth. More vines went flying as one jumped atop the warthog's back and grabbed it by the ears.

"What's he doing?" I asked the elf warrior woman beside me. But she was already on her feet, her eyes flicking between the battle and me, her legs bouncing as if itching to jump in despite being ordered to watch me.

"Go ahead," I said. "Unless that giant pig says otherwise, I'm not going anywhere."

She hesitated, looking at her king. He cried out as something soared past us, dropping his hand to cradle his arm and cutting off the flow of vines from his direction.

121

"Your Majesty!" cried the elf woman, and she no longer needed to be told twice to get a move on. I slipped back into the cover of the bushes, observant, but eager to get out of the path of the battle. Even if I'd had hand-to-hand combat skills, I didn't know what I could do in this situation.

Fuck, I wish I had Nash or Jayden or even Zander—

"Finally!" shouted Zander over the bond. *"I've been trying to reach you since you vanished. I've been talking in your head—your boost is still working, so I didn't even need you to think about me for it to work, but you haven't been focused enough."*

Well, excuse me, I thought. *Been a little busy.*

He grunted across the bond. *"That was a really stupid thing you did—"*

Can you still reach Roulette? I asked.

"No," he said. *"I thought maybe your boost was wearing off already, but I didn't know. We were in mid-conversation—I told her about Darien's return—when she mentioned a princess and it cut out."*

Alanna must have taken her powers away, I thought. *And even if you have yours, they can't reach through the nullification Alanna does to a person—I've noticed that before.*

"Shit," he thought. *"Where's this princess now?"*

A great, echoing pig squeal rang out behind me and I turned to find the giant warthog ridden by an elf and being redirected—from heading in the opposite direction to being turned around and headed straight for where I lay.

"Shit!" I muttered, pushing down for the moment the panicked, soft cries of *"Darlin'?"* in my head. I stumbled to my feet.

"Aurora," Alarik called out, raising a hand and lowering it as if to tell me not to move.

Not to move? When that thing was about a minute away from tumbling straight through me?

Alarik's arm was bleeding, his other hand still holding on to the wound tightly.

What had wounded him anyway?

The elf woman who'd abandoned me moved to support her king, but he gently batted her away and stood on shaky feet.

"Brother," said a voice, though it was deep and resounding, not at all the light tone of Alanna. An elf man broke through the forest flanked by four other elves, including another woman grabbing hold of Alanna by both arms.

Alarik gritted his teeth, cursing, and as the princess was forced to move closer, the remaining elf shooting out vines from his hand stopped all at once.

So her presence had removed his abilities.

Zander? I called out in my brain. No surprise that he was cut off, too.

"You're no brother of mine," spat Alarik to the elf man.

"I will be once your sister and I wed," said the elf man. He was tall and handsome, perhaps a little broader in the shoulders than the other elf men around him. He gazed at the captive princess—and he didn't look cruel, as I expected. He seemed… loving. She looked pointedly away, though, so I couldn't tell what she thought of him. Though being dragged like that was probably a clue.

The giant pig squealed again and pivoted slightly, the tension in my shoulders easing somewhat as it seemed less likely it'd plow right through me.

Instead, the rider aimed the warthog beside me, behind me. I glanced over my shoulder. Mere feet away, hidden behind a canopy of trees—there was a cliff. I hadn't noticed it at first.

"Of course, she'll have to forgive me for only spending some of my time with her even after the ceremony," said the man confronting Alarik. "Her powers are extraordinary, but alas, I don't think I can truly be so self-less as to give up mine for eternity to be in her presence always."

The warthog struggled a bit, trying to fight its way backward when it seemed to realize where it was headed. It started spinning in circles as the elf man on top narrowed his eyes and tugged the creature's ears harder. The movement kicked up some wind and I stumbled back.

"You'll never wed my sister, Xerxes!" Alarik cried out. "You'll never use that as an excuse to be king—"

"I love her!" said Xerxes, tossing his shoulders back. "I've always loved her and you know it!"

Alarik choked on a wry chuckle. "It's just so convenient to you that if I died and she became queen, that as her husband, you'd rule at her side, then, right?" He turned to his sister, though she wouldn't meet his eyes. "Because we both know she's more likely to do what you say than to obey her own flesh and blood, her rightful king."

At that, Alanna's head snapped up. "I asked Xerxes to stop, Alarik. Really, I did—"

"I don't care!" shouted Alarik. "You always disobey me because *Xerxes* has ideas. *Xerxes* would be a better king."

"I've never said that!" snapped Alanna.

Apparently, things were more volatile on their home turf than we'd ever thought.

I lost track of their squabbles, though, as the giant warthog let out what could only be called a death knell and went charging—again straight at me—as if determined to flick the elf on its back down the cliff behind me and to bring me with him for good measure.

"Aurora!" shouted Alarik, but I was already running deeper into the forest, continuously skirting the cliff's edge as that wayward pig seemed to anticipate my every movement.

It was fucking *chasing* me now. I'd never done anything to it.

I skidded to a stop at the very edge. "Shit!" One foot went flying off and I grabbed on to the nearest thing above my head—a vine twirling through the tree tops, maybe left there during the elves' initial battle against this creature, as it hardly seemed at home naturally growing out of the tree above it.

It worked, but my arms wrenched and I screamed. My body was still sore from the battle earlier—had it really been this morning? I wondered if I'd ever see another day. If I'd ever see Zander and Nash and Jayden again.

The warthog skidded to a stop right in front of me, bucking its head, and the elf man went flying, his screams echoing as he descended down to the misty fog and the tops of the trees below.

The warthog's breath made the air grow hot above my head.

"Your Majesty!" said someone, but I couldn't look to see who.

A man cried out and Alarik appeared atop the creature's head, stabbing a dagger into its eye.

It shrieked and bucked, stumbling down over the cliff.

"Your Majesty!"

"Alarik!"

Panicked voices echoed numbly from behind where the pig had been. As the pig stumbled and started drooping, Alarik jumped off and grabbed the vine I was clinging on to right above my head, his body sliding into place behind mine.

I cried out at the impact of his weight, though he was lighter than I'd expect from a finely toned man, even if he was less bulky than Nash or Zander.

"Hang tight," he whispered in my ear.

I chortled wryly. "You think?"

But my laughter cut short as what could only be described as a ripping sound echoed out above me.

The vine.

"Oh, shi—" I started, but the rip grew louder, then stopped as the vine broke free, Alarik's injured arm wrapping tightly across my breasts, his other still clinging to the vine above us as we began falling.

"Alaaarikkk!"

The last thing I saw was Alanna reaching over the edge of the cliff, as if the small length of her arm could ever hope to catch us.

CHAPTER TEN

AS THE MIST ENGULFED US, ALARIK PUMPED THAT VINE LIKE A lasso and he flung it. Miraculously, it hooked on something and he yanked us back toward the cliff.

I screamed at the sight of the rock face rising up to meet us, but he tugged hard on me, causing my own hand on the vine—which I hadn't even realized was still gripping it for dear life—to slip as we moved down the length of the plant, ripping off little sprouting leaves as we fell.

I kept screaming and screaming and then we tumbled forward—into a hole in the rock face. We ran out of vine to slide down then and we still had to jump a couple of feet, stumbling, Alarik grunting as he wrapped himself around me with both arms and we rolled, tumbling and tumbling until stopped by a wall.

It was finally over. But my insides hadn't gotten that memo. My heart racing, I gasped for shallow breaths, finding each one harder and harder to form.

"Aurora," said Alarik. Seizing up, he let out a little grunt of pain as he shifted behind me, gently pushing me forward to put some space between us. He rolled me over so we were lying on the hard ground face to face. He took my cheeks in his hands, his one palm slightly rubbery and rough—the one that'd slipped us down the length of the vine, no doubt. "We're alive," he said. "We made it." His voice was soft, like a mother trying to console a panicked child.

Closing my eyes, I counted my breaths. Despite the pain I felt at each inhale, I told myself I could still breathe. I just had to believe I could make do with the air I could get.

His own breaths were shallow beside me and we both lay there, quietly breathing for a while longer until I felt a light touch on my forehead and I opened my eyes to find him pulling his lips away.

This guy was nuts on so many levels.

I sat up, groaning as my head spun and I cradled it. "I can see in here," I said, blinking. A violet light radiated from shiny spots along the walls.

Alarik shifted to sit up beside me. "There's starlight in this mountain," he explained.

"Starlight?" I asked, confused again by his reliance on that word. He'd compared my hair to starlight before.

He grunted and turned a hand toward the wall just slightly. "It's what we call the sparkling crystals," he said. "Since it reminds us so much of the sky at night." He stared at me then, and I could *feel* the way he looked at me —not necessarily that he was undressing me with his eyes, but that he was just in awe of me.

I had no freaking idea why, though.

I took stock of my clothes and popped a boob half-tumbling out of the too-small tank top back in place. Alarik's gaze lingered there as I did and I sighed, shifting my front away from him and hugging my legs to my chest. "Did you know this cave was here?"

"Not this cave exactly, no." Alarik cleared his throat

and shifted, his hand clutching at his arm. "But the mountains are peppered with them and I thought it best to see if we could reach one."

"You're hurt," I grunted, not sure whether to care or not. He'd saved my life, but I wouldn't have been in this position in the first place if he hadn't kidnapped my friend and blackmailed me into joining him.

He pulled his fingers away from the wound and I was somewhat surprised to find he bled red like us. "It's just a scratch," he said, wincing.

I crawled closer to him to take a look. It seemed pretty deep. "If Roulette were here, she could heal us both in a snap," I said, pushing aside the leathery material around his wound.

"Why do you think I kept her?" he said.

I poked him in the wound—a little too hard. His eyes closed and he took in a sharp breath.

"Oop, sorry," I said wryly. "The thought of one of my best friends being held captive just makes me lose focus."

He rolled his shoulder away and stared at me, his brows furrowing. "We haven't hurt her."

"Oh, that's a relief," I said. "And here I thought you tortured her or her boyfriend into revealing information about me—"

"Ah, the ghostly man," he said, nodding. "We could tell he'd paid her a visit in her head as well." He bit his lip. "We have a truth-puller among us. You saw him. He only needed to use his powers on her to get her to speak."

"Zander said she was *frightened* into talking."

"So she must have been." He shrugged. "That's a little how his powers work."

Shaking my head, I let my lips grow thin.

"Your friend has amazing abilities," he said. "Not just the healing of our kind—but the healing of our vines. She promotes quick and bountiful growth, though when we saw the growth wasn't as fast or as bountiful as it had been back on your planet, Xerxes demanded she tell us why and she spoke of your boosting powers." He took a rattling breath as he shifted to pull what appeared to be a length of plant-like gauze from a pouch at his waist. "I knew once we had the both of you, our limited journeys to Earth would be a success. We could achieve our goals much more quickly." He winced as he unrolled the green gauze with one hand.

"Let me," I snapped, snatching the gauze from him. He watched me cautiously, but I stayed true to my word and unrolled it, tearing off a small piece to dab at his wound before wrapping it. He clenched his teeth, drawing in a breath through them. "It's not *that* bad," I said, beginning to roll the remainder of the gauze around his bicep. "So what *is* your goal exactly? What are you doing on my planet on a daily basis sending vines every which way and destroying buildings?" I tucked the edge of the gauze inside the wrap.

"Our vines, given the right environment, can grow into trees," he said. "They encourage native plant life to grow as well. We're trying to return your land to what it's meant to be."

"So you're an ecoterrorist?"

He was framing his actions as if they were noble.

His eyebrow quirked. "I don't know what that is, but if it means encouraging a planet to heal from damage done by its inhabitants, then yes."

Chewing my lip, I thought about it—it wasn't that I wasn't into protecting the environment, but this... "You don't care if people get hurt?"

He grunted and shifted his butt, leaning up against the

cavern wall. "We try not to hurt anyone. But we know it's inevitable."

I thought back to Alanna rescuing me—but then the image of the boy with his bone sticking out of his arm in the middle of the tissues aisle flared brighter. My eyes narrowed. "Damn right, it's inevitable. I don't think anyone's died yet—but let me tell you, that's an outright miracle. People have gotten hurt. And you just took away the best healer my town has."

A hollowing echo resounded and a burst of wind flurried past, sending Alarik's long locks twirling above his head, but he didn't flinch. I scrambled to keep my own hair from flying, covering my exposed ears with my arms to dampen the roaring noise.

"What was that?" I asked, breathing deep as the cavern quieted once more.

"Winds," he said, as if it were obvious. Okay, so it was in a way. "It can get cold up here."

"Tell me about it," I said, shivering and running my hands up and down my arms, which did nothing to ease the goose bumps popping up on my skin. Once the adrenaline of the almost-fall had worn off, I supposed my body thought it time to react to the fact that I was still in this skimpy, too-small outfit I'd borrowed from Lila—and now I was lost in the middle of a cold cave in a cliff side with no hope of helicopters or rescues or anything.

Alarik moved to unfasten the knots threaded through loops that acted like buttons on his jerkin.

"What are you doing?" I asked, an accusatory tinge to my voice.

"You're cold," he said, sliding his injured arm out of a sleeve and wincing.

His jerkin was open now down the middle, his thin torso strangely *extremely* well-defined and muscular, even if he didn't reach bodybuilder levels of arm and torso thickness.

After drowning in how buff both Nash and Zander were, and even Jayden when I got a glance, I was surprised to find that *Mama likey* was the first thing to pop into my mind.

He took his other arm out with less obvious discomfort. "Here," he said, handing the jerkin toward me with one hand. His hungry gaze sized my own torso up and down, lingering on the u-neck of my top where my breasts threatened to pop out again. "Your people let you walk around like that?"

Snatching the jerkin away from him and sliding an arm through, I growled. "Nobody *lets* me do anything," I said. "I decide what I want to wear, just like any woman should." I didn't add that I wouldn't have *decided* on wearing this, per se, but... After sliding on the second sleeve, my hand lingered on the blood-stained hole in the fabric and my gaze darted to his bandage. It didn't look like it was bleeding through, but...

Damn, if I didn't want to slide my fingers all over that hairless chest.

Alarik smirked and tilted his head back.

"What?" I asked, quickly fastening the knots to close the jerkin. The second knot down just popped right back out and I tried a couple more times before giving up. My boobs would not be confined within this slender man's clothing.

"I don't know if you think you're hiding it," he said, "but my people have an innate sense of the pheromones that exist between two or more. My sister knew just as I did the moment we met that you and I were meant to act on the attraction between us."

Wait, what? And did he say two...or more?

Leaning away from the wall, he grabbed my arm and moved closer, his lips beside my ear. "Don't deny that you want me."

I ripped my arm out of his grasp as another blast of cold air sucked its way through the cavern and I shrieked, tumbling into his arms and slamming us both against the cavern wall before I even realized what I was doing.

He grunted as his injured arm hit the wall, but he took me roughly into his grasp, my face flush against one of his pecs. The warmth of his strange but smooth skin on mine did wonders to warm the iciness that the wind had caused to burrow into my flesh.

The gust died down and I was left with the hastened beat of his heart beneath my ear. Absentmindedly, I traced a finger beside my cheek over his chest at the sound. So they bled like us and they had hearts like us, too. The only difference seemed to be their ears, their slightly rubbery skin, and their powers—oh, and their desire to see my world turn back to prehistoric days.

Alarik's little peal of laughter then was throaty and sent a hot, burning shiver roaring to my groin. "I see I don't have to argue with you about this. Your actions speak for themselves."

I darted up, some sense slapping into me. Gripping the open jerkin partially over my breasts in vain, I did my best to cool the wild ache stirring in my groin. "How do we get out of here?" I snapped. "So I can see Roulette."

"So eager to return to your friend, are you?" He shifted, bringing one knee up, and picked at a loose thread on his pants. His pants were *tight*, his thighs thicker than I'd noticed, leading to a rather big bulge between them.

He snickered again and this time I saw his face as he laughed—knowing, cocky. Monstrously sexy, goddammit.

"Yes!" I said, back to the conversation that mattered.

"You know I never promised to let either of you go home," he said.

My tongue traced circles under one of my incisors. I'd known that. But I'd thought maybe once I was near her, we'd figure it out. Jump through the next portal they opened. Take someone hostage and *make* them open a portal. I didn't know. Something.

"I imagine a hundred scenarios to secure your freedom are racing through your head, but I assure you, not a single one will work." He tapped the side of his head with a long finger. "I'll outthink you at every turn." He leaned closer, his voice growing huskier. "So why not just give in to me?"

Scoffing, I shuffled backward, noticing too late that squirming my butt only drew his ravenous eyes that way. "Fuck off," I said. That only seemed to make him happier. Then, because I wanted to make him *consider* backing off, I added, "You didn't seem to *outthink* that Xerxes dude back there."

He scowled, pulling back. "Don't speak of what you do not understand."

It was my turn to laugh. "Sure, sure, Your Royal Asshole."

He snatched my arm again then, pulling me closer. His nose twitched slightly and then he moved his head down the side of my face, down to my clavicle, hovering above my breasts. "I can smell the desire on you, starlight."

Fuck. Fuck, don't let it be true, I willed to myself. *Stop getting turned on, you horny traitor*, I added to my nether regions.

But there was no helping it. I was already buzzing down below, moisture clawing at the insides of these dumb leggings that would probably be the death of me when another blast of cold wind froze them to my pubic hair.

"All right," I said, snatching my arm away from him once more. He looked amused but didn't try to grip harder to stop me. "Then enlighten me on whatever it is you think I don't know that would change my mind about you."

"Oh, I'd love to *enlighten* you, starlight," he said, his eyes drinking me in from top to bottom. "I bet whatever kind of mating ritual you've done on Earth, there's *plenty* you don't know."

Fuuuuuck… Back to that again, were we?

Still, the comment was like an unintentional blow to the amazing experiences I'd had with both Nash and Zander, so I felt a little twinge in the back of my mind at the idea of even someone ignorant insulting my men. My *men* in the plural. Apparently.

But I had a singular goal now. Learn what I could and figure out how the hell we were getting out of here.

Tugging the jerkin tighter, I put on my game face, all-business. "How did you find Earth to begin with?"

Alarik leaned back, clearly amused. He rubbed a thumb and forefinger together as he leaned his forearm on his knee. "We've always known about your world since the dawn of our history. Our history tells of how it was once a beautiful place—bountiful and plenty—and that it was ruled by giant beasts—so much bigger than our biggest creatures, taller than the tallest trees—that roamed the lands."

"Dinosaurs," I said, pinching my lips. His people were *old* if they were cognizant enough to write histories of our world all those millions of years ago. "But it wasn't us who did away with them. It was a meteor or an ice age or something. We're not sure."

"But it was you who rose from the ashes of their reign,"

he said. "And you, not they, who took such poor care of the planet."

I shook my head. "Since we look so much more like you than dinosaurs do, you'd think you'd feel some empathy."

"Oh, we do," he said. "We know you're too stupid to think outside of your own immediate needs." He slid closer another inch and his voice went low and sultry. "That can be a positive in certain situations, too."

Quiet down, I shot to my libido. *And learn when it's appropriate to get turned on already.*

"However, we—that is, some of us—*are* fascinated by what kinds of tools your kind creates," he said. He dropped his hand off his knee and dug into the little pouch at his waist from which he'd drawn the leaf bandage. He held out a battered off-brand MP3 player in his palm and I had to cover my mouth to keep from showing the grin that appeared on my face. It didn't stifle the giggles, though.

"What?" he asked, fishing out a pair of earbuds and bouncing the MP3 player in his palm. "Some of this stuff is quite riveting. We have music here, but your planet has such a vaster array." He plugged the earbuds in—*look at him, the little expert*—and put one in his ear. Then, without asking, he leaned forward and put the other in mine, drawing us close. My palm fell from my face and his hand slipped behind my head as he laid his forehead gently against mine, closing his eyes. He hit a button on the MP3 player and even as another gust of wind made me jump, he gripped my head harder, keeping me riveted to the moment. I didn't know what song I'd expected him to start playing, but it certainly wasn't "Unforgettable" by Nat King Cole.

As the wind died down, I felt the warmth of his breath,

heard the small punctuations of our inhales between the words of the song. When it ended, he hit another button and pulled the earbuds out of both of our ears, sliding the earbuds out and back into his pouch.

I felt cold at the absence of his nearness, even though he hadn't pulled a great distance away. "Where did you get that?" I asked.

"I picked it up during one of our trips to Earth."

"Where, the dump?" I asked. When he seemed uncertain as to what I meant, I felt it a bad idea to explain to an ecoterrorist that there were places where we just piled our garbage.

"I don't know," he said. "It looked like a home. It was in a cabinet my vine had grown through." He fondled its surface. "I know... I know your people manipulated the natural resources of your planet to create such a thing." He turned it over, then brought it to his lips, biting it, and I burst out laughing.

"What are you doing?" I asked. "You can't eat that!"

His eyebrow quirked. "I wagered. Nor would I want to. It's just..." His lips soured. "I've never tasted anything so vile. So unnatural."

I rolled my eyes. "Then maybe don't eat plastic and metal."

He didn't seem to like the sounds of those words. "It's beautiful," he said, holding it up again. It was a sleek, red color. "But wasteful. Soon it will no longer play a song. It keeps beeping and warning me that it's almost out of... bat-te-ry."

"Well, back on Earth, you can recharge it," I said and that caused him to look at me with eager eyes. "With electricity," I added.

He frowned again. "That stuff created by putting poisonous gas in the air."

137

"That's a byproduct anyway," I admitted. "Though we have completely clean ways to generate electricity. Some people *do* do it that way—just by absorbing sunlight or the strength of a gust of wind."

Alarik shoved his player back into his pouch. "Then why in the great mother Nelia do you not *all* do it that way?"

I sighed. "Honestly? I couldn't explain it. You're right. Sometimes we're greedy, selfish creatures. Not everyone likes how things are exactly, but pretty much all of us benefit from it in one way or another."

"But you have powers," he said. "For the first time in tens of thousands of years, your people are developing powers of their own—and a much wider variety of them than the Nelians. Why not take over from the people who do these stupid things for greed?"

Maybe he and Zander would get along more than they thought. "It's not… It's not that simple." I bit my lip, then thought about changing the conversation. "So all your people have powers? More than just the vine growths?"

He bristled. "The *vine growth*—vine life—has helped us cultivate a beautiful and rich planet for millennia, I'll have you know."

Sooory.

He swallowed. "But yes, not everyone has that power. Most do, but… Quite a number can create portals to your world. Our people were flummoxed as to the point of such powers, but eventually, we knew it was because we must have been destined to watch over your baby planet. To nurture it when its own residents might not."

"Then why, if you're so disappointed in us, did you wait until a few months ago to attack?" I asked quietly.

"I thought it time," he said. "Before your race became overrun with power-users…"

"Natches," I said.

"Natches," he said, his mouth curdling at the word. "Before you could effectively fight back."

"But we've been fighting back anyway," I said.

"True," he said. "Though I cannot imagine you'll win."

That had gotten dark fast. "So there's the truth-getter, too," I said. "And your sister can take away powers for a time."

"Yes, there are rare cases when elves are born with powers that don't match either the vine life or the portal creation." He sneered. "They get treated as rather special anomalies, sent from the mother goddess for specific purposes." He looked me up and down. "My mother and father wondered what could have been the purpose of a child like Alanna," he said, and the way he phrased it seemed so cold and calculated, "but when I became king, I knew. That is… *Xerxes* had an idea." He swallowed visibly. "If she could take away our powers with mere proximity, perhaps she could do that with your planet's Natches— give us the edge we needed to fight before your numbers became too great."

I seemed to remember him being quite *disappointed* she'd turned up during an assault the first time we'd met, but I decided not to push him on the whole Xerxes-and-Alanna thing. I knew enough to report back to Veras—if I ever got a chance to report back anything. Alarik went quiet, the perfect image of a brooding man as he stared off into the darkness of the cavern, and I decided to lighten the mood. I patted my leggings-covered hips for pockets where there were none. I kept forgetting my phone wasn't there. "We have little *tools* like that player you like now— maybe a bit bigger—that play music, allow you to talk to someone on the other side of the planet, and act as a way to send written messages—and look up almost any information on Earth."

His eyes widened and he looked contemplative as he sunk back against the wall.

"Though I don't think all of those functions would work here anyway," I said. "You have to have satellites." I pointed to the star-like glittering of the cavern ceiling. "Tools we put amongst the stars."

He gasped and his nose wrinkled as he looked up. "You would defile even the stars themselves?"

"Well, not me personally," I said, swallowing. Why on Earth was it up to me to defend my people when I knew we hadn't exactly done the right thing a lot of the time? Maybe even most of the time. "Look, I can't explain to you the entirety of human innovation or even try to defend any damage it's done—both to the planet and to other people—in a cold cavern in the side of a cliff with no hope of rescue. I just... can't. But for all the bad our technology has done, there's been good, too."

Alarik flicked his palm out in front of him and focused on it, but nothing happened. "Once Alanna's nullification powers wear off me, I'll create us a vine to climb up," he said.

That harrowing prospect was a kick to the stomach, even if the knowledge we might move on at some point was a bit of a relief. "Climb up?" I asked. "Not down?"

He pointed up. "My village is up there," he said. "And if I'm presumed dead, Alanna and Xerxes may be taking over. That... would be even less beneficial for you and your Earthlings."

I clenched my jaw. *Worse than destroying city blocks with vine growths?* I shuddered to think.

"They won't send someone to rescue you?" I asked. "Their... king?"

He grunted. "They'd assume I couldn't have used my own vine since Alanna had robbed me of powers," he explained. "And probably doubted I could control the one we were using well enough. Xerxes and some of his followers would be happy to leave well enough alone, call it destiny and dwell no more upon it."

I had so many questions, I barely knew where to start. He stood, leaning against the wall to steady himself and wincing a little. Then he walked toward the front of the cave and the muted, misty light outside. "Where are you going?" I asked, getting to my own feet. "Are we leaving?"

He looked over his shoulder at me and drank me in with his eyes, following the curve of my hips in particular. "Patience, starlight. I need time." I hung back as he reached his good arm out the cavern entrance, fishing around the edges. I hesitated, knowing I couldn't hope he'd fall since he was my ride out of here. I slipped my arms around his abdomen from behind.

The smile that appeared on his face as he glanced over his shoulder at me was like the grandma-eating wolf coming across Little Red Riding Hood. "Is this really an appropriate moment?" he asked.

Rolling my eyes, I puffed out a blast of breath to keep the lock of hair that had fallen across my face out of my line of sight. "Just don't want my ride out of here to fall into the abyss, thanks."

He chuckled even so, stretching and then grunting as something snapped. He shifted back around and tossed a handful of small branches on the ground. "Just gathering material for a fire," he said. He shifted entirely so that it was his back my hands were clasped around, my chin coming up to his clavicle. I stepped back probably a little too late and he wrapped his own arms around me, pulling me back against him tightly and guiding my cheek to rest

141

on his bare shoulder—the one without a wound. "Or we can stay warm in other ways," he whispered—darkly, promising.

I dropped my hands and pulled away, bending to pick up the sticks. "A fire will do," I said, heading back to the depths of the cave before another gust of wind toppled us both over. His laughter echoed down the cavernous opening and I tossed the branches down, slamming my butt on the ground beside the stone wall. I pulled my thighs up against my chest, telling myself that if he fell out of the cavern entrance, it was just my destiny to die at this point. Maybe that would teach my libido to get over itself already.

Another gust of wind brought a chill and Alarik back to my side, more branches in his hand.

I kept my chin parked atop my knees as I watched him gather the branches together and place them in a small alcove surrounded by walls on three sides.

"The fire won't even last with this wind," I pointed out.

"It should here," he said, striking a rock against the cavern wall. Sparks shot out from the friction. "If we both sit on this side of it and block the wind." The sparks set the branches alight. He had a far easier time of it than I'd ever had. Before I'd met Nash and his instant fire fingers, of course. I sighed at the thought of maybe, just maybe, never seeing my horny best friend again.

But he was more than just a *best friend* to me. I just hadn't ever been able to reconcile the fact that I was in love with more than one person with what society expected of me. Even without my weird Natch power excuse.

"Come," said Alarik, gesturing toward me before crossing his arms tightly across his bare chest. I wondered if he really was freezing and too macho to admit it. Shivering, I somewhat reluctantly obeyed. The fire immediately sent waves of relaxation across my body, loosening stiff muscles and curling my toes.

"Our backs may be exposed, but I still propose we solve that with a little body heat." He slipped a hand under the jerkin and around my waist, pushing up the tank top to put skin against skin.

I shrieked—at the coldness, at the boldness—but Alarik just leaned closer and rested his forehead on the top of my head, his lips hovering over my ear. It took a moment more, but the iciness of his soft skin faded and I felt warmer than I had before.

"We're alone here," he said. "Stop talking your heart out of what it wants—what it *needs*. There is nothing to do just now but wait."

Sighing, I tried to focus on my breathing, my eyes fixed on the fire. Ignore the temptation. *Ignore it.*

He pulled his head back, but not his arm. "I may need your help regardless," he said. "I may need to be inside you before we escape."

That was a slap of cold against the warmth. "What are you talking about?"

"I know how your powers work, remember?" he said, studying me. I turned away. "We're both weak. We can't make a climb like the one we need to, even when I can create vines again." He grabbed another lock of my hair and shifted it to the side of my face. "I want to see if your boost will work on a Nelian as well."

I didn't like that idea. Not one bit. It might have proved necessary to get us out of here, but if my boosts worked on the Nelians, what hell was in store for Earth? Maybe—just *maybe*—I could keep him occupied enough for one day afterward so my boost wore off, then get Roulette and hightail it before he could test his boosted powers on Earth.

But what if I failed? Or worse, what if I *liked* it? I thought—I knew—that I would. Would I be sane enough to stay away from ever giving him a boost again? Would he *let* me stay away or would he... Would he *take* what he wanted from me?

I swallowed as another burst of wind flew through the cavern and Alarik used my distraction to force me closer to him. His lips pressed against mine and I felt the buzzing rumble of the apex between my legs.

I pulled back. "I've probably lost my powers regardless," I said. "Your sister's power seems to work on mine."

"I don't care," said Alarik. "Not right now." He kissed me again and this time, it was greedier, taking my lips between his teeth just roughly enough so it didn't do more than sting. "I need you," he breathed. "And you're going to give yourself to me."

CHAPTER ELEVEN

I WANTED TO LAUGH, TO SHOW HIM WHAT A JOKE HIS WORDS were. If he truly needed my boost—assuming it worked on him—to get us out of here, that was one thing. But I wasn't going to *give* myself to him happily.

Right?

There might have been a small part of me that was glad for an excuse. But my brain knew that boosting an otherworldly invader wasn't a good thing, libido be damned.

Can't you be satisfied with two? Some people don't get half as many.

Instead of laughter tumbling out, though, I opened my mouth and my throat just went dry.

Alarik slid his hands around my cheeks, cupping my face. "Do humans taste better than elves?" he asked—which should have made me laugh. Damn, that should have made me laugh.

But the tip of his tongue went sliding over my lips, and I moaned.

"Why are you so excited about making love to your enemy?" My voice was raspy and quiet. Almost as if afraid someone might overhear us.

He leaned back somewhat, his grip still gentle—but firm—on my face. "I told you," he said. "I knew the instant we met we were compatible—more than *compatible*. Meant to be." There was a slight twitch in his jaw as his gaze drank me in. He moved in to kiss me again—hungrily—as the small fire crackled beside us. He pulled away, dropping his hands and wiping his lips with the back of one like he'd just gorged. "Since discovering what you can *do*, I know precisely why the mother goddess made us as one."

I shook my head. "I have to disagree. My powers are *precisely* reason number forty-eight why I shouldn't go anywhere near you."

"You can't have *that* many reasons."

"*Slight* exaggeration, then." I tucked my hands between my thighs, squeezing hard, both to warm them and to attempt to focus on something other than the feelings stirring inside me. I stared at the diminutive flames, crying out as another gust of wind blew through the cavern.

Half-naked Alarik didn't even flinch. As I brushed my hair out of my face, he watched me, bringing his knee to his chest and resting his wrist over it. He leaned forward, tracing the tip of his thumb over his lips.

"If your powers haven't returned yet, then mine haven't, either," I said, stiffening and moving to tuck my hands back between my thighs. "So this"—I gestured between us—"is pointless."

He caught my hand before I could slide it between my legs and yanked me forward. Stumbling, my other hand shot out and landed between his legs, my breasts skirting his raised knee as he lifted my arm high above his head. He moved his lips toward mine with the promise of a kiss, but he stopped just short. "I don't need your powers to enjoy this. And I *will* enjoy it, the moment you do as you're told." He shifted his mouth to my ear. "Remove your clothes." The husky tone of his voice sent shivers down my spine, my arm holding up my body weight beginning to quiver, the slight ache being overrun by the adrenaline of desire.

He let me go and it took me a moment to pull back, scrambling to sit up again. "It's cold," I whispered, meaning to be louder. "If we *need* to do this, I'm keeping as much on as possible."

"No, you're not," he said. He wasn't angry when he spoke, and his voice didn't even quiver.

Cocky, this asshole. Why did that rev me up? He stood then, taking slow, soft steps toward me, dragging the fingertips of one hand along my back, then grabbing hold of the jerkin and yanking it off my shoulder, the fastener keeping it tied at the top ripping at the seam, not allowing me to fasten it again, not even if I wanted to. My body palpitated at the force of his movement. He bent down, moving his lips toward my ear. "Show me your breasts, starlight. Make me shiver in anticipation of fucking them senseless."

No one had ever fucked my *breasts* before. There'd been no reason to when my cleavage offered no way to boost.

I squeezed my legs harder together, taking a deep breath of cold air into my lungs to try to ignore the tingling moisture escaping my pussy. The thin yoga pants may as well have been made of paper for what good they were doing me at this point.

Alarik stepped behind me, his back to the fire. In the dim cavern light and the glow of the flames, he looked every bit a king. One arm rested akimbo on his hip as he gazed down on me through lidded eyes. "Starlight," he said, his chin jutting upward slightly. "I will take you to realms of pleasure you could hardly have imagined existed. But I want you at my feet first. I want you *begging* for me."

That cocky son of a bitch. If he thought for one second I would *beg* for this—from *him*... A gasp escaped from between my lips.

"Take the jerkin off," he said. There would be no arguments. "Do as I say and I promise you won't be cold for long."

With shaking hands, I slid the other sleeve off my shoulder, then pulled first one and then the other arm out of the jacket, tossing it to the side, away from the fire.

"Good girl," he said, leaning forward to take a strand of my hair in his hand. He let it slip from between his fingers like grains of sand through an hourglass. His other hand remained on his hip as he thrust his pelvis toward me. "Now the shirt."

With the touch of nullification, there was no hope of Zander reaching me, though my boost that allowed him to reach this far would only last so much longer. No, nothing. No sound from my constant brain companion.

We were here alone, and no one need ever know...

My heart hurt at the thought of keeping it from Nash— if he'd barely been okay with Zander, what would he think of this? And there'd be no keeping it from Zander, not for long. I could already picture the disappointment on Jayden's face, and after I'd finally tasted his kiss.

My pinky traced my lips as I stared straight ahead, right at the bulge in the form-fitting leather-like pants.

He grabbed the back of my head—just rough enough

to get my attention, and not so much that it hurt me. "Shirt. Off," he said, letting go.

Grabbing the bottom of the tank top and rolling it up, I flung it up over my head and tossed it beside the jerkin. Shivering, I pressed my forearms against my breasts, my mind racing with the fact that I'd just done that, had just willingly exposed myself on his say-so.

The fingers on one hand lightly traced down my cheek to my neck. Trembling, I felt a fire roar up from below. "Drop them," he said, his fingers pausing atop one of my arms.

I hesitated.

"Did I *tell* you to cover yourself?"

My hands dropped.

His voice went low. "That's better." The warm tips of his fingers moved to circle the top of my breast. "On your knees," he said.

I was sitting on my calves already.

He took my left breast tightly into his hand, the flesh spilling out between his fingers.

My heart hammered. I didn't—I couldn't. I wanted to blame some power for all of this—after all the Natch powers I'd seen, seduction couldn't be out of the realm of possibility—but I knew there was nothing more to it than I just *wanted* this.

Despite everything my brain knew to be true. Right now, away from it all, I would turn off my thoughts and just *feel*.

He jerked a knee in place as he gave my breast a squeeze. "I *said*, on your knees."

I sat up, balancing on my knees and bringing my face up to his abdomen, my breasts in line with his crotch.

"Good girl," he said, softer. His hand wove through the

hair on the back of my head again, soft, but possessive. The other loosened its hold on my breast somewhat, shifting, running a careful thumb in circles around my nipple, caressing it to stand erect.

"Exquisite," he said huskily, dropping his hand and pressing his bulge against my breasts. It grew firmer at the contact and I wanted—*needed*—his pants off. Gasping, I leaned my forehead against his hard abdominal muscles.

"Not yet," he said quietly. He dropped his hands. "Lie down," he said, the snap of the fire behind him accentuating the words.

My thighs weak and straining, I gladly obeyed, resting my head atop the pile of clothes I'd left behind. My breaths hitched as I stared up at Alarik, who placed both hands on his hips. He watched me intensely, but he didn't look winded at all. Fuck him and his cocky demeanor.

A gust of wind passed through again and I seized up, arching my back and closing my eyes as a little gasp escaped my lips.

"That's a start," he said, sliding off his pants with a flourish and stepping out of them. His bare legs were thick, though not so big as to offset his svelte frame. Still, there wasn't an inch of muscles that wasn't defined, not a centimeter of his pale brown skin that wasn't blemish-free —even the bandage seemed only to add to his mystique, his aura like that of a conqueror.

And under a sheer layer of soft, pale green curls was a thick, long cock, starting to stiffen but infuriatingly taking its time to get fully erect.

I wanted him inside me *now*.

Lowering himself to hands and knees, he crawled toward me as my breaths grew shallower, louder. He positioned himself over me, his mouth greedily taking my lips between his teeth, parting my jaw wider and inserting his tongue inside, tasting me, devouring me.

He backed up and I mewled a little, trying to keep quiet, but the sound sent a satisfied smile to his face. He stared down at my breasts and took both between his hands, forcing them together as his thumbs moved in synchronized circles over my nipples.

"What do you say?" he asked. It was *infuriating* that my breaths kept getting heavier while he remained so calm.

Infuriating but hot.

My eyes darted downward. "Please?" I asked.

Shifting to saddle himself above me, his thighs hugging my sides, he dropped a hand from my breast to his erect shaft, which he guided between my breasts before resuming his hold on either side and squeezing them together. My pussy ached for his touch, but my back arched at the friction between my tits as he slid back and forth, straddling me. My sides were alight at the pressure of his thighs and I had to bite down on the side of my index finger to keep from crying out.

He tugged my arm away. "Cry out," he demanded. "There's no one here to hear you but me."

I did, at first guiding my shaking hands to his hips, only for him to swat those away too, his chest puffing out as his booming laugh echoed out among the crackles of the fire. "Do not presume to touch royalty without first being asked," he said, and part of me wanted to smack that satisfied smirk right off his face, but I was too far gone to cloud my head with anything other than the moment. I tilted my chin upward and swept my hair away, granting him access to my neck.

He grinded on me, squeezing me harder, grinding and

grinding until he came over my chest and I cried out at the slick seed on my skin.

Before I could so much as speak, he withdrew and bent over, peppering my neck with kisses. My groin burned hotter and hotter with the *need* for more, but I held tight to my hair, writhing beneath him.

His lips touched mine and in an instant I knew—my powers were back. And they worked on him.

He pulled himself up, settling himself lightly on my abdomen, laughing and clasping a hand to his chest. He was finally starting to breathe a little harder, and my pussy purred at the thought of me doing that to him, even if it might have been just because of the power of my lips.

He aimed his other hand above my head and a vine shot out, thin and long—not as thick as the ones that had terrorized my city.

Squirming, I let out a shrill cry and after a few moments, the vine stopped.

"This isn't to hurt you," he said, picking himself off me and standing. "I was just testing things out." Without much circumstance, he grabbed hold of my leggings and ripped them down my legs, stopping only to remove my shoes and socks and then sliding each foot to his cheek and kissing it before removing the sopping leggings entirely and tossing them aside. My groin quivered with anticipation of him taking me, but he just let the second leg fall and backed off, offering his hand to me. I didn't want to move. If I moved, I might start to think, and then I'd realize what a fucking idiot I was being.

A fucking happily horny idiot.

"Come," he ordered, shaking his hand for emphasis, a pinched expression clouding his face. "Unless you prefer writhing in the dirt at my feet."

I took his hand and he pulled, bringing me to stand

beside him. Our naked forms were mere centimeters apart, but the hands were our only point of contact. He leaned in, teasing me with the promise of his lips as he nuzzled his head against the side of my face. Then he leaned back. Dropping my hand, he pointed to the vines behind him. While I'd been panicking, I hadn't noticed he'd hung them across the cavern like a hammock. He took wide steps to the side of the makeshift bed and sat down on its edge. He sat with his legs splayed apart, his back straight, one elbow resting on a higher part of the hammock as he tapped the tips of his fingers against his mouth and looked down at me with a smirk. "Come," he said, patting his lap with his other hand.

I shuffled toward him, shivering at even the short distance put between us and the fire. I went to sit on his lap, but his head shook back and forth and he placed a gentle palm on my abdomen. "Be a good girl and prostrate for your king." I wanted to laugh, but his hand slid down between my curls, a single finger running teasingly between my lips and back up to circle my clit.

My knees buckled as my breath caught in my throat.

His other hand slid behind me, grabbing hold of my one of my buttocks and squeezing it greedily.

I moaned, about to lose my balance. His hands went to my stomach and the small of my back and he bent me over, hanging me off either side of his firm thighs, his penis growing hard against my belly button as his hand retreated out from under me. Blood fought to both shoot to and drain from my head as desire waged with the downward angle of hanging over his lap.

His hands moved in careful motions over my ass, gently prying my legs farther apart so they could access me from behind.

A blast of wind roared through the cavern again, and

though he didn't flinch, my hand shot out to grab hold of the vine hammock beside me.

"I've got you," he said quietly as the wind died down. He nudged my elbow until I let go and then secured one arm beneath me, his wrist across my left breast as he grabbed firmly to the right.

His other hand moved between my labia, circling my clit again as my toes curled, my legs growing taut as I tried to keep from screaming out in ecstasy. His forefinger took over the gentle circles as his thumb went inside me—as far as it would go up inside me—and then retreated out again, meeting up with the finger to caress my slit.

I did scream this time, my breaths growing haggard. He laughed then—booming, commanding—and I could feel the surge of power that had passed between us even with that motion.

Nash might have been right about a finger inside me. He'd never had patience enough to try himself. Not that I'd wanted him to—he got me hot and bothered fast enough that any waiting would be torturous.

The hand retreated entirely, making me gasp at the sudden coldness, and his palm smacked firmly on my ass cheek.

I cried out. It stung for a second, but it also sent the blood raging to my pussy with desire. Any more of his teasing and I would burst. "Why...?" I breathed. Why spank me, why draw this out, why were we doing this? That single word was supposed to ask all of that, but it was all I could get out.

"Your pheromones shifted," he snapped. He leaned closer, hovering over my head. "You can desire as many others as you please, but it is a Nelian custom to give the one you're with your full attention." He leaned back. "I won't have my efforts remind you of *anyone* else." He spanked me again and I buckled, rocking my abdomen against his erect penis, the tingling at my apex skyrocketing as a fresh wave of moisture exploded from my vagina.

"That's better," he said, tossing his shoulders back. But then he smacked his palm against my ass again. "Tell your king you're sorry," he said.

Clenching my hands into fists as they dangled over the side of his legs, I stretched my legs out, trying to shift my abdomen to feel what he'd so far denied me against my belly. "I'm not…" I breathed. "I'm not… sorry."

He laughed, one of his knees bouncing. Then he smacked my ass again. "I like a challenge," he whispered, his hand prying apart my cheeks again to slide between my labia as his other squeezed my breast tighter. Two fingers dipped inside my pussy as I mewled in excitement, and then he pulled them out, smacking his palm against my ass cheek again. "Beg," he said. "Beg me to forgive you."

"No…" I breathed, though I had to fidget and stretch and arch to stop the madness inside me from making me flail at his feet and beg, beg him to put an end to this and grant me the release of his cock inside me.

Smack. Hard, always a bit hard, but never too painful, the sting sending me into convulsions of desire.

His penis dug against my abdomen, harder, harder and I writhed into it, taking it where I could get it.

"Beg," he said again.

"Smack my… Smack my fucking ass already," I spat, barely getting the words out.

He snickered then, almost losing his kingly character entirely, but he smacked me again and I screamed in delight.

"I think you just begged me to spank you," he pointed out.

"Oh, fuck you..." I said between gasps of air. "Take me, please. I'm fucking begging you." I rolled over and he swooped in to catch me, his other hand shifting behind my head, so I lay with the small of my back over his lap, my legs kicking outward for lack of something better to do without his penis inside me.

Our eyes locked. "I'm sorry," I whispered. "I'm sorry, Your Royal Highness. Fucking take me—please."

His eyes probed mine as a smirk lit up his face. "That's better," he said. "Starlight."

He stood, making sure to keep me from sliding off him and shifting my back toward the makeshift hammock. It wasn't perfect—there were gaping holes between the vines, but it would do.

He took hold of both calves and yanked me closer to the edge of the hammock, hooking my ankles up around his neck, my legs burning—aching, but in a good way—at the stretch. My pussy was hot and wet and ready for him as my hands gripped the vines on either side of me. He stared down at me and his smug smile went slack as he flipped his long hair over his shoulder—tickling my calf—and he rubbed his thumb over his lips. His breaths were shallower, but mine were about to burst.

"Please..." I said again, my voice cracking.

He stroked his cock a few times as he stared down at me. I writhed a little, clenching my jaw. He'd been hard enough, surely. But my movement only made him stroke harder.

Then he shifted, sliding his throbbing cock inside me. I yelled in delight, the tight muscles all over my body seeming to melt at the movement. Grabbing hold of my thighs, he thrust even deeper and the power between us was overwhelming. I screamed out his name, a name I'd never had cause to address him by. "Alarik!"

He withdrew a bit and then thrust back in, pounding me over and over as my voice caught in my throat, my animalistic cries the only thing escaping from my lips. The wind blew through again and I hardly even flinched as the vine hammock rocked—both from the gust and his movement—the chill unable to penetrate the extreme, tingling heat overtaking every cell in my body.

CHAPTER TWELVE

I'D EXPECTED HIM TO RETREAT THE MOMENT HE'D FINISHED spilling inside me, preparing for our return to the top of the cliff, testing out whatever bonuses my power gave him.

I'd expected to be slapped with the cold, hard truth then, at the sight of what my folly had wrought.

Instead, we lay together on the hammock, my cheek on his chest, his hand woven through my hair as his other moved in soft circles over my arm. The activity, his nearness, the slight life of the nearby fire, was enough to lull me to sleep.

I woke, though who knew how much later, the firelight out and a chill raking through me, even as I felt the warmth of his skin against mine. I bolted upright, a hand flying to my mouth. I stared down at Alarik, who slept peacefully, his breathing light.

"Finally!" said a voice in my brain.

Zander.

"Damn right, it's Zander. And before you tell me you weren't thinking about me, believe me, I've been extremely aware

of that…" His voice went quiet. *"Your boost is wearing off,"* he said, causing my heart to thunder even more. My "day long" boost after sex wasn't a perfect science, but that meant it definitely had to be about a day since then.

I gnawed at my knuckles, trying to calm the tension in my chest. Shivering, I jumped off the vine hammock and pattered to pick up my clothes near the smoky ashes of the fire's remnants.

"Yeah, I saw… I saw that," Zander said over the bond. *"I was trying to reach you forever—"*

Alanna blocked me with that power of hers, I sent back.

"Yeah, well, I figured that was why, but I kept trying. And trying. Because I was fucking worried about you, darlin'. Then…" His voice cut out as I slipped into my ridiculous filthy pants one leg at a time.

Zander? I asked, wondering if he wouldn't be able to find me in this other dimension when my boost wore off him.

"We can talk about you fucking him later."

My gaze flicked upward to the sparkly, shiny cavern ceiling as I shook out my tank top and slipped it over my head. *Can you see through my eyes?* I sent over the bond.

"No, but I sure as fuck heard your thoughts about him. I didn't need you to be thinking about me as long as the boost was working—remember? I can even reach people I've never bonded with. But thoughts were enough. It didn't take a genius to figure out what was going on between you. More or less."

So he didn't know the *details…*

"Do I even want to?" he asked. I could almost hear the sigh over the bond. *"Never mind, darlin'. I said you could fuck who you please and it wouldn't change how I felt about you."*

Gathering Alarik's pants and jerkin in my hands, I

slipped into my boots and took careful, quiet steps back toward the hammock.

"Doesn't mean I have to approve of you boosting the other-worldly invaders, though." There was a rumble over the bond, like he was mentally clearing his throat. *"Tactics and all that. I... I may have told Jayden. And your boy toy was there. And he—to put it lightly—flipped out. Wouldn't stop saying it was hard enough you were fucking one enemy, but now another... Jayden, well, Jayden was Jayden about it. Grim and taciturn. But I know what he was* actually *thinking."*

Great. Sighing, I looked down at the lithe, naked form of my captor—reminding myself I was using him every bit as much for sex as he may have been using me. That whatever I may have felt was there between us had just been some wild fancy, my libido overtaking my brain.

"You're getting weaker in my head, darlin'," said Zander over the bond. *"So let's touch base."*

The bond wouldn't let us speak across dimensions, then, once my boost wore off. Not without my kiss.

"Or, more accurately, your juicy pussy," he purred.

My ears flushed hot.

"Later," he said. *"Because there* will *be a later. You need to be back here."*

Nodding, I sent my affirmation through the bond. *That's the plan. I'm here to grab Roulette through the first portal we can.*

"Stay focused," he said. *"Darlin', even if—"*

But whatever else he had to say, I felt the chill in my core, a bleak mark of his absence.

Zander? I pushed through the bond. To be extra sure, I closed my eyes and pictured him taking me in the tub, pictured his roving hands, his feather-light touch.

Nothing.

Alarik's voice rang out through the cavern. "You're up early."

I opened my eyes to find him sitting up, stretching one arm high above his head, his long, thick cock hung brazenly mere centimeters from my legs.

Swallowing, I gritted my teeth to keep that traitorous groin of mine in check and shoved the pile at him. "Let's go," I said.

He fussed with his hair, drawing it in front of his shoulders and running a hand up and down it to smooth out what little frizzes there were as he spread his thighs apart wider. "You sure you don't want to go again?" he asked.

I dropped the clothes atop his lap. "Take me to Roulette. Now."

"I should spank you for that tone," he said, making a big spectacle of sliding one leg through his pants.

My lips parted as I silently choked on my retort, my ass tingling with the memory of his touch. Finally, I got my head back to the moment as he stood and readjusted his pants. They hugged his butt cheeks tightly and I resisted the urge to grab one in each hand. "Let's go and I'll give you an extra boost with my kiss," I said. "The sex boost should still be working," I added, before he could start the ball rolling on another round. Better that the clock keep counting down on that boost—better to stay away from fucking him ever again so he never had the chance to try out these newfound powers back on Earth.

I shivered as I squinted and tried to gaze through the bright mists gathered at the entrance to the cave, plastering myself against the stone wall as another blast of wind hurried through.

"You want my jerkin again?" he asked as he padded over, fastening the bottom of the item of clothing in question.

The tip of my tongue darted out to slide against my lips as I shook my head and looked away.

He took my face in one hand, his grip firm around my chin as he turned me back to face him. "Don't look at me like you want me to fuck you again, then look away. I won't be teased without satisfaction."

Was it that obvious? Fucking hell.

His grip loosened as his lips dove to meet mine, only they stopped before we came in contact. He pulled back a little.

"What do you say?" His voice was stern.

My throat went dry, my mouth still just a little hard to control with his hand on my chin, even if it'd loosened.

"If you don't kiss me, you might not have enough power to get us out of here." I spoke through gritted teeth. My hands balled into fists and I ground them into the wall behind me, daring myself to *try* to let my libido run wild with this arrogant ecoterrorist again.

His eyes gleamed. "You *are* a stubborn one," he said. Then his lips moved closer to my ear, his husky voice lowering to a whisper. "The most satisfying to break."

His other hand slid down the front of my pants, a finger charging straight between the lips of my pussy. Startled, my eyes flitted to look at what he was doing down there and I cried out as his finger danced, but it was more like a moan.

The hand on my chin squeezed—not at all painfully, but firmly, directing my gaze sharply back into his eyes. "What do you say?"

"Please," I said quietly, hating myself for loving this.

"Please what?" he asked, a finger jutting up inside me.

"Please kiss me," I said, groaning as my knees went weak. In and out. In an out. Just near the entrance. He stared at me, clearly expecting more. "Please…" I said. "Your Majesty."

He did then, shifting his full hand inside my pants to move his thumb in a teasing circle over my clit as another finger joined the first one up my pussy.

I felt the stirrings of an orgasm as he finger-fucked me. Deeper, harder—teasing my pleasure point harder and harder. It was more distracting than the shift of power flowing between us as his lips nibbled mine greedily, his tongue dancing around mine.

Oh, shit. This was giving him more of a boost than I'd intended.

I gasped, taking my face from his. He let it go, dropping his grip on my chin.

His fingers withdrew and he took a careful step back and rubbed his forearm over his mouth before licking his fingers. "Pure starlight," he said. Then he flinched, his chest hitching as he went unnaturally stiff.

It took me until then to remember his injury—dark blood stained the bandage.

He lifted his chin. "All right, starlight," he said, acting as if he hadn't just finger-banged me near a perilous cliff and left me clutching the wall. "Let's see what I—what *we* together—can do."

He motioned for me to step back and I did on jittery legs.

He raised his palm out upward and the vine he produced went soaring—larger, stronger, faster than before.

His laugh echoed through the cavern as he slammed to his knees, startling me. He hollered into the misty air, his cries ringing like a wild animal's. He closed his palm and stared up at his creation—the vine must have hitched itself somewhere up out of sight. He tentatively aimed his palm at it again and instead of another vine shooting out, the dangling one swung back and forth, as if a giant's hand had swatted it.

He shouted again, jumping to his feet and running to me, sweeping me up into his arms. Even the flash of pain that crossed his face as he lifted me a few inches off the ground and spun me around wasn't long-lived as he peppered kisses all over my chin, my neck, my clavicle.

What in the ever-loving hell…? So much for his royalty routine.

But as he lowered me a little, his hands sliding down to cup my buttocks, his lips greedily slamming against mine, I felt my pussy become wet entirely. Dominating or exhilarated, this fucking otherworlder could turn me on like a faucet.

He finally pulled his lips away but wouldn't let go of his greedy grip on my buttocks. "I can control it," he said.

"What…?" I asked, and my stomach sank.

There was no containing the grin on his face. "With your power, I can control it. Before we had to aim with our hands, but now…" He shifted to lower my feet to the ground and turned one palm toward the cavern opening as the other gripped me tighter against him. The vine shot toward us and I cried out, but he laughed as it slid gently around our waists, acting like a belt tying us together. "I've got you," he said, his voice loud and forceful. "And I don't know if I ever want to let go."

Before I could reply, he waved his hand and the vine tugged on us both, whipping us out to the canyon at a pace outrunning the shriek that escaped my mouth at the sudden movement.

THE VINE HAD CARRIED US UP THE CLIFF IN A FLASH, depositing us safely at the top before I could even think about what was happening. I'd pounded on Alarik's chest, unleashing a string of curses that he was *never* to do that without warning again, but his lips took mine before I could finish my protest and we were off, bounding through the forest on his newly-formed vines, moving almost at the speed of sound, every short break in the action punctuated by another kiss before I could steel myself up to complain. At last we arrived before two elves who stood at attention on either side of a gaping, door-sized hole.

"Your Majesty!" they said in unison, dropping to one knee.

"You startled us—" began one.

"We heard you'd perished," said the other.

Alarik, true to his word that he didn't want to release me, waved one hand lazily at them as he guided me through the hole, his arm wrapped tightly around my waist. "Well, obviously, you've been misinformed." He turned to one. "Bring Xerxes to the throne room immediately."

The two guards drew to their feet, their weight shifting awkwardly in place.

"Your Majesty," said one. "Xerxes is *in* the throne room—"

Alarik didn't wait to hear more. He stormed ahead, shifting his hand from my waist to my hand, tugging me after him. I was so keen to not stumble that I didn't notice at first, but as we made our way up half a flight of wooden stairs that looked almost like they'd *grown* out of a winding tree trunk, I tugged back as my mouth went slack.

My head shook slowly as I took in this elvish kingdom.

It existed in symbiosis with the trees, dwellings carved into tree trunks with thriving leaves overhead, a stream weaving through the town. Little shops had been made out of tree trunks and with roofs that resembled giant mushrooms grown five thousand times too large. The town went back as far as I could see, dwellings alit with candlelight, the elves moving to and fro, stopping to laugh with their neighbors or fill up their baskets with goods.

"Right," said Alarik behind me, clearing his throat. He took a careful step back to join me on the landing I'd found myself on without even fully taking in the surroundings at my feet. I couldn't look away.

He moved closer and planted a kiss atop my head. "Welcome to the heart of Nelia, starlight," he said. "Welcome home."

I was too flabbergasted to argue.

His hand fell from mine, and I felt him turn beside me, his voice directed elsewhere. "Tianah," he said. "Perfect. Come here, please."

"Your Majesty," said a soft voice behind me. I finally turned to see a beautiful brown elf woman—small and willowy-thin and oozing femininity—curtsey before giving me a clearly puzzled onceover. "We heard—"

"You all heard wrong," Alarik snapped. Then he sighed and put a hand on the small of my back, directing me toward her. "I have business to discuss with Xerxes," he said, gentler this time. "Please get her clean and into something warmer." He sized me up and down. "But not *too* warm," he added, grinning at me.

Rolling my eyes, I let my hair whap across my face as my head moved back and forth. "I'm going with you," I said. "I'm here to see Roulette."

"Get cleaned up first," he said, taking a step toward the

rest of the staircase. "Then we'll discuss our future conquest."

My blood ran cold, reminding me I had no business boosting this cocky asshole's powers.

But damn, did his royal ass look fine as he climbed the stairs away from me.

CHAPTER THIRTEEN

Elvish wear was luxuriously comfortable. I supposed I could have come to that conclusion when borrowing Alarik's jerkin, but away from the biting wind and fresh from a steaming hot bath, I could finally appreciate the soft material of the form-fitting dress. The velvety, colorful material actually *glowed* like magic in the light. It melted into my skin like I was wearing nothing at all without feeling tight and constricting like Lila's too-small outfit. The elf maiden handed me a pair of long, green arm warmers to wear along with it, and I shuddered at how soft they were as I slipped them on, my hands poking through freely. Minutes later, I tapped my feet impatiently as Tianah moved a brush through my thick hair, then insisted on weaving what appeared to be dried, silver twigs through the tresses.

"I appreciate the help, but I really need to see my friend," I said at last as she wove in the fifth or sixth twig. "The other human?"

But Tianah hadn't had much to say at all the past hour or so. Just enough to relay instructions.

"His Majesty will send for you when he's ready," she replied.

Sighing, I sunk into the chair. The seat and back were woven with what appeared to be dried grass, the frame made of branches, any jabbing edge worn down and smoothed.

Zander? I tried again. But naturally, there was no reply. Tianah kept weaving her twigs through and I zoned out a little.

"His Majesty awaits," said a new voice some time later. I jumped in place.

Tianah stepped back and bowed her head to the newcomer—a handsome elf man who looked familiar, but then again, there wasn't one who wasn't handsome.

He stared at me expectantly and I stood. "Thank you," I said to Tianah, though I'd much rather have been scouring for Roulette than getting pampered. To be fair, I sure felt a hell of a lot better after getting pampered. I'd been sore in so many ways, and the warm waters had eased the tension in my muscles.

The elf who'd summoned me didn't speak as he led me through the Nelian village, up to the staircase where I'd parted from Alarik and farther and farther up what I realized to be a giant tree. A giant freaking tree encircled this whole damn village.

Gasping, I stopped to look at it from above once more. The man stopped several stairs above me. "Your Excellency," he said, and I had no idea where he'd gotten that title from. "Please." He gestured upward.

Sighing, I tore my eyes away and followed after him. "What's your name?" I asked because why the hell not? I'd already fucked an enemy king. May as well get to know a few others.

169

"Normak, Your Excellency," he replied. His jaw twitched just slightly.

"'Aurora' is fine," I replied.

"Not so long as you are the royal consort of choice."

The... what? "What do you mean?" What had Alarik said to these elves in the hour or so we'd been apart?

Normak clasped his hands together and said nothing more. We walked in silence a bit longer, the melodic trickle of the river below at least keeping the quiet from being excruciating. At last we reached the top of the staircase, where the gaps in the tree branches grew wider and the whole thing plateaued to what seemed like a cavernous room, though the floor and walls were all worn and uneven, as much a part of the tree as anything. The back wall was lined with elves at attention, the branches making up the ceiling latticed to let wisps of sunlight inside. I wondered if it was lit by moonlight at night.

"Your Majesty," said Normak, taking a knee before the wooden seat at the center of the back of the room.

Snapping to attention, I found Alarik seated there, shirtless, his arm unwrapped and being held gingerly by...

"Roulette!" I shrieked, running past Normak to throw my arms around her.

Her eyes widened as she looked between Alarik and me, but she said nothing.

Frowning, I leaned back to better take her in. She was dressed in colorful elven clothing like I was, even down to the twig highlights in her hair—only hers were golden, and they popped out among her fiery red tresses and dark roots like gold dust.

"Starlight," came Alarik's voice from beside us. A sharp intake of breath from him drew my attention as Roulette released her hold on his arm, his wound healed.

He drunk me in with a thirst that needed quenching—

despite the gallons he'd metaphorically drunk the night before. The heat rising to my cheeks was too damn distracting right then in a room full of other people. My hand found Roulette's and I squeezed, hoping she could pick up on some of my confidence—that I had a plan. Sort of.

"I'm sorry," she whispered to me. "I didn't intend to tell them about you, but something—"

Setting my jaw, I shook my head. "You couldn't help it," I whispered back, but that was as far as our conversation got.

Alarik stood then and opened his arms toward us both. I slunk back, thinking he might embrace us, but he turned and spoke to the room, his arms still open wide. "And these two humans—these Natches—my citizenry, are how we will accomplish our goal on Earth."

"You would use a defiler to atone for defiling?" asked someone from behind Roulette and me. I whipped around along with Rou, and she instinctively pulled me backward toward the wall as a handsome, dark-skinned elf strode toward Alarik from the corner of the room, flanked on either side by soldier elves. It took me a second to recognize the tall, muscular elf—that Xerxes, who'd confronted Alarik in the forest. I searched around for Alanna but didn't find her, though I remembered quickly that Roulette had just used her powers, so she must not have been nearby. I knew from the incident downtown that her nullification powers had a range. Xerxes crossed his arms and jutted his chin toward Alarik. "I suppose it has some poetry to it, but I caution against relying on the enemy in such a manner."

Forcing a laugh, Alarik held his arms to either side and two elf servants seemed to take that as their cue, stepping out from the shadows to drape their king in a new jerkin.

This one was similar to the other, like those the soldiers wore, earth-tone and form-fitting, but it had silver threads woven throughout, an echo of my hair. He nodded at them after one finished fastening the front and pulled first on one sleeve and then another. "I have promised victory, and I will deliver it."

Xerxes looked over his shoulder, then turned around, gesturing casually to either side and then resting his hands above his belt. "And you have promised us such before. I do not see a parade of triumph about to begin in your honor, Alarik."

Narrowing his eyes, Alarik took a seat again and curled a finger around the edge of the armrest. "You've made no secret that you think you could do it better," he said. "Be grateful I don't have you banished from my sight for your insolence. Were it not for some misguided affection on the part of my sister—"

Xerxes took a bold, quick step forward. "Were it not for the love of that same sister, I'd have ousted you years ago."

Alarik snapped up to his feet, his nostrils flaring. "You would dare? After the mercy I just showed you for—what did you call it? Keeping my throne warm?" He turned to some of the elves beside him—they'd already stepped forward.

"I wouldn't do that if I were you," said Xerxes. "Not if you ever want to see your sister again."

Raising a hand in the air, Alarik stopped the movements of his guards with one gesture. "Where is she?"

Xerxes rocked back on his heels. "You're the one who never wants her around. You should thank me for keeping her out of the village."

"I only ever said that because..." Alarik's clenched fists shook at his side. "If you've hurt her—"

"I wouldn't," said Xerxes, his voice going quiet.

Letting out a clipped laugh, Alarik smiled. "Then what do I have to fear from you?"

"Just because I wouldn't hurt her doesn't mean I'll let her go free," he said. He pointed to the two men behind him, who hadn't moved to subdue him when the others had. "Nor does it mean you can count on every Nelian to aid you. Some are more than ready for a change in leadership."

Alarik's glare to the elves behind Xerxes was cutting. "Until I have children of my own, Alanna is my heir—not you. I don't care if you fuck her. You'll never be king."

"Children of your own?" The belly-shaking laughter Xerxes offered did nothing to release the clear tension in the cord in Alarik's neck. Roulette's hand went clammy and she squeezed my palm harder as Xerxes took a few steps toward us. "Do you intend to have children with this 'consort' of yours? This filthy human consort?"

Alarik moved between Xerxes and me, and the guards on the king's side took a few steps toward us. "You stay away from her."

Of course. Consort. Me. Maybe if I told him I couldn't have kids, he'd—

Alanna's powers. My fingers tingled at the idea of putting Wade and Jayden's theory to the test, of staying around his sister for nine months and then—

"What are you so afraid of?" asked Xerxes, a thin, false smile appearing on his face. "I've no interest in your human animal."

"Then. Stay. Away." Alarik planted his legs wide as he raised a trembling hand.

"I just worry," began Xerxes, taking a step back and seeming to speak to the room at large, "what danger the king could be putting us all in by keeping these women hostage? Does he honestly think they'll willingly assist us in reforming their planet?" He turned his nose down on Alarik. "How much time do we need to waste on a slowly-dying rock when we have Nelia?"

Alarik crossed the space between them in a flash, shoving at Xerxes' chest. "You're the one who told me to invade," he said. "*You're* the one who told me my reign was time—"

Hands in the air, Xerxes shook his head. "You misunderstood me, brother."

"I did not!" said Alarik, winding up a fist. "You lying, foul—"

Xerxes sidestepped Alarik's blow and spun, grabbing my arm and tearing me from Roulette's grasp.

"No!" Rou screamed.

I didn't have a chance to think about why she might have been so afraid before a wave of fog came over me and I went slack in the elf's arms.

"Unhand her!" insisted Alarik, but two of the elvish soldiers who'd stepped away from the wall grabbed his arms instead.

I could barely register what was unfolding before me, my brain was such a fog.

"What's your name?" asked a voice beside me. The hand grasping my wrist was cold and clammy, the voice familiar and causing bile to rise in my throat, but its question *demanding* an answer.

"Aurora Haddix," I said, feeling sick.

"Xerxes, if you hurt her—" Alarik. I thought. My head was swimming.

"And do you have plans of escape from your elven captors, my dear Aurora?" asked the voice. Xerxes.

"Yes," I said before I could stop myself.

The rumbling voice laughed, and I felt myself swaying

on my feet. "You have no intention of helping us destroy the accomplishments of your own people, do you?"

"No," I said.

"Aurora," said a familiar voice—Roulette, I thought. She was fuzzy, though. Everything was fuzzy.

"And what about Alarik, our elven king?" asked the echoing voice in my ear.

"Xerxes, I don't know what you think you're going to accomplish with this," said that same elvish king. I giggled. It was like I was getting drunk. But it hurt, too. My head throbbed.

"This king is besotted with you," said the voice—Xerxes. "I can sense you feel an animalistic attraction to him, too."

Snickering, I tried to hide my smile behind my hand, but I tugged and forgot someone was holding tightly to my wrist.

"But do you love him?" asked the voice. "Can you see yourself willingly giving him heirs to the throne?"

"Yes and yes," I said, then I giggled again.

Murmurs floated throughout the room, gnawing at my brain like buzzing bees.

My wrist went cold and I collapsed to my knees, my brain suddenly snapped back to life like it had been doused with cold water. Palms on the cold dirt floor, I took a deep breath, filling my lungs.

"Aurora," said Alarik at the same time Roulette spoke. Roulette appeared at my side and Alarik struggled to get out of the hold of the two soldiers keeping him at bay.

"Starlight," he said, his voice wavering somewhat.

"Confine them," said Xerxes as he strode over to the seat in the tree wall I'd assumed to be a throne. Leaning back in the chair, he stretched his arms high overhead before gripping the armrests.

Two more soldiers surrounded Roulette and me and I cocked my head at her, as if to ask why she didn't see if her powers would come up "harm" and blast these suckers away. With her flaring nostrils and tense muscles, though, she didn't need to say a word. She just squeezed tightly to my arm and that was enough.

What had they done to her?

Alarik didn't stop screaming about traitors and injustices the whole way as we were dragged down a flight of stairs and along a winding, wooden hallway.

ALARIK PACED THE ROOM, HIS LIPS FLAPPING AND SOUNDS coming out on occasion, but nothing intelligible. For the first time, I wondered why this alien race seemed to converse in perfect English, and whether that was a show all for our benefit—highly unlikely, considering there had been plenty of opportunities for them to speak another language and keep us out of the loop.

Not that I wasn't grateful they hadn't.

Perhaps this dimension was simply one of infinite possibilities where humans had evolved into elves, keeping their love for nature at the forefront of their hearts, and cobbling together a language eerily similar to ours through a series of events…

I didn't know. I wasn't Wade.

"Your brother-in-law started a coup?" I asked.

"He's not wed to my sister—yet—but yes," snapped Alarik, intelligible at last.

Gnawing on her lip, Roulette leaned back against the headboard. I'd surmised from Alarik's ramblings that this was his bedroom—perhaps they had no need for prisons here. Usually.

I'd confirmed for her that Darien was safe at home, and she'd relaxed somewhat. Zander had told her as much when scouring Nelia for me in his mind last night.

"So tell me what he did to me again?" I asked, looking at Roulette as much as Alarik.

Shuddering, Roulette waited to see if Alarik would answer, but he'd taken to clutching the bedpost now—a bedpost that looked like the trunk of a small birch tree.

"His power is to compel the truth to be spoken," said Roulette quietly. "With a touch. That's how he got me to speak about you. At least… I figured out as much."

Alarik seemed to come to life then, scrambling around the side of the bed we Natches were both seated on. He took my hands in his and went to his knees on the floor beside my calves. "Aurora, my starlight," he said, now the gallant knight. He kissed my knuckles. "The one good thing to come of this—you… You feel it too."

Face flushing, I pulled my hands away from his grip, glancing at Roulette guiltily. She seemed unnaturally stiff as she narrowed her eyebrows at me. "They… When they asked me about you, he and his sister spoke of an attraction between you." She looked to Alarik for confirmation or denial, but he said nothing, just hung his head low. "They said they could *feel* such things, though they didn't feel anything between Darien and me."

I glared at Alarik then. "Because humans and Natches don't give off tangible pheromones like wild animals," I said.

"Well, they said *you* did." Roulette hugged her arms tight across her torso.

"Rou," I started. "Don't give credence to—"

"And now the truth guy, whose powers I *know* work, gets you to admit you're actually *in love* with him?" asked Roulette, her voice rising as her lips flattened into a curl.

Roulette looked as if she wanted to smack me—and Alarik gazed up now from his position at my feet, his lips parted slightly.

"I—no," I said. "I can't possibly love someone so fast—never mind the fact that he keeps leading the charge into my city and uprooting buildings, putting people's lives at risk." Looking down at wide-eyed Alarik, the tiniest bit of pain in his beautifully deep brown irises, I had to tear myself away, rubbing my forehead between my fingers.

"And what about Nash?" asked Roulette, letting out an impatient huff. "And Jayden, for that matter?"

Why does everyone insist there's something between Jayden and me? Rubbing a finger over my lips, I remembered that kiss we'd shared at last and I mentally kicked myself for having *zero* self-control.

Good thing she didn't know about Zander to boot.

"And what do you mean, you want to have his kids?" said Roulette, her voice growing louder. "When you thought you just *might* be pregnant with Nash's, you said you weren't ready—"

"Who's this Nash?" demanded Alarik, rising to his feet.

Smacking my palm against my forehead, I shook my head, trying to shut them both out for a second. "I never thought about having kids, okay? When Wade figured out I couldn't—I don't know, I figured I'd deal with that some-day, if I was ready to adopt... I just... Look, I never said I wanted this guy's kids right now, right? Please give me a break. I don't... I don't even know what I want myself." My lips dry, I pulled them in and ran my tongue over their surface before locking eyes with Alarik. His knees seemed to wobble, his tight expression softening, and he took a seat beside me at the edge of the bed. Roulette drew her legs closer to herself, pulling them against her chest and

178

resting her chin on her knees. Her narrowed eyes didn't leave Alarik.

This was as good a time as any to explain to everyone present that this was impossible—and also, that we had more important things to deal with just now.

"Look, okay? You want me to be honest? I slept with this asshole last night," I said, looking at Roulette more than anything. A slight shake of her head was all the indication she gave me that she'd heard.

"Starlight," began Alarik, but I put a finger to his lips. Startled, he actually went quiet.

"And just so *you* know, that even if you weren't my enemy, I have other men I'm attracted to—ones I can actually say I'm in love with and not question my sanity. As much." I dropped my finger from his lips and set my jaw. "Multiple men."

A tiny scoff from Roulette was expected, but I didn't imagine Alarik simply shrugging his shoulders. But that was what he did. "And this is this odd to you?" he asked. "My people believe in loving everyone they feel attraction to." He rubbed a hand behind his neck, unsettling the silky green hair that hung over his shoulder. "I just... If you were pregnant with another man's child, I wanted to know. It would affect succession."

There were so many things wrong with that sentence, I barely knew where to begin. "First, I probably—*probably*" —I emphasized, sending Roulette a careful look not to get into that just yet—"can't get pregnant. The other time was unlikely and just a fluke."

Alarik shifted to cross his arms and hung back a little, as if observing me.

Sighing, I continued. "And secondly, I'd say you have more of an issue with holding on to that throne at the moment than you do worrying about your future line of succession, don't you?"

As if that served as a harsh reminder, Alarik took a sharp intake of breath. He shut his lips tight and looked to both Roulette and me. Then, tossing his shoulders back, he grabbed for my hand.

"I love you," he said, sending a tightness through my chest and a rumble between my legs. "I don't care if you have others, but I've never felt this way with any of my lovers before. I don't know... I don't even know if I ever want to take another woman, elven or human."

Roulette snorted and I had to shoot her a look to get her to stop rolling her eyes. At the enemy confessing his devotion to me. Okay, it *did* seem ridiculous. That is, it would seem that way to me, too, if I didn't feel what I felt...

Clenching my other hand tightly against the soft blanket beneath me, I steeled myself to get him to drop the subject, to focus on something that really mattered.

"I don't care if you can't bear children," he said. "I don't care if you can and simply don't want to..." He put his free hand to my cheek, the soft touch sending shivers down my spine. "You're right. I'll worry about succession later. After putting Xerxes in his place. I just want you to know—I love you. And you can always be with me, even if you always need to be with others, too."

I opened my mouth to speak and then shut it. There were so many things wrong with what he was saying— what I apparently felt myself when compelled to tell the truth.

"I won't help you take over Earth," I said. "And by the way, I don't know if you're aware, but you've been attacking the same moderately sized town over and over— it's like one-ten-thousandth the size of the whole Earth." I looked to Roulette for confirmation, but she shrugged. "Or even less, I don't know."

Alarik dropped his palm from my cheek and I snatched it, giving both his hands a squeeze. "So you had *a lot* more work to go. Not to mention, the military is probably working on ways to stop you whenever they can figure out where exactly you'll appear and how long you'll be there. And they—they can do so much damage to the planet in their efforts to stop you."

Roulette guffawed wryly. "You think he cares about…" Her eyes narrowed as she looked at Alarik. "No, seriously? That's what you were doing? Going on a crusade for Mother Earth?"

"I…" Alarik's bravado had waned more and more in the past few hours. He swallowed visibly. "I knew the planet must be large, and I knew you had technology that we don't have…" He dropped one of my hands to pat the pouch at his belt, where I knew he'd stashed the MP3 player. I found myself smiling, and he met me with his own weak grin. "But I… It can't be so hopeless," he said, his voice growing quiet. "I have you two now—"

"*Ha*," said Roulette, and it was clear she didn't find this very funny. "Not me. Not willingly." She looked to me and I nodded. "And even if she *wants* to fuck you, she's not going to do it again while it stands to potentially benefit an attack on our planet, *right*?"

Reluctantly, I nodded, biting down on my lip. Yes, reluctantly. *What is wrong with me?*

"Not even if I order you to?" said Alarik, his voice practically purring, his hand growing warmer and wetter in mine.

Startled at the shot that sent to my groin, I gasped and pulled back out of his grip.

"Oh, brother," said Roulette.

Clearing my throat, I stood. "Okay, enough of this. Rou, you can still use your powers, right? Alarik, you too?"

Roulette flicked her palm lazily at a tree trunk table and shot it with what turned out to be a white light, causing the dead lumber to burst forth with flowers. "Yup," she said, quickly closing her hand and shutting off the light.

"That means Alanna isn't nearby," I said, looking to Alarik. "Right?"

He nodded, his face grim. "She could be somewhere in the village—she must be, surely, Xerxes wouldn't be so cruel as to send her away—but she's not within five hundred tree limbs of us right now. Or we'd lose our powers."

"Tree limbs?" I asked, wondering how they determined the average length of something that came in all shapes and sizes.

He nodded. Okay, so there was *something* different about the language.

"So what are we waiting for?" I asked. "I can boost..." Roulette shot me a look before I could continue. "I can boost one or both of you—it's just for a few minutes, Rou —and then we'll get out of here."

"And go where?" asked Roulette. "In case you didn't get a good look, this whole planet is full of giant warthog creatures out to get you. There are no other places to go."

"No other cities?" I asked Alarik, who looked confused that I'd even ask. "No other elven settlements?"

He shook his head. "Nelia is the heart of Mother Nelia as a whole. And it belongs to the mother goddess. My people are just caretakers allowed to live in it."

Hmm, well, that was more admirable than the positions humans took—but then again, there were far too many of us to attempt to squeeze all together in one giant tree.

"But so what?" I said. "At least we'll be away from here, away from the coup. Maybe we could just rough it in the wild."

"Even if that *were* tempting, and it's *not*," said Roulette, leaning back against the pillow and crossing her hands beneath her breasts like Sleeping Beauty, "it wouldn't be home. It just... wouldn't be home."

You'd think she'd been imprisoned here for years instead of two days. I pounded a fist on the soft blanket, but it didn't make much of an impact. "Then what do you propose we do?"

"Don't ask me. You're here to rescue *me*, aren't you?" She frowned. "Or maybe you're just here to fuck him."

"*Rou*," I said, urging her to heed the warning.

There was a knock at the door and Alarik shot to his feet, his hands reaching for a dagger that was no longer there. His traitorous guards had taken it when they'd shoved him in here with us.

"Your Majes—er, Alarik," said a voice, soft and familiar.

"Tianah?" he asked, striding to the door. He opened it. It wasn't even locked.

Oh, my freaking god. He—and Roulette—really didn't believe there was anywhere to run, did they? Had no one ever heard of camping?

Tianah carried a tray of food past two guards at attention, followed by another—Normak, who had his hands similarly full. Alarik shut the door behind them as they made their way to the table that had grown a few new blossoms.

Tianah gasped, her cheekbones becoming prominent as she put the tray down. The liquid—in a wooden cup—

sloshed slightly and I noticed her limbs were trembling. "It's beautiful," she said.

Alarik's fast-paced strut to her side startled Normak as he nearly mowed the other elf man down. "Isn't it? And that was before the healer got my consort's boost."

"I have a name," said Roulette, not even bothering to lift her head from the pillow. "And Rora hasn't agreed to be your consort yet, buddy."

Normak put his tray beside Tianah's and I shrugged, figuring at least Xerxes didn't wish us to go hungry. Alarik gestured wildly, practically bouncing on his feet. "You see how my plan to take over the human planet could work—"

Roulette shifted to lean back on her forearms. "Hey, I *just* explained to you that I have no interest in helping you. Can't speak for Aurora, apparently—"

Gaping, I shook my head and rubbed a careful hand up my neck. I wouldn't help Alarik take over Earth. That much should have been obvious.

"We have to at least *try*, though," said Alarik, his voice going hoarse as the smile vanished from his lips. "Right?" Was he seriously asking that? I didn't know how he expected to force Roulette and me to try his boosted-vine-growing plan. If we ever even got back to Earth to begin with.

The two elves exchanged a glance.

"Your Majesty," said Normak quietly. "We can send you there."

Alarik blinked. "You would do that? Against the order of Xerxes?"

"Xerxes is not my king," said Tianah, her shoulders pushing back as she tightened her fists at her sides.

Alarik studied them and then nodded, running back to my side and yanking on my arm to pull me around the other side of the bed, where he tugged on Roulette's arm, too.

"*Hey,*" she said as she stumbled up and to her feet.

Tianah and Normak stepped several feet apart and opened their arms wide, as if holding on to an invisible circle.

"What?" I said, my brain slower to catch up than my eyes.

These two were portal creators. And Xerxes had not only not locked the door, he'd let them walk *right into* our room.

The air crackled between them as their lips went thin, their eyes focused on the shifting light.

"Come on," said Alarik, tugging on us both. He stopped right before charging through, causing both Roulette and me to stumble against his back. He didn't flinch, though. "Thank you," he said to both of the servants.

They nodded.

"Go," Normak whispered.

Alarik tugged on us again and we went through, the air sizzling as we stepped from one dimension to another.

CHAPTER FOURTEEN

IT TOOK ME A MINUTE TO RECOMBOBULATE MYSELF TO MY surroundings. Someone screamed and I turned to find a few people running through the parking lot we'd found ourselves in. One guy was pointing a phone in our direction and a girl beside him was typing furiously on her own.

We were in a grocery store parking lot. I blinked. We weren't too far from Veras headquarters. I could even pick up some milk before we headed back.

I laughed out loud.

Roulette looked at me like I had a screw loose. "Right, so..." She patted her waist, but there weren't pockets in these elven dresses. She stared at me. "Do your brain bond thing," she said, glancing out over the crowd. "Before things get hairy and our own teams descend upon this place ready to blast us into oblivion."

Right. The Nelian tracking apps. Wade must have been watching, must have been alerted to us by now.

Zander? I thought over the bond.

Alarik stood stock still beside me, clenching his fist at

his side, as if struggling to stop himself from shooting his vines out as usual.

Roulette grabbed his arm and yanked him toward the sidewalk, and I followed suit. She looked much more herself now, less hopeless and more at home.

"Darlin'?" came Zander's voice in my head. *"Thank God. How? No, never mind—where? Where are you?"*

Save 'n Buy, I told him, referring to the grocery store.

"Wade is—right. He caught that on his computers. Did you sneak along with elves on a Nelian attack?"

We are the attack—well, Roulette and I are back. We could use a ride.

"That's my girl! Let me relay the news—"

"It's fine," shouted Roulette to a crowd of onlookers. "Nothing to see here." She gestured like an air traffic controller. "Go about your business. Thanks."

Alarik's forehead wrinkled as he watched her.

Zander, I thought again, waiting for the update.

"We're on our way," he said. *"Hang on, darlin'."* He sent a picture of me splayed before him on Jayden's bed, my hands in embarrassing places. *"Can't stop thinking about you,"* he added.

Blinking rapidly, I meant to explain the situation with Alarik as best I could when Zander projected himself right in front of Rou.

"Damn!" she said, a hand to her breast. "You scared me, Renegade." She shifted into a fighting stance, though the form-hugging elvish dress gave her less room to stretch than usual. "What's on the menu today, huh?"

"Relax," said Zander's projected form, smirking. "We're on a temporary truce while we scrambled to find a way to bring the both of you back. We're all on our way."

His gaze fell on me—and Alarik beside me. His brow

wrinkled. "You brought a prisoner? No... You brought *him*, didn't you? The one you..."

"The elvish king," I said, tossing my hair over my shoulder. "Or the former one...?" I looked to Alarik for confirmation.

He scowled a moment and nodded, cradling one elbow with his hand. "For the time being."

Zander's projected form laughed. "That's a story that needs telling." He turned over his shoulder. "But perhaps we should wait until we return to your headquarters." He nodded at Roulette. "Ice-Blast is insisting I tell you he's relieved you're safe."

She beamed, clasping her hands behind her back. "Tell him I can't wait to squeeze those fine-ass butt cheeks."

Zander's lips clamped together as he gave a slight shake of his head. In the time it took him to zone out— probably communicating Roulette's message—I grabbed Alarik's hand.

"Darlin'," said projection-Zander. "We're just around the corner. I—" His eyes darted to my hand in Alarik's, then with a frown, he was gone.

The Veras van pulled up a moment later and Roulette didn't hesitate to run toward the sliding door, jumping up into Darien's arms before his hands even left the handle. He put his feet on the ground and hoisted her up so she could wrap her legs around his waist as she peppered him with kisses.

Zander stepped out after him, followed by Jayden. Wade waved from the driver's seat. Nash was either still home or deep within the dark recesses of the van—and he didn't come out. I remembered that Zander had told me his reaction to the fact that I'd slept with an elf hadn't been... ideal.

Shifting to put myself somewhat between Alarik and the approaching men, I found him squeezing my hand gently and taking a step forward.

"What in the blazes is going on here?" asked Jayden, seemingly taking painstaking measures to keep his voice even. I tried to meet his gaze, but he pointedly refused to look my way, staring straight at Alarik.

Scoffing, Alarik dropped my hand to slip an arm around my waist and pull me against his side. "We won't be parted," he said, as though that even *began* to approach the more important subjects at hand.

Roulette slipped down from around Darien and they both glanced over at us, frowns appearing on their faces.

Pushing myself slightly away from Alarik, I ignored Jayden's pointed glare and settled on pleading with Zander. "Can we discuss this elsewhere?" I jutted my chin toward the onlookers. "We're drawing a crowd."

Something silent passed between Jayden and Zander—perhaps a conversation in their heads—and he nodded. "Okay," Zander said, reaching forward to slide an arm through mine, ripping me completely free of Alarik's grip. He leaned down to kiss me atop the head as he directed me toward the car. "You look stunning," he said and I saw we caught Jayden's eye at that, though he quickly turned to focus on the ground instead. "You'll have to tell me how to get that slinky dress undone, though," he purred directly into my ear, and a tingling shot up from the back of my neck to my cheeks.

———

THERE'D BEEN NO TIME TO FIGURE OUT HOW TO GET OUT OF this dress—though I figured it went over the head like it had when Tianah had slipped it on. Roulette and I both sat around the conference room table in our elven attire, the place packed with Veras and Renegades alike. Lila shifting one leg over the other as she sat at the edge of Wade's console kept drawing my attention, my brain urging me to flee from this room before it broke out into Natch-on-Natch fireworks.

Even if the four men who'd each taken a piece of my heart were all here, too.

Especially if, maybe.

Nash had given me a quiet hug as soon as we'd arrived, but when I'd opened my mouth to speak, he'd just put a finger to my lips and shook his head. "Not now, angel," he said. "Give me a little time to process this."

And that had been it. He leaned against the wall opposite me now, Chastity—looking much better after Roulette's touch—beside him. She cracked her knuckles, her gaze pointedly on Torynt, who seemed to be amusing himself with a little tornado in his palm in the opposite corner.

Kouta was actually in our kitchen making dinner—despite the seriousness of the situation, despite the shaky alliance bringing us all together. Lila had sworn she'd fill him in and we wouldn't regret letting him focus on food.

My growling stomach had to agree with her—we hadn't even gotten to eat anything Tianah and Normak had brought for us.

Roulette finished speaking about what had happened to her since Darien's departure—he'd filled the rest of the group in on what had happened before then—and fortunately, it hadn't been much. She'd seen Xerxes acting like a substitute king. They'd provided her with a room, reminded her she had nowhere to run—and she'd obeyed, fearing the sickening touch of Xerxes' power.

Alarik tried to speak to explain more about Xerxes, but Jayden had sent him a cutting glance to shut him up, which had caused Alarik's hand on the table to clench into a fist as his lips grew thin. He looked to me, as if to ask permission to let loose with his powers.

As if.

I filled the group in on what had happened to me—skipping the details, acknowledging only that we'd needed his boosted powers to escape the cavern—and after explaining the rest, that brought us to this moment.

A disquieting silence fell over the room. Zander wouldn't stop looking at me—Nash kept stealing glances —and Jayden pointedly stared at his white knuckles clutching the table's edge.

"Nelia is beautiful," I said then, surprising even myself. "It's lush and symbiotic."

Lila snorted. "You said there were giant, bloodthirsty warthogs."

"Yes," I admitted, nodding. "I didn't at all feel like the dominant being there. But that doesn't change the fact that it's… it's beautiful." My eyes met Alarik's and for the first time since he'd sat down, his expression softened. "I understand where the Nelians are coming from, even if I don't agree with it."

"If they're really just all clustered in one village smaller than our Podunk town," said Torynt, closing his palm and letting the little tornado dissipate, "then I say the plan is we jump through one of these portals the next time these fuckers appear and see how *they* like it when Natches tear *their* shit up." He rubbed his palms together gleefully.

"Torynt," snapped Zander, sighing. "Not helping."

But Alarik was already on his feet, Chastity at his side letting her crackling light color her fist.

"Stop!" I shouted, jumping to my own feet. Jayden had

191

pointedly directed me away from sitting beside Alarik, so there was no way I'd reach him in time to stop either of them.

"Settle down," said Jayden to Chastity first. "Our goal isn't to decimate another civilization, even if they attacked first."

"Typical Veras limp dick," huffed Torynt, leaning back in his chair.

The mouthwatering scent of something cooking wafted into the room from down the hall and my stomach grumbled very audibly. Lila snickered as I retreated back to my chair. Alarik followed suit and Chastity backed up beside Nash, exchanging a quiet word in his ear. My mouth went dry as I sent him a silent plea to not act rashly.

"We won't attack the Nelians on their planet," said Jayden, and he looked at Zander, as if daring him to contradict him. "Unless they take more of us hostage again…" He turned pointedly to me.

Hostage. I *was* a hostage, even if…

I let out a deep breath.

"It's a moot point regardless," said Wade from his computer keyboard. I'd almost forgotten he was here, he'd been so quiet, but the screen behind him and Lila kept bringing up and closing windows, so he'd been hard at work on something the entire time. "I still can't predict the portals' appearances."

"That's because there's nothing to foresee," said Alarik, folding his arms over his chest. "There is no pattern to most of our appearances—we don't care where we appear, so long as it's here." He nodded at me. "The time we appeared here, at your headquarters, the one exception. But that was difficult for the portal creators to pull off."

"You needed to get in and out real fast to pull off that kidnapping, didn't you?" snapped Nash, his lip trembling.

"We could wait until after we arrive on a scene and jump through the portal then," said Chastity quietly. "Then conquer these would-be conquerors."

Jayden stared at her as if she'd recommended we all split our guts then and there. A corner of Zander's lips twitched and I didn't need his voice in my head to know he was delighted Chastity was seeing the light of the Renegades' more forceful ways.

"I prefer to think of them as the more practical ways, more likely to get fast results," he purred to me over the bond. *"Jayden's having a fit, mind you—internally. In so many, many ways."*

Just slightly, I shook my head at Zander, silently telling him to not distract me just then, and rose to my feet once more.

"We don't need to attack such a beautiful place," I said. I gripped the silky-smooth material of my dress at both thighs and I had to flit my gaze away from Nash's—then away from Zander's—away from Alarik's... They all proved too distracting.

Jayden swallowed visibly, but he was the one I needed most to convince. "Capture this Xerxes—end his rebellion. Then Alarik will step back into his role as king."

Zander scoffed. "And this helps us how?" He gestured at Alarik beside him. "He's the one who started the assaults on our city, isn't he?"

This time I met Alarik's gaze, pouring every ounce of determination I had into the action. "Because if Alarik resumes his throne, he'll give up his quest," I said. "If he ever wants me to willingly give myself to him again."

I didn't know how his lust for me stood in the face of an age-old goal his people had to turn our planet into an echo of theirs, but I had to hope I had some sort of power over him.

Alarik's intense gaze met mine, a slight twitch in his jaw as he flipped his long, green hair over his shoulders. "Agreed," he said.

And that caused the entire room to burst into argument.

CHAPTER FIFTEEN

A<small>FTER THE MEETING ROOM SETTLED, PEOPLE BROKE OFF INTO</small> groups to come up with strategies for what they knew about Xerxes. Wade insisted on Alarik staying behind to tell him everything he knew about the rogue elf—every little detail, starting from childhood. He input the information into his computer, running a program to determine strategies or something.

My strategy? Kick Xerxes' butt and take him hostage. According to Alarik, Xerxes didn't have the vine power at all. It was just that uncomfortable truth-telling thing, apparently. So without his followers, he was nothing.

Even if he brought Alanna with him, I was confident our fighters could take him out without their powers.

Alarik seemed less certain.

Exhausted, I left them to it and went to my room, intending to take a short nap.

I woke up, groggy, and finding it difficult to reorient myself for a moment. I'd collapsed on my bed, the long arm warmers off, but the elvish dress still on, the dried branches still in my hair. My fingers made them crinkle as

I ran a hand through my knotted tangles. The bedroom light was even still on.

Fighting against the desire to just lie back down—I needed to know how long I'd been out and what had happened in the meantime—I leaned up on my haunches and searched for my phone on my bedside table.

Right. Lost it somewhere downtown during Alarik's assault... a day ago? Two days ago? Who knew at this point? I rubbed my eyes and stood, padding across the room to my shared closet to put on some of my own clothes.

Raised, muffled voices carried through the hallway, and the exchange, whatever it was, was tense.

Quickly tossing the beautiful dress over my hair and swapping it for sweats and a trainer's jacket after putting on a sports bra and some boy shorts, I headed to the hall-way, pulling at the branches in my hair as I made my way toward the sound.

Even the aroma of something new cooking—how long had I been asleep?—did little to deter me as I made my way to Jayden's office, his door slightly ajar.

"Will you stop pretending I can't fucking see inside your head and just tell me what this is really about already?" Zander. There was a coy stirring over our bond in my head at my recognition of his voice.

"You need to stop confusing impulses for some sort of indictment on character." Jayden. "It's a person's actions and words that comprise who they are. Thoughts are irrelevant so long as a person is able to focus on what really matters."

Zander scoffed at that and I felt the desire to turn tail and stay out of it. It shouldn't have surprised me to come across the two of them arguing. It'd just been a while since they'd met to exchange verbal blows instead of physical ones.

I could have asked Nash for an update—or Roulette or Chastity. Anyone. But here was where my feet had taken me.

"Aurora, darlin', come in here," said Zander out loud, his voice raising a decibel.

Shit.

"Not 'shit,'" said Zander over the bond. *"Just get that sexy butt in here."*

Sighing, I pushed on the partially-open door and let myself in. Jayden leaned against the front of his desk, shuffling his feet and pushing his glasses up his nose, then crossing his arms and clutching his elbows a little too hard. His gaze was all over the place, too—though I didn't know why. I was probably in the least revealing outfit I'd been in in days.

"I wish you wouldn't do that," said Jayden to Zander.

Do what, I didn't know. Surprise him by sensing me nearby? Say something dirty in his head?

"Pretty much on the mark on both accounts, darlin'," Zander said over the bond. He sent me a playful grin as he crossed his own arms and leaned back on the bookshelves he'd once slammed me against in our first throes of passion together.

"Only our first?" he asked over the bond. *"I'm hurt. I seem to remember something wild passing between us at the first kiss."*

Clearing my throat, I took a seat on one of the chairs in front of Jayden's desk, shifting it at an angle so it would face toward both of them. "How can I help you?" I said, folding my hands over my knee and preparing to get down to business—to go over anything I might have learned about Xerxes or Nelia or whatever we needed to get out of this mess.

"You don't really think that's why I called you in here, do you?" said Zander, and it took me a moment to realize he was talking out loud. He chuckled. "We've got Wade and everyone else on it." His eyes flit to Jayden, who placed a hand on the edge of his desk and stared down at a paper weight beside his thigh. "No, we'd just reached the part of these little peace-while-at-war talks where it cycled back to one of the causes of our rift. As it always does."

Looking between Zander and Jayden, I waited for more explanation—though I felt myself squirming in my seat because I had an idea.

And Zander wasn't jumping in to tease me for once, so I knew this time was different. This time he wasn't taking Jayden's weaseling for an answer.

But I wouldn't let him force the guy into anything he didn't want to do—whatever it was that was apparently in his mind. Jayden was right. It was a man's words and actions that mattered, not some repressed feelings.

Standing, I made my way to the door, but Zander shot away from the bookshelf and got there first, slamming it closed and resting his back against the knob, embracing himself and narrowing his eyes over my shoulder.

I looked to Jayden for help, for him to tell Zander to fuck off already, but Jayden just sighed and pushed away from the table, his eyes meeting mine just briefly—long enough to send shivers down my spine. He tucked his hands in his pockets and walked around the desk, staring out the window. It was twilight—and I wondered if it was dusk or dawn at this point, if the meal out there was dinner or breakfast.

My stomach rumbled and Zander laughed, destroying some of the tension hanging in there.

"Sorry, darlin'," he said, stepping away from the door to slide his arms around me and yank me closer to him. He kissed the top of my head. "I'll get you something to eat."

"I'll just go with you," I said, placing my hands on his chest, so fucking broad and fine even through his T-shirt.

There was laughter over the bond, an amused smirk on his face in front of me. "Nope," he said. "You two"—he backed up some to send a glare at Jayden, even if his back was to us—"are getting over this hang-up *now* and you're going to boost Jayden—*fully* boost him—because I've spent the last hour or so explaining to him that a super-boosted earth power will prove *invaluable* in a fight against mostly plant-users. That, and he's dreamed of fucking you almost as soon as he saw you anyway."

Jayden cradled his forehead in one hand. "Zander, please. Just stop."

I noticed he didn't deny it, though.

Zander leaned in my ear. "I fucking mean it. I'm going to leave the food outside the door for when you're done."

Tittering, I shook my head. "I'm too tired to even think, Zander, let alone—"

"Then I will fucking walk in here and hand-feed you grapes until you get your engine started," he said, a little louder this time. "I mean it, Jayden. Get your fucking act together already."

He gave me another kiss atop my head—not even breaking his tightened expression—and pushed me lightly in Jayden's direction, slapping my ass and making me let out a little chirp of surprise at the action—even if he'd immediately revved up my engine.

"Noted," said Zander over the bond, chuckling. *"I'll make use of that in future lovemaking sessions."*

199

Face reddening, my mind tried to go as blank as possible while he kept mentally laughing as he opened the door behind me and slammed it closed.

The room went quiet without him, and for once, he wasn't bugging me in my head, either.

"That's a relief," said Jayden, still staring outside. The bird's nest on the tree outside his window showed three little slimy baby bird heads straining to call for their mother.

"What?" I asked, my voice catching on the dryness of my throat.

"The quiet," he said, tapping a finger to his head. "He left me alone. You?"

"Yeah," I said, tucking my hands inside the pockets in the jacket over my abdomen. "But I don't... He's not boosted," I said. "The only time he can talk to us is when we're thinking about him."

Jayden turned, a weak smile attempting to break onto his lips. "You don't think I do? I think about him. And I often think about you—which almost always makes me think about him more."

It took a solid moment for my brain to catch up with what he'd said.

"What?" I stupidly asked.

Sighing, Jayden turned back around and took a seat in the squeaky chair behind the desk—just another meeting with one of his subordinates, a teacher with his student. I sat numbly in the chair across from him, ready for a lecture I hadn't been expecting.

"Do you ever wonder why his telepathy only works on you and me?" He threaded his fingers together and rested his elbows on the desk.

"He has to... feel an emotional bond with someone," I said, trying to remember what Wade had said once.

200

"And yet he leads a team devoted to him and he doesn't feel close enough to them to be able to use what would be a very convenient power relaying instructions to his team?" Jayden leaned back and gestured to either side of him.

"We don't *know* if he can't communicate with any of them—"

Jayden shook his head. "Zander may be many things, but he's not a liar. I know it's just you and me—unless he's boosted, of course."

Biting my lip, I picked at the cotton in my jacket pocket. "He loves… us," I said.

Jayden nodded, and there was a slight tremble to his fingers as he pushed his glasses up, a slight twitch in his jaw.

"He, but—he wants to have sex with you too?" I asked.

That actually made Jayden crack a smile. "I don't… I don't think so," he said. "Though I've wondered if he has certain… wishes."

Well, that was about as clear as a fogged-up mirror in the middle of a dust storm. I shook my head. "You'll have to be more specific than that."

"He wouldn't be against observing us copulating," he said, making the sentence as unromantic as humanly possible. "Though he wouldn't even have to be in the room, considering he could project himself into it. Or simply rewatch the scene in one of our minds later."

My jaw dropped open and I struggled to speak—but I had no business getting embarrassed or even, damn it, aroused just then. Especially not when I had three ungodly handsome men who wanted to fuck me and were all—in their own ways, though I did have to have a talk with Nash again—willing to share me.

I did not *need* a fourth man in this mix, but fuck me, I would never stop wanting Jayden.

My fingers had left one of my pockets and were tracing my lips then, the memory of our too-brief kiss taking over my mind.

"I love him, too," said Jayden, sighing.

That bolted me back upright.

"What?" I thought I was breaking a record for saying that word at this point.

A tear trickled down Jayden's cheek, and he ripped his glasses off his face, wiping his eye with his forearm as his other hand held on to the temple of his rims.

"*Jayden,*" I said, surprised at the huge crack in the façade. I leaped to my feet and crossed around the table, putting a hesitant hand on his shoulder.

Oh my god, was he gay? What the fuck was all that stuff Zander had teased me about then?

Emitting a weak laugh, Jayden removed his arm from his eyes and went to put his glasses back on, but I took careful hold of them and put them down between a photo frame and a pencil holder. Damn, he looked hot in and out of those glasses, his green eyes wider and more vulnerable right now.

My hand clanked against the photo frame and I picked it up, looking at it. It was a house in a suburb, a little ostentatious, but not obscenely so. Two boys were running in the background, a toy plane in the dark-haired one's hand as the blond boy chased after him.

"He was my best friend," said Jayden, his voice wobbling at the past tense. "And I... We... I lost him."

A shadow passed over his face then, his Adam's apple swallowing as he seemed to summon the power to shove the tears down. Only I knew that must have caused a headache—the straining, the trying to shove it all down.

And for the first time, I really understood what Zander meant. Jayden was hurting himself keeping this all inside.

Gently, I laid the photo frame on the desk and took a seat on the edge, my knee unintentionally knocking into his hand as it gripped the armrest of his chair.

"We all thought…" I tried to think of how to word this. "We knew Zander walking out on the team hurt you, Jayden. You don't know how bad I felt—"

"It wasn't your fault," he said. "He was never mad at *you*. Never frustrated that you couldn't agree with him."

Ouch. But yeah, I knew what he meant. Whatever was between the two of them, it was older and stronger than whatever role I played.

"We thought maybe you weren't interested in sex," I said. "Not just because… I mean, I didn't want to *force* you to be with me, I knew you weren't interested—"

"I was," said Jayden, a wry laugh escaping his lips. "Hasn't he told you half a million times already? I always have been."

Swallowing, I went to speak but found no words escaping my mouth. "Are you…?"

"I don't know," said Jayden, shaking his head. "I've always had other things on my mind—except for you. For the both of you. I love you, Aurora." The chair let out a groan as he swiveled it to be closer, to take my hand between both of his. "I have since the moment I saw you, but you were a kid, and I was taking you under my wing, and I…" He chewed his lip as his gaze dropped to my hand. "I was angry Zander felt no qualms about pursuing you. Jealous. Even when he backed off just a bit because he *knew* how I felt, he got annoyed that I didn't disregard my principles and pursue you myself, so he… He ran out of patience and then I lost… I lost you both."

Pulling my hand from his, I took his face between my

palms, tired of his wandering eyes looking anywhere but at me. "You never lost me," I said. "Never."

"But Nash..." he said. "And Zander... And now that, that elf..." He shook his head. "I know you're with me. I know you're with the team when you could be out there with Zander or even with these Nelians apparently, but..."

I jumped down from the desk and put my lips to his. The surge of my power flowing between us, soaring from my core to his, made me forget all about the emptiness in my stomach, the promises I'd made to myself not to force anything on him.

I pulled away, never once focusing on anything but his deep green eyes. "I love you, too," I said. "I love... In a way, I love all of you." I didn't know whether or not to count Alarik in that number, even though I had to chomp down on my bottom lip to stop myself from thinking about our wild night in that cold cavern. "And I understand if you don't want to be with me, knowing that—"

With a loud, grating squeak of the chair, he jumped to his feet, slamming my chest against his, his lips hard on mine again, his tongue grazing over my teeth like he was savoring every centimeter of me.

He took a deep breath. "I need you," he said, peppering my forehead with kisses, moving down to my cheeks, his tall, muscled form hunched over as he tried to reach me. "I've always needed you."

This barely felt real, but I wasn't going to let reality ruin the moment I'd been dreaming of. I laid my own lips against his jaw, his neck, moving my hands to the top of his button-down shirt, ready to rip it off—

His hands grabbed hold of mine and flung my arms tightly behind my back. It didn't hurt, but it was clear he was exerting pressure—that I'd struggle to break free unless he decided to let me go.

"What…?" I numbly said again, but he swallowed, holding his eyes tight to mine as his delicious lips parted and he panted.

"I've imagined this for so long," he said. "Taking you over my desk, bending you over backward…"

Zander hadn't been kidding that Jayden was hiding some filthy thoughts about me.

"Okay," I said quietly, suddenly feeling meek. Now it was my turn to find my eyes roving wildly, unable to hold his gaze, my knees instinctively locking together.

He thrust forward, using one of his own knees to pry my legs apart.

Even with my clothes still on, my legs turned to jelly and I stumbled back against the desk.

He dropped my hands from his and went immediately to the zipper on my jacket, pulling it down before I could so much as blink. I took my arms out of the sleeves, and then his lips were on mine again, his fingers crawling up under my sports bra as he tugged that up over my breasts and paused, pulling back with bated breath as I wiggled my arms out of that, too.

"Perfection," he said, taking hold of my breasts in his hands.

My legs really did lose all control then and I stumbled back against the desk, trying to take a seat, but Jayden quickly dropped hold of my breasts to maneuver his hands beneath the elastic waist band of my sweats, beneath the boy shorts to the skin of my ass.

I mewled as his hands went exploring to the front and as I gasped, he yanked down on my pants and underwear both, dropping them to my ankles as I stumbled back onto the desk.

He dropped to the floor and started pulling one pants cuff off my foot, pausing to lay a kiss on my inner calf as he did. He repeated the motion with the other foot and I collapsed back onto the desk, my butt digging into the photo frame and my mouth making noises I tried to stifle, lest the whole place heard.

Jayden stood again, and I felt vulnerable before him, naked, bare—especially with him still fully clothed. I ran my hands over his shoulders, teasing my fingers into the collar of his shirt, feeling the hot sensation of his skin on mine. He stood back and ripped his own shirt off, quickly chucking his white tank top beneath over his head. He kissed me again, hardly leaving me time to drink in his form, my hands wandering over his back, one of his hands on my own back, the other roving over my front, over my breasts, teasing my nipples.

I gasped, and then his mouth was moving down my neck to take a nipple between his teeth as his fingers traveled down between my folds, causing my thighs to squeeze together.

"Jayden," I whispered, my voice cracking. If this was a dream, I didn't want to wake up. He stepped back and put firm palms on either side of me, pulling me away from the desk.

I opened my mouth to speak, but he surprised me by sweeping an arm across the surface of the desk, sending a mug, a pencil cup, the photo, his glasses, a paper weight, a lamp—*everything* to the ground in a huge crash.

"Jayden! What if someone heard that?" I hoped he hadn't shattered his glasses while he'd been at it.

"I don't care," he said, breathing hard. He took hold of my sides again and spun me hard, fast, making me cry out in giddy surprise as he bent me over the desk, laying my front gently onto the hard surface. His hand squeezed my breast again once more before I heard him fumbling with his zipper, saw him flinging off his pants and underwear as I turned to look over my shoulder.

God, he was thick and long—glorious.

He shook his head and laid a hand over one of my shoulders. It was forceful but not painfully so. He leaned his form over mine, spooning me, sending tingles from my crotch to my toes. "Let me take you," he whispered in my ear.

I nodded numbly, my cheek flat against the cold, hard surface of the desk.

He backed up and his hand went to work between my ass cheeks, traveling frontward to my clit and rubbing in gentle, teasing motions until I cried out, my toes curling as my feet flung out behind me.

His cock slid between my ass cheeks—not penetrating, but like they were meant to fit it like a glove, his long, thick girth teasing across my entrance, and I screamed. Happily, achingly, but I screamed. "Please!" I said, my voice hoarse.

He took hold of each of my butt cheeks and pushed them tighter against his penis, massaging the cheeks and grinding, his cock growing harder and harder with each strike until it felt so hard, I couldn't take it anymore, its teasing presence gliding the length of my labia. "Please!" I begged again, a shower of moisture coating us both and demanding he come inside.

He released some of the pressure on my ass to back up and then slide inside my pussy, the friction almost non-existent. I cried out, groaning, an orgasm already nearly at its apex as he pushed all the way in—slowly, forcefully, but reveling in every second of it.

Then he pulled out a little again, his breath so hot and heavy, I could feel it across the length between his head and my back, and he plunged in once more.

I shrieked in ecstasy, my feet completely leaving the ground. "Yes! Please! Yes!"

Then he went faster, pulling out and then pushing in, the movement causing me to bounce and grind against the desk, the pressure on my breasts beneath me increasing, the only way I could keep from trembling to exhaustion by gripping the edge of the desk with both hands above my head. The slap of his cock withdrawing and plunging into my insides, the rhythm of the motion, the surge of power pouring out from every fiber of my being into his every molecule... I was going to die. I couldn't handle this much pleasure—couldn't take the idea of this ever ending.

I moaned again, not even caring that the whole place was sure to hear it.

"That's my girl," said Zander—and at first I thought it had to be across the bond. But he was there—his projected form—in front of the door, a lascivious grin on his face as I shifted my face to watch him. My chin and throat were flat against the desk as Jayden kept pumping.

"Dinner's outside the door," he said, and Jayden didn't even comment. "But it'll keep until you're ready."

And with that, he vanished back into air.

CHAPTER SIXTEEN

Our bellies fed, we'd continued our dance, moving to Jayden's bed. I rode him this time—he'd had his fantasy, now I got mine—my thighs aching as I bounced up and down, but my body wracked with pleasure despite the soreness. My hands gripped either pec as his palms rested on my ass, our eyes locked the entire time. I could feel the sweat flushing from my body, hear the gasps of pleasure pass through my deep breaths, but I kept going. The power flowed from my sex to him again and again—not that he'd needed another boost so soon.

And maybe Veras needed its leader. Maybe I needed to talk to Nash and boost Zander and figure out where Alarik fit into all this—but right now, I just needed this.

We just need this.

Tossing back my head and shutting my eyes, I let out one more scream of pleasure, adding, "Jayden!" as I dug my fingernails into his chest, my thigh muscles giving so I could bounce no more. His seed responded in kind, shooting out just at the moment when I'd hit my apex and I moaned, taking it all in, breathing hard—hearing his own deep breaths. And then, ages later, I shifted to slip him out and collapsed at his side on the bed, wrapping an arm around his front as he encircled me in his arms entirely. He kissed my brow and took a deep breath, as if imbibing the scent of our workout, the proof of the two of us together.

We didn't speak. It was wondrously silent with Jayden, asking permission and shrieking names the only words we'd exchanged in hours. We'd even eaten silently, his hungry eyes devouring my naked form the whole time.

But there were things I needed to get straight. "You're okay with it?" I said, clearing my throat, finding my voice hoarse despite the lack of use.

He coughed as well. "With what?"

"This," I said, tapping a finger softly above his nipple. "Us. Me with... the others."

Squeezing me tighter, he laid another kiss on my forehead. "I love you, Aurora. I always have—I didn't think I ought to, but I have."

Tears streamed down my cheeks and I didn't even know why. "But you knew I loved you," I said. "*Everyone* seemed to figure that out."

"I know," he said, "and I thought Zander told you the truth about how I felt."

"He did," I admitted. "But I thought he was just teasing me—it didn't seem to match your actions at all."

"Zander doesn't lie," said Jayden softly. "It's the one thing about him you can believe in."

Chewing my lip, I slipped my hand down his side and rested it on his sharp, jutting inguinal crease. "I love fucking him, too," I said. "It makes no sense and I... I never want him boosted when we're about to face him in battle, but... I love him, too."

"And Nash as well," said Jayden. It wasn't a question —and there wasn't anything accusatory in it.

I nodded, my cheek grazing his shoulder.

"But what about that elf king?" he asked. "How did…?"

"I don't *love* him quite like I love the three of you," I said. "I mean, I hardly know him. And he's… he's a former enemy—probably still would be one if his friend hadn't taken his throne." My hand dug into Jayden's skin a little. "But there's just some kind of… animal attraction there, and Jayden, I can't picture giving him up, either." Sighing, I screwed my eyes shut and buried my nose against the crux of his arm. "I suck as a member of Veras. I suck as a Natch. I suck as a human being."

"No," said Jayden, petting my hair softly. "You are who you are, Aurora. And I love you for it. I wouldn't ask you to change that."

I was honestly the freaking luckiest woman in the world to have four hot guys eager to step up to the job of fucking me—and not that combative about sharing the load. My groin tingled at the idea and I buried my face harder, telling my accursed libido to quiet the hell up already.

She was already getting every single fucking thing she desired.

"Beyond you and… Zander… There's no one else for me, though," said Jayden quietly, continuing to pet my hair. He stopped suddenly and I heard a crinkle, so I turned and saw him picking silver dried branches out of my hair. I snickered. I hadn't gotten all those. And cripes, I'd come to Jayden in my messiest state possible and he'd still splayed me over his desk.

I settled my cheek against his chest and he squeezed me tighter against him, one of his hands cupping my butt cheek.

"I'm not going to be with Zander… like that," he said. "If you're wondering."

"I…" I hugged him tighter and then lifted my head so I could peck him on the chest through the blond fuzz of hair. "I love you both," I said. "So I couldn't ask you not to love each other."

He laughed as I shifted to straddle him more, my chin on his chest and gazing up at him. Even from this awkward angle, he sent shivers down my front. "If anything, he might be up for a three-way—since he's already tried observing." He shook his head wryly and I wondered how long Zander had watched in the end. I'd been too caught up in Jayden. "But… there's way too much to worry about to consider something like that right now," he said. "Besides, Zander… wants you. Only you. He's sent me images of me inside your pussy with you splayed on your back over the desk, your legs around me, and his cock in your mouth on the other side, his hands massaging your breasts as mine dig into your ass cheeks."

My body stiffened. I didn't think anything Zander thought of could surprise me at this point, but it was prob-ably mostly the fact that *Jayden* was saying it.

Besides, Zander had never included Jayden *in* those images he'd sent me.

"Oh… okay…" I said, clearing my throat. Rolling off his body, I slid in next to him again, finding my place in his spooning embrace.

"If you don't want to—"

"I didn't say that," I snapped, my traitorous libido purring wildly at the thought. I laughed. "Sorry…"

He chuckled, too. "For now, I want you all to myself," he said. "When we're together anyway."

I nodded against his chest and closed my eyes. The simple rhythmic rise and fall of his chest lulled me to sleep.

Light was once more breaking through the window

when a fast pounding at the door brought me back to consciousness.

"Jayden!"

It was Nash's voice.

The door—not locked—swung open.

"They're here," said Nash. "And they…" He swallowed noticeably as he took in the sight of Jayden and me splayed together, entirely naked, not even a blanket to cover us. His body heat and the workout had been enough to lull me to sleep. Nash shook his head slightly and I realized he carried something over his arm—a number of things.

He tossed one at the bed. It was a battle suit. A man's suit.

"The elven king's usurper is at the marina," Nash said. "And his people seem less concerned with minimizing human injuries than they were before."

His eyes grazed over my body before he shifted slightly and stared out the window. He still held two more battle suits.

I stuck an arm out for mine as Jayden jumped off the bed and started suiting up, crossing the room and looking at the pile of broken and disheveled desk knickknacks until he found his glasses. It was clear Nash wasn't going to hand me anything, so I stood up as well, at least looking for my pants.

"Wait," said Nash as I found my sweats on the other side of the desk.

I stood, my pants in my hand, my head cocked to Nash.

His eyes flit between the suited-up Jayden and me. Nash was in his tank top and gym shorts, and I was the only one butt-naked. Even if the both of them had seen this all by now…

"Boost me before we go," said Nash.

I silently checked with Jayden. "Nash—"

Jayden flexed his hand and laughed, reaching over the desk to peck one more kiss on my lips. His glasses bumped my brow, but I just chuckled. "I'm good," he said. "Definitely boosted." His smile practically reached his ears and he kissed me atop the head. "I need to get everyone ready." He stormed out of the room, shutting the door behind him, and I was left staring at Nash, my pants in my hand, the chirp of the birds through the window behind me the only sound for a moment.

"We don't have a lot of time," said Nash, gently laying two suits on the back of a chair. A woman's and a man's. His and hers. He quickly chucked his tank top over his head.

"Wait, Nash," I said, holding my pants up over one breast, like that afforded me any modesty.

He paused, both hands gripping the elastic waist band on his shorts, frozen in the moment as he stared at me. "Yes?" he said after a bit when it was clear I had nothing more to say.

"I don't want…" My mouth was dry. "I know this is an emergency of sorts, but I don't want… I don't want things to be awkward between us."

"Why should they be?" asked Nash, and he finished removing his pants. His sizable cock drew my eyes immediately and I had to mentally slap myself to lock eyes with him instead. Good thing, though, because his hand was already going to work on himself and my groin was moistening at the realization, my knees going weak. Jayden's chair let out an oily squeak as I slunk into it.

"Angel," said Nash as he grunted and his arm moved faster. I couldn't look down or I would melt right then and there. "I was the one who recommended you boost as many people on our team as possible before a fight."

"Yes, but..." I had to bite my lip—hard—as he made his way around the side of the desk. "I don't want—I don't want to be some pussy factory every time there's an emergency."

Nash tittered. "I was going to recommend you boost Zander, too. Maybe even that asswipe elven king if you're so sure we can trust him."

"What?" I asked, my jaw dropping.

He was standing in front of me now, his erection impossible to avoid, his breath shallow and his skin flushing with sweat. "We need as many boosted fighters right now as possible," he said.

"But I..." I fought the urge to leap out that window behind me and run and run and run until my libido cooled the fuck down, even if I was butt-naked. I'd had them all —in pretty fairly fucking short succession—but one after the other in a hurry was just...

It was just...

Nash pulled me gently to my feet and I let him take hold of me. He pulled me toward Jayden's bed, but we didn't even get that far when he put his hands on either side of my waist and lifted me up until I got the hint and wrapped my legs around his waist. He shimmied to get his cock lined up and I grinded against him at the movement, taking it in my hand for just a moment to help slide it in.

He slammed me—though not too hard—against the wall as his mouth parted and his tongue darted out to lick his lips.

"Angel," he breathed. "You drive me wild, and I don't even care... I don't care who else you fuck, as long as you still joyfully fuck me."

I crashed my lips against his in answer and he pulled out partway again, slamming hard back in, over and over as I started moaning, my fingers digging into his back.

If this was what being a pussy factory felt like, fuck my inhibitions—it felt great.

It ended far too soon, but that surge from inside me had passed to him and he ejaculated inside me, taking a deep breath and pulling out as he gently maneuvered me back to my feet. I opened my mouth, but he took my face between both hands and laid a long, deep kiss on my lips before turning around. He grabbed his battle suit off the back of the chair and put one leg in.

I grabbed mine, too, and he froze, staring at me. "I wasn't kidding," he said. He nodded toward the door. "Zander and the elven king are both eager to get a boost before we go."

"What...?" I asked, my hand going numb as I dropped the suit back on the chair. "But do we have time...? And... I mean..."

But Nash was already fully in his suit, zipping up, and pressing his communicator to check in with everyone. "Okay," he said. And I realized I'd been so dumbstruck, I hadn't even heard what had been communicated.

He turned to me, taking my hand in both of his. "Angel, the first team is about to go out. I'm going to go with them." He kissed me on the top of the head again. "Boost everyone else you want to and then I'll see you there."

I was cognizant enough to tell him to be careful and he grinned before exiting out the door, passing Zander on his way in.

"You have to be fucking kidding me," I said, my mind scrambling for some logic in what was happening.

Zander shut the door and tossed a hitchhiker's thumb

over his shoulder. "Should I just go?" he said. "I'm not a ton of help on the battlefield without your boost, but my team could use me to help with strategy." He didn't sound angry—on the contrary, he shrunk back and slouched just a little, almost like he was worried he'd upset *me*. "I don't want to wear you out…"

Rapidly blinking, I shook my head and got it in the game. "Come here," I said, gesturing for him to come closer. "The pussy factory is open for business."

His eyebrow cocked as he neared. "Is that what we're calling it now?"

"Yup," I said, wrapping my arms around his neck. I pecked him on the lips, and a tiny firework of power transferred between us. "And we're on a schedule, no?"

"Yes, ma'am," he said, chuckling. He stood back to slip out of his pants as his eyes roved all over my naked body. "*Damn*, darlin'," he said, his cock already twitching. He moved a hand along his thigh and grabbed hold of it, pumping furiously. His chin nodded toward the desk, barren of any impediments. "Can I have you like Jayden did? I want to play with those fine ass cheeks."

Swallowing, I raised an eyebrow and moved toward the desk, though on the other side from when Jayden had taken me there. My groin was still hot and slick, my thighs trembling as I bent over. "Just how much did you see?"

"Plenty," he said, slipping up behind me, the slap of his hand on his penis getting faster. "I had to find a quiet place to rub one out and couldn't watch the rest, though." He bent over and breathed in my ear. "But I'll be peeking inside both of your minds plenty to see what I missed."

His knee went between my legs and spread them farther apart. Before I could even retort, his fingers were racing up and down my labia and I mewled in pleasure as his cock slid in.

My power surged once more, flowing from me to him and back again as he massaged my ass and shoved in as far as he could go. My toes curled as I pressed my breasts hard against the table, screaming out.

Then he was out a little again, and back in, over and over until my pussy was soaked to the point I thought I was going to leave a stain on the floor. He kept going and going, saying "darlin'" all the while and I could hardly breathe, my body about to collapse with all the orgasms it was apparently capable of producing one after the other.

He released inside me and I screamed, my legs curling up behind me. Breathing hard, he pulled out and then smacked my ass playfully. "We need to take our time next time," he said, wiping his groin with a tissue from a box on the floor amongst the desk's knickknacks and pulling on his pants. I rolled over, gasping for breath as I watched him dress.

He stared at me a moment and then squeezed his eyes shut. "Damn it, darlin', I'm trying to get back out there," he said, then over the bond, he sent me an image of myself naked on the desk, breathing hard, and I realized he was sending me an image of exactly how I looked to him right now. And he wanted to go back at it.

He settled for crossing the room and laying a kiss on my lips. "Later," he said. "I mean it. And… I love you. Thank you. Thank you for letting me back into your life, however you see fit." He cleared his throat and headed toward the door, not giving me much time to process his vulnerable moment. "The Renegades—we have our own car here—so we're going out next," he said. "Catch a ride with the last team and I'll see you soon, okay?"

I nodded numbly, choking out an *I love you, too* over our bond in my mind. He smiled, then he opened the door and Alarik stepped inside, the two of them staring each other down, something unspoken passing between them, until Zander nodded and left, pulling the door closed behind him.

Oh, my fucking god. Were they serious? Could we trust Alarik? Even if his boosted vine powers would come in handy against other vine users in service of Xerxes…

Fuck that. He was *mine*. And I was ready for this.

My head lolled back as my breaths continued to come in and out shallowly, my eyes focusing on the chirping birds in the nest behind me. Their mom was there this morning, passing out a long worm amongst her babies.

"Ready and waiting," purred Alarik as his form drew closer. "Just how a king likes it."

"Oh?" I asked, looking up at him. "I think I missed something because I thought you were no longer a king."

He bent over and I realized he'd quietly removed his clothes when I hadn't been looking at him. His naked, lithe form somehow drew even more moisture from my nether regions and this was it—I wasn't going to make it to the battlefield, because every ounce of my strength was being expended here in the pussy factory.

Alarik's hand cradled my cheek and then his finger moved lightly down my neck, tracing around one breast and then the other as he moved in position in front of me.

"What do you say?" he said, his finger stopping at my belly button.

"Maybe *you* should say 'please,'" I said between breaths. "Since you need me."

"Oh, I do, do I?" His finger moved closer, teasing just above my clit. "Seems your other lovers thought it wise for me to be boosted for this fight," he said. "I *could* just work with what I have to help save your community."

His finger drew away. *Oh, fuck.*

His games were driving me wild, though we had no fucking time for them.

I closed my eyes and swallowed hard. "Please," I whispered.

His finger went back to my groin, this time slipping between the lips. "What was that?" he asked, the movement stopping.

"*Please*," I said, louder this time. "Please, Your Majesty. I want you inside me."

His finger worked faster, sliding up and down and pushing just slightly up inside me. As if I needed any more teasing. I was ready to go last Sunday at this point. My back arched and I moaned, unable to take it with him so near and teasing me and not giving me what I wanted.

"Maybe I don't want to give you what you *want*," he said, his voice husky. "Maybe I'll only give you what you *need*." His finger plunged all the way in and I moaned.

"Please," I said, sort of hating myself but letting myself go wild. "Please, I fucking *need* you inside me, Your Majesty."

"That's better," he said, grabbing hold of both of my thighs and practically yanking me down toward him. His thick, hardened cock was already ready and he slid inside me—hard—the pleasure equal to the shock I felt as he and I became one, the power from me surging into him. His hand gripped my butt hard as my legs wrapped around him.

He spanked me underhand, not too hard, but hard enough that I gasped.

"That's for your sass," he said, his voice low.

He pulled out slightly and then pushed back in, spanking me again. "And that's for making me have to remind me that you fucking *need* me inside you."

He pounded again and again and he kept adding some

ass slaps in there. I shrieked in ecstasy, the power long since transferred, his own boosted, but both of us unable to stop.

Finally, he came inside me and I tried to dig my fingers into the hard desk, and I almost felt like I'd gotten the strength to do so, the tingling was so intense everywhere throughout my body.

He pulled out, and his own breaths were shallow now —I could hear when my moans were finally quieting. "We need to go," he said, rubbing his forearm over his mouth as his deep brown irises stared down at me. He turned on his heel, as if that were the only way he could tear himself away.

I nodded numbly, sitting myself up on my forearms, my legs jelly as I tried to sit back down, my groin so sore but still tingling with so much pleasure, I thought I might die.

What a way to go.

Alarik appeared beside me in his clothes again, my battle suit over his arm. "Come on," he said, taking my hand and letting me collapse against him. His lips grazed my forehead, his long, green hair falling over my face. "I'll help you get dressed," he said, so much softer and gentler now.

And he did, even helping wipe some of the mess from my groin with the tissues beforehand. And with wobbly legs and a face flushed with heat, I walked side by side with him, his arm through mine like I was some kind of god damn debutante at a ball, as we went to join the last of Veras waiting for us.

I'd boosted four men, but there were still my lips for additional boosts. And I sure as hell wasn't staying behind for this, not even if they'd asked me.

CHAPTER SEVENTEEN

WADE IMPATIENTLY TAPPED THE STEERING WHEEL OF THE NEW used car Jayden had authorized him to buy in my absence —another van, may the jeep rest in peace—as pedestrians who'd been enjoying a sunny morning at the marina and who now abandoned their cars to the endless traffic poured through the streets on both sides of the road.

"We have to get out," said Rou. She was particularly antsy since Darien had gone in that first wave with Chastity, Jayden, and Nash.

People screamed as another giant, green vine shot up above the few-story buildings dotting the beachfront about a half mile ahead.

"Okay," said Wade, shutting off the engine and pocketing the keys. As we all jumped out—Alarik included—Wade turned around and patted the hood of the vehicle. "Hope you make it through," he said. I knew why. One look ahead and it was clear that the roadblock had been caused by overturned cars, the vines growing too big to be contained between them.

"That goes for all of us," said Roulette, grim. Her head turned as if in answer to a scream and she ran toward the sound. I knew she was off to see who she could heal. I turned to Wade and Alarik, taking Alarik's hand in mine and giving it a squeeze.

I felt better—less sore, and more focused to boot because right before we'd jumped into the car, Roulette had healed whatever soreness and aches I'd experienced, a wry smile on her face, her eyebrows lifted, without saying a word.

"I should go with her to offer a continuous boost." My eyes flitted to Alarik. "Please…" I left the rest unsaid. Please don't betray us. Please stay safe. Please don't hurt any of my other friends and lovers.

Wade nodded and took off at a run down the block. Alarik spoke quietly, running a hand along my cheek. "I want you with me," he said.

"You're already super boosted—for a day." I swallowed. "I can do the most good with Roulette, helping her heal people."

Alarik's gaze wandered over my head, his expression tightening as he took in the destruction his people had unleashed around us. It wasn't like they'd done much differently when he'd been at the helm.

"I told them to be careful of the humans," he said as a group of them dashed past us. "I… I'm sorry, starlight." He bent to put his lips to mine. "I'm sorry about everything." He stepped back, dropping his hand from mine. "But I *will* take control from that traitor and make sure my sister is safe and then… get the Nelians and humans to work together differently." He turned then, taking off after Wade, shooting out a smaller, thinner but long vine from his palm as a bigger one slithered down the block—successfully knocking it out of the path of a group of fleeing civilians.

"Rora!" My name echoed out from down a nearby

alley. I bolted for it, dodging hazardous vines and upturned asphalt along the way.

I skidded to a halt when I found Roulette bent over a man who was dripping blood from his head, a woman with a blood-soaked leg on the ground beside him. Rou's hand was extended, the bright white light pouring from it. I quickly crouched beside her and turned her head, pecking her on the lips. The light shone brighter, the healing worked faster, taking care of both of them.

"What the...?" said the man, clutching his head. He turned to the woman with him. "Did they just kiss?"

"Natches," said the woman, shaking her head. Like we were always making out in the street. "Thank you," she added, her voice faltering.

Roulette nodded and we both jumped to our feet, heading closer to the waterfront.

"She's here!" spoke Zander over the bond—no, to everyone he wanted—*anyone* he wanted. Roulette frowned as she skidded to a halt, tilting her head like she was trying to drain Zander's boosted voice from her head like water logged in the ear. *"The power-nullifier. Radius one block east and west of 4th Avenue and 21st Street intersection. Steer clear."*

Zander, I thought back. *Keep an eye on Alarik. He wants to find his sister—but he'll lose his powers if he gets too close.*

"Sister. Right." He sent the warm, fuzzy feeling I got from one of his grins. *"Looking good even in clothes, darlin'. Though, admittedly, they're skin-tight, so..."*

Not now, I sent him, groaning out loud. But then I added in my head, *Love you. Stay safe.*

"You too."

"So what's the plan?" I asked Roulette aloud. We were still some distance from the nullification area Zander had reported, though I wasn't sure about the rest of our team and the Renegades.

"We follow the screams," she replied. As if on cue, shouts rang out in the air as a huge pillar of fire shot upward, turning a burgeoning vine to ash.

"Nash," I said. His boosted powers were truly something.

We ran in his direction, checking for injured people all the while.

At one point, a vine started growing and Roulette whipped out her palm, getting a lucky destruction red light on the first try.

The jutting edge of the vine turned to smoke, the vine's progress halted.

"Veras," cried Jayden over our communicators.

"What's up?" asked Roulette, hitting hers casually like she hadn't just saved our butts from becoming pierced by twisting tendrils.

"The Renegades are closing in on this Xerxes, we think," he said. "He's behind the nullification barrier, so we're all trying to congregate just outside of its range and come up with a plan of attack."

"Where's Darien?" Roulette asked.

"Here, babe," Darien grunted over the line. A sound like ice cubes dropping on a hard linoleum floor echoed over the comm. "A little busy," he added.

Chewing her lip, Roulette looked to me, as if to ask what we should do. I shrugged, then hit the comm. "You guys said they're being less careful with injuries. Where should Rou and I go so we can heal them?"

"Aurora," said Jayden into the comm, a softness to his tone. Roulette just shook her head. He cleared his throat. "Just a minute."

"Here," said Wade over the line. "I found a condo

complex that took some pretty bad damage. Just outside the nullification radius. Maybe, maybe... Damn it!" he shouted and both Roulette and I jumped back. "I think the elf princess is on the move because I can't turn invisible."

"Fuck," said Roulette, not even into the comm. "How can we go there to heal people if I'll lose my powers as soon as we get there?"

"Can anyone be moved?" I asked into the comm.

"Not a great idea," said Wade. "Some bad injuries and... I can't bring them all with me."

"Jayden, what are Nash and Chastity up to?" I asked.

But he didn't answer at first. Then a few blocks down, I saw a rock the size of a Porta Potty rise up from the ground and smash back down. He really was boosted. Some ice and crackling light shot up as well.

"I take it they're all down there," said Roulette, taking off at a run.

I stumbled over a vine but did my best to keep up, leaping over an overturned mailbox and twirling to avoid being hit by another screaming, fleeing person.

Zander! I screamed in my head. *We've got a problem—Alanna's moving and Wade says he's at a damaged condo complex with a lot of injured residents and if Roulette and I try to get there to help them, we'll lose our powers and won't be any help.*

"Kind of... busy, darlin'," he said, though not unkindly, over the bond. A moment passed. *"Lila keeps taking Kouta and Torynt to different spots around where we perceived the bubble of her influence,"* he said. *"And damn it—wait!"*

I didn't know whom he was talking to just then as Roulette and I padded up to most of our teammates exchanging blows with Nelian attack forces.

"Lila, Torynt, and Kouta all got caught up in it," said Zander over the bond—and from the way Roulette's head

picked up, I realized he'd sent the message to us all. *"They're powerless for however long that lasts…"*

Over an hour, I told him. *See if they can help Wade with the injured people.* I sent him the general area Wade had communicated—then told Roulette what I'd suggested the Renegades do.

She nodded. "Sir?" she asked Jayden as he ran past.

He looked over at us, a wary smile on his face. "We can still win," he said. "We have four boosted fighters… right?" He looked to me for confirmation.

I nodded, numbly, my knees knocking together. But Alarik…

"Has anyone seen Alarik?" I asked, but everyone else was rather busy flinging their powers to and fro.

"Wade?" I asked over the comm. "Is Alarik with you?"

"What?" he asked back. "Oh. No… Geez. The Renegades just appeared and I almost got ready to karate chop them. Allies, allies. Temporary allies…" He seemed to speak the last few words mostly to himself.

Zander? I asked over the bond. *Is Alarik with you?*

"No," he said sourly—out loud. He projected himself in front of me then and looked at the chaos unfolding around us. "I can't reach my team anymore with my boosted telepathy so long as they're in the princess' bubble."

I held up my wrist. "I can talk to Wade with this."

"Okay," he said, and for the first time, he seemed a little on edge as he instinctively jumped when a vine went by—even though it couldn't hurt his spectral form.

Darien took a tumble a block down, bouncing down the length of a giant vine—I hadn't noticed how he'd gotten there, if it had simply grown and picked him up along with it—and Roulette shrieked beside me, running forward.

"Rou!" I shouted, following suit.

"Darlin', watch—" said Zander's projected form behind me.

But neither Roulette nor I got far as she slammed right into an elf, who appeared from around a vine to grab her by the arm, spinning her in front of him and drawing his blade against her throat.

Stumbling, I screeched to a halt. Zander's ghostly form was at my side.

Then I blinked, recognizing the elf taking my friend hostage. "Normak!"

He looked from me to the struggling woman in his grip and I shook my head at Roulette, who had her palm out and seemed ready to gamble on whether she'd shoot out destruction or healing.

He cleared his throat and dropped the knife, shoving Roulette forward. She stumbled and spun, lifting her hand like she was ready to smack him one anyway, but I darted to her side, lowering her arm.

"I didn't know how else to get you to stop," he said. "And how else to find the two of you who'd recognize me anyway."

Roulette's eyes kept darting to the skies behind Normak, and I knew what she must have been looking for, but there was no sign of ice shooting out anywhere.

"You know this guy?" asked spectral-Zander.

"Yeah, he helped us get back," I explained. "He's loyal to the true king." I hoped.

Zander flicked out of existence, but not before letting out a startled cry and his projected form darting backward —a sign his actual body required all of his focus and was most likely in danger.

"Zander!" I screamed, then emphasized his name in my head.

But there was nothing.

Normak wasn't the least bit concerned. "Xerxes is here, but he's keeping Princess Alanna with him," he said. "I don't know how you hope to take him down."

Roulette snorted, though her brow wrinkled, her attention still drawn behind Normak. "Figured he wouldn't care about losing his useless power on the battlefield."

As someone with a pretty useless power on the battlefield, I begged to differ. "No, this is good," I said. "If she weren't nullifying his power, if any of us got too close, he could grab hold of us and put us in that painful, dream-like state. Now he has virtually no defenses."

"Yeah," said Roulette, aiming her palm high above as a vine went past. It shot out white light and she closed her palm, cursing. "And neither do we."

I clicked on the comm button. "Wade. Zander should have been on the outside of the nullification area, but he went quiet."

"He's not here," said Wade's voice amidst some static. Sounds like rumbles and murmuring carried across the comm link. "We're treating everyone we can, but— dammit!"

"Wade?" I asked. Screams were my only reply.

Roulette hurtled forward. "Let me through," she said, pushing aside Normak. It likely wasn't Wade's distress call so much as needing to check on Darien.

Normak and I stared each other down, and I clenched my fists at my sides. "Are you one of the portal creators for them this round?" I asked.

He shook his head. "The portal has to stay open on the other side. Every mission, we bring some portal creators along to try to create a portal here to home, but it never works." A rumble of vines from behind him, followed by another shot of fire, made me jump, but it didn't seem to bother him. Normak grabbed me by the arm as I moved. "That's why we have a limited amount of time here. The portal creators can only hold it open so long, and if they try again, they're unlikely to open it in the right place because the air doesn't seem to like two portals in proximity at once. Forgive me." He yanked me toward him and pressed his lips to mine, cold, quick, and utterly surprising.

He let me go, and I wiped my lips, too stunned to confront him. He pointed his hand away from me and a small black hole with fuzzy forest images on the other side appeared. He smiled thinly, and the hole grew bigger. "It works on this side with your power boost." He struggled to stand as the hole grew larger and larger. "I can even make it big enough on my own without a partner..." His eyes narrowed as he focused, and I had an idea.

"Let's go," I said to him.

He shook his head. "Portal-creators can't travel through their own portals, even with this boost..."

I nodded, seeing how he struggled to keep hold of it. Then, flicking on the comm and saying, "Trust me, I have a plan," I bolted through, ignoring the cries coming over the comm as I leaped.

I TUMBLED INTO LUSH FOREST, ONLY ROLLING TO A STOP WHEN my ass smacked against a giant tree trunk. "Ouch," I said, rubbing my sore behind and reorienting myself.

Standing, I took a look around—my muscles tense as I scanned for giant warthogs or whatever it was that might kill me. It didn't take long to spy the entrance to the heart of Nelia some distance away down a forest path almost clear of debris, though it would take me a bit to walk there and I didn't have a lot of time to spare, not if Xerxes himself was counting down the minutes until his way home expired.

Cursing myself, I thought about what a stupid risk I'd taken—though as long as I found Tianah, I might be able to get home—but it might be too late. I didn't even know how I'd get past the guards at the gate.

A rumbling snort echoed over the air and my heart leaped out of my throat as two giant warthogs ambled over the horizon, down the path toward the Nelian village. I ducked into the foliage, unable to hear at first over the pounding in my ears.

Then I realized the warthogs were walking rather slowly, swinging their little tails behind them without a care in the world. And behind those tails were wagons, stuffed full with something that looked like piles of cotton or maybe wool. Two elves rode atop their backs like horse riders. If there were no other elven settlements, it was likely they were headed to the village. Taking a deep breath, I waited until they passed, then darted as quietly as I could and crawled beneath the layers of fluff on the back of one of the carts.

If they were the only humanoid creatures on this entire planet, they were unlikely to expect an enemy to sneak in this way. They hadn't even had a prison for their king during the coup.

I wondered if the guards at the gates were more cere-monial than anything.

Sure enough, the warthog riders and guards seemed to exchange nothing more than greetings as we passed through the giant arch to the village. I watched from a hole I poked in the soft, fluffy material. Then before the cart could take me to the market or wherever it needed to go, I rolled out at the sight of that endless staircase, bolting up, feeling the burn in my thighs as I ran to the room where Tianah had bathed and dressed me.

"Damn it," I shouted when I skidded to a halt, gripping the frame of the open door. No one was in here.

"Who are *you*?" said a voice from behind me—an elven woman whose snow-like face paled beneath her green updo when we locked eyes. She took a step back as I ran to her, clutching her by the shoulders. She cried out.

"Where's Tianah?" I demanded.

"I—uh—are you that human King Alarik fell in love with?" she asked.

I shook her. She wasn't dressed for combat, so I'd have to hope she wasn't about to slam me against the wall with a shooting vine. "I need Tianah," I said, not answering her question.

Her brow furrowed, the shock slowly melting off her face. "She's making a portal right now for Xer... For King... For Xerxes," she finished, her head slowly shaking. Maybe Xerxes' support wasn't so widespread.

Double dammit.

"Well, that portal needs to close," I snapped. "Take me to her."

"They'll never let you—"

My eyes narrowed. "Then I guess I'll need your help, won't I?"

CHAPTER EIGHTEEN

THE ELF WOMAN, WHOSE NAME WAS FLORA, LED ME UP several more flights of stairs, bowing slightly to any elf we passed who looked at me funny. But no one questioned why I was walking side by side with this elf maiden. *Alarik really needs to work on security*, I thought. I probably could have waltzed right past the guards at the entryway to the village with just a *hello*.

When we approached the throne room, she told me to hang back in an alcove—that Xerxes' most loyal followers would be guarding the portal home.

If I had any power other than succubus lips, I'd be right there, pummeling the lot of them. I whispered to Flora, telling her what to say to Tianah—that she had to shut this portal down and then she *had* to get me close enough. That her real king's life depended on it.

She nodded and straightened her back, smiling as she approached the two elves in front of the door. I watched from the shadows down the hall.

Flora went inside. I waited and waited. Dammit, my plan got stupider with every second. I just had to hope

Veras could hold its own, especially with the Renegades and Wade and maybe Darien down for the count.

And I had *no* idea where Alarik had gone.

Then there were cries and shouts. The elves in front of the throne room door bolted inside and I ran after them, peering in.

A portal sputtered and fizzled as one elf man tried to hold on to it—his partner, Tianah, now lowering her palms, Flora at her side.

Elves charged at her and I bolted in, yelling, drawing their attention as I body-slammed into the other elf barely holding open the portal, causing it to close as we both tumbled to the ground.

"What in the mother's name…? Are you mad?!" shouted one elf guard, both to Tianah and myself.

He turned on her. "Now you have to try again, try to get it somewhere nearby. I know if you portal morons focus hard enough, you can picture a place to open it—"

"No!" I said, jumping to my feet. The portal-creating elf I'd landed on top of looked up at me, running a hand over his sore shoulder.

"Who the root are you?" said the elf man, striding toward me.

"She's our queen consort," said Flora, speaking loudly. "And you will obey her."

"The sediment I will," he said. "I follow Xerxes, and he's to wed Princess Alanna—"

"Her Royal Highness won't wed him," said Tianah, tossing back her head. "She told me so herself. She loves him, but she knows that much power isn't good for him. And she's never been as devoted to him as he has been to her—because he's too blinded by his ambition."

Well, that was a revelation. That did me little good at the moment.

"Send me to Xerxes," I said to Tianah, stepping forward to snatch the dagger from the angry elf man's hilt at his waist. He looked flabbergasted as he darted forward to snatch it back, but I jumped away.

"I can't do it alone," said Tianah. She looked around the room. The other elf soldiers bounced and shuffled and looked all around the room, as if to ask one another which side they should be on.

Even coups were too new to this place. Xerxes could only inspire so much loyalty when the mere idea of revolt was foreign to them.

"You can do it with me," I said, stepping toward her. The elf soldier whose dagger I'd stolen leaned toward me again, but another elf soldier jumped out of line, her own dagger shooting toward his neck. "Let her go, Thorn," she said. "Let this be over…"

His eyes widened, but he didn't move.

"Tianah, with my boost you can send me *right* to him," I said. "I know you can." A lie, but I had to sell it. "I got here because Normak used my boost to create a portal from my Earth to your Nelia."

Gasps echoed around the room. Flora grinned, then curtsied toward me. "A human truly worthy of being queen consort."

If she needed to believe that for everyone to help me on my way, so be it.

I continued, the mental clock running down in my mind. "If Alanna is with him—and she's likely to be—I bet your portal will fail almost the instant it appears, because the princess nullifies your powers." I straightened my back. "But I need you to do it anyway. I need to jump through the instant it's open and I need to surprise that motherfucker and put an end to this."

Tianah bit her lip but nodded.

"Thank you," I said to her, to Flora, to the elf soldier who'd kept that disgruntled elf at bay. "Please... don't participate in a coup again."

"What's a coup?" asked Flora, cocking her head.

But I didn't have time to explain. I pushed forward and kissed Tianah, letting the power move between us, then stepped back.

She squeezed her hands into fists, trembling at the feeling coursing through her, then with a slight jut of her head, she raised both hands at me and screamed, shooting out the wavy, shimmering black light.

She'd shot the portal right at me.

BLINKING, I STUMBLED, MY FEET ECHOING ON SHINY WHITE tiles that seemed to be decorating an office building lobby.

Focus! I shouted in my head and I spun, just taking in the sound of my name as my leg came into contact with something hard with a thud—someone's broad calves— and I flung the dagger I was still holding high, slamming it right into the back of a set of broad shoulders.

Fuck me, I was trusting that Tianah had been able to send me literally right behind Xerxes. I could have been stabbing an innocent stranger for all I knew.

A shriek echoed across the wide-open space and I realized Alanna was right beside me, her hands going to her face as she trembled. But I was wrapping my legs around the form in front of me, shouting and digging the dagger into his shoulder as the green-haired elf man below me choked and gurgled and blood started flowing out from his wound. I saw his face for the first time—Xerxes all right.

Thank the fucking universe.

Not that I'd wanted to *kill* him, but I couldn't be sure I hadn't with the random movement of my blade. And the blood loss. I shrieked again and pushed harder at the dagger, and we both fell to the ground, his blood pooling and staining the white floor.

"Aurora!" said a voice again. A familiar voice. But I was lost, panting loudly, growling like an animal, sitting up on the fallen back of my prey.

"Starlight," said the voice, softer now. Alarik crouched by my side, his eyebrows drawing together as he took me in.

My breaths quieted and I stopped making animal noises, my shaking hand letting go of the dagger. I stared at it. It was covered in blood.

"Enough!" shouted a woman—Alanna. She'd clearly been crying, her voice wavering. "Enough, you fools! Call this off!" She looked down at her brother and I realized his arms were tied behind him with green vine.

"Do it!" he shouted over his shoulder and there was a flurry of footsteps, but I couldn't think beyond what I'd just done.

Sniffling, Alanna bent over and removed a dagger from her own belt, sawing at the vines holding her brother captive. As soon as his hands were free, he put them to either side of my face and planted a kiss on my lips. "Starlight," he said soothingly. "How…?"

But I shook my head numbly.

"He's still breathing," said Alanna, panic in her voice. She pushed at me gently and Alarik sent her a withering look, but I complied and shuffled off Xerxes' back.

My wrist comm crackled with static and voices and I realized I was really back. I was really here. I lifted the comm to my lips, Alarik's hands falling away. "Hello?" I called out.

"Aurora?" said Jayden, his voice shaking.

"Angel!" shouted Nash. Things must have calmed down enough for him not to be fighting.

"Let the elves go if they don't put up a fight," I said, exchanging a look with Alarik, and he nodded. "They have orders to stand down. They should be hearing from their comrades soon."

Alanna slowly flipped Xerxes over. His eyes were closed and blood pooled.

"Roulette can heal him, maybe," I told her. "But you have to be far enough away to not nullify her powers."

Alanna sobbed, bending over her sort-of lover. "I can't do anything!" she wailed. "I can't help him, I can't help my brother—all I do is take and take away!"

"Aurora, we can't get home," said Alarik, grim, as he stood and walked over to his sister, tugging on her head gently until she buried her face against his knees.

I stood, too, trying not to look down at Xerxes as my knees shook. "You can. With a boost, your portal creators can open on this side," I said. "It's a long story, but... that's how I threw together this plan."

Alarik drew me to him and kissed my forehead. "My love," he said. "You are... You are the reason for all of this. I know it. With you, we'll find a way to approach this more peacefully."

I raised an eyebrow as I took in his musky scent, not wanting to contradict him, and with more pressing things to worry about.

"Alanna, I'm sorry," I said, "but if you want to try to save him, you need to move. Then I can tell Rou where to come."

She nodded and stood, letting her brother support her. I took her other side and we headed toward the doorway, our footsteps coated in blood half the way.

When we hit the sidewalk, I relayed my plan—promising to explain everything in due time—to Jayden and Roulette, relieved to hear that everyone on Veras was okay—that Rou had healed Darien and that no one else had sustained too heavy an injury.

"Elven messengers seem to be talking to these other soldiers now," said Jayden. "A cease fire."

About goddamn time. Alarik and I kept shuffling, practically dragging Alanna farther and farther away.

"We need to get her away from the worst of the human injuries, too," I said, directing them down a relatively clear alleyway. There were fewer vines here, which made sense in Alanna's bubble of movement, I supposed.

Alanna kept crying. "I'm sorry. Brother, I'm sorry…"

"Hush now," he said, reaching across himself to rub her head with his free hand. "We'll talk about everything later."

"Rou's aware Xerxes' injuries are bad," I said, causing Alanna to hiccup and tumble between us. I hadn't meant to make it worse. "So she agreed to see to him first." Although that had taken some convincing. The cool breeze from over the waters danced across our faces, ruffling our hair, and if I squinted, I could almost believe I was out for a stroll with two pointy-eared tourists.

After walking several blocks, we came across a playground, empty of children, with equipment designed to resemble forest animals—frogs and weasels and rabbits alike. I jutted my head toward it and Alarik and I directed the crying Alanna toward a metal tree-stump-like chair.

"Aurora?"

I turned as I let go of Alanna to find Zander, sitting atop a rock overlooking the waters some distance away.

"Zander!" I cried, running toward him. He took me in his arms, lifting me off the ground, and kissed me while I wrapped my legs around his waist. He kept peppering kisses all over my face.

"What the hell happened?" he asked. "I lost my power"—he glared over my shoulder at the elven princess as he set me down—"and I felt useless, so I decided to look for any injured people, see if anyone came this way." He looked around him. "And it was just so damn peaceful, so for a moment I zoned out."

I filled him in on as much as I could, though I had to interrupt him every few minutes to touch base with Jayden over the comm.

Zander used my comm to speak with Lila via Wade's comm and confirmed the Renegades were all okay, if still powerless. They'd been helping with the injures at the condo complex and my eyes widened at the thought of those rebels helping Typical humans with *anything*.

"Aurora!" called Alarik from behind me and I grabbed Zander's hand, pulling him toward the waiting elven royalty.

Alanna hiccupped as I approached. "I can't go home," she said.

I looked to Alarik as I spoke to her, confused. "Yes, you can. You might not have heard before, but I can boost Normak or any other portal-creator you have here and make it so you all can go home." Not to mention, I was sure the elves back in Nelia would create portals to send a search team.

She shook her head again. "I *could*, but… Someone needs to knock me out. I have to be unconscious for portal-creators—for anyone—not to lose their powers around me."

"Hey," I said, dropping Zander's hand to give her shoulder a comforting squeeze. "It's okay." So there *was* a way around her powers... I looked up at Alarik. "Is that how you got her back the first time?"

His face went grim. "Yes."

"Well, we..." I looked to Zander and he shrugged. "We can knock you out as gently as possible, Alanna."

She sobbed, cradling her face in her hands. "I can't go back. Not if Xerxes is being taken there."

Alarik nodded. I didn't know whether to push—but I had my own ideas why the prospect of going home might bother her just then.

"All right," I said. "We'll figure out a place for you to stay here, okay? Don't worry about it."

"Thank you," said Alarik softly.

The comm burst to life with Jayden relaying the news that Xerxes was fully healed but restrained, and I allowed Alarik to speak through it to explain his plans.

We had a lot of cleanup to do. The buzzing of helicopters overhead reminded me that there were bound to be a lot of eyes watching, too. Nice of them to show up when it had all calmed down. "I'll hide her," said Zander from beside me. "I'm useless enough at the moment as is."

I gave him a quick kiss and nodded, sending Alanna a sympathetic look before I took Alarik's hand in mine, heading back into the fray to get our new coexistence started.

EPILOGUE

"Strip poker," said Nash, drumming his fingers on the meeting room table as I flipped lazily through news stories about "our new Nelian diplomatic relations."

Oh, the controversy it had caused when Alarik had started talking to people—the mayor, the governor, the president. He wanted to help the environment—he'd *insisted* we cooperate—and he had the full support of the Renegades, who were demanding another look at Natch-targeting crimes, too. Lila's teleportation had been coming in handy for moving Alarik in and out of diplomatic meetings, letting the powers-that-be know they weren't to be messed with.

And of course, his portal-creators had to stop by Veras headquarters for a boost before they could send him home to Nelia between visits.

Though he made sure to stay for dinner—and breakfast—at least once a week.

"Angel, I'm talking to you," Nash said, waving a hand in front of my face. "Hello? Where's Aurora's trademarked righteous indignation over the fact that I just suggested we pass the time by playing to remove one another's clothes?"

Letting out a deep breath, I shoved the tablet away. Alarik had already convinced Congress to enact an immediate massive investment in clean energy, with promises to shift current power works jobs to the new facilities. Damn, things were much easier when a threat dangled over these politicians' heads.

Now I sounded like Zander. He'd pounced on Alarik as the face of a—to put it lightly—dictatorship when it came to certain causes.

"Welcome to the dark side, darlin'," Zander sent me over the bond.

I sent him an image of the two of us going at it in a room with all the lights dimmed. *"Only interested in joining you in a dark room,"* I sent back.

I'd kept my boys in line to make sure nothing went too far and nothing implicated Veras. We still had work to do, even if our two enemies were no longer a direct threat.

In exchange for allowing me to keep them in line, I allowed them to exert all manner of control over me behind closed doors.

My groin rumbled as my toes curled.

"Okay, I'm just going to start stripping and see if you notice that," said Nash, jumping to his feet and peeling off his T-shirt.

I laughed, finally bringing myself back into the moment. "If you think I'm going to stop you, guess again." A wry smile darted over my lips as I took in his chiseled chest, bringing myself to my feet and running my fingers up and down his pecs.

"Chastity, have you seen—? Oh, sorry." Jayden cleared his throat and pushed his glasses up his nose. "I thought she was in here."

"She wanted to go to town and I offered to monitor things for her," I said. I kissed Nash on the nose for his silliness and then crossed the room to Jayden, wrapping my arms around him and pecking him on the cheek. "What's up, sweetheart?" I asked him.

He swallowed visibly and my heart sunk. Was something wrong again—after everything going so right for months now?

"I was actually looking for you," he said. He nodded over my head at Nash behind me. "And you, too. Wade needs to talk to you."

"Okay...?" I said, but he didn't offer anything more, just stepped back and slid his hand through mine.

He led me down the hall to Wade's lab and I exchanged a grin with Roulette and Darien as we passed them in the guys' dorm room, so entwined with one another, it was hard to tell where one ended and the other began. She giggled and shut the door so I couldn't keep waggling my eyebrows at her as we passed.

Wade was typing furiously on his computer as we entered the lab and Jayden directed me to the seat beside our resident scientist. "Sit," he commanded.

I did as asked and exchanged a look with Nash, but he shrugged, crossing his arms over his chest as he took position behind me.

"Aurora," said Wade seriously, removing his glasses and placing them next to his computer keyboard. He clasped his hands together and put them between his knees, leaning forward as if he were my physician about to deliver devastating news.

My heart jumped out of my throat. In effect, he *was* my physician, and this, for all intents and purposes, looked like he *was* about to deliver bad news. I'd just had my first full-body scan this morning since... Since, well, before this mess had all started.

"I'm sorry I told Jayden first, I just... It tumbled out of

my mouth when I was looking at your scans and he was in the room with me."

Jayden squeezed my shoulder and I looked up at him, my body trembling. Nash must have noticed the mood of the room, too, because he came closer, putting a hand on my other shoulder.

"Well, out with it, doc," he said. "Don't keep us in suspense."

Wade took a deep breath. "You're pregnant."

My eyes started blinking a mile a minute. "What?"

"You're pregnant. With twins."

"*What*?"

Wade shifted his computer monitor so I could see what he was looking at—it sort of resembled those ultrasound pics the Typicals relied on when looking at embryos, but it was more detailed, the images of two tiny, tiny fetuses entwined with one other as clear as day.

"*What*?" I shrieked, jumping to my feet. I stumbled, and both my men currently present swooped in to support me on either side.

"I'd say about two months in," Wade continued.

"*How*?" I demanded, my jaw agape, looking rapidly from Wade to Jayden to Nash and back, demanding an answer.

"I don't know," said Wade. "We'll have to run more tests. And keep a closer eye on your condition, obviously." He looked to me. "That is… if you want to have them."

My legs weak, I sat back down, slowly, my mind racing. "I… I… Are they safe?" I asked, my fingers racing to trace my abdomen. My period was late—okay, way late, but too much had been going on for me to worry about it. "What about my power?" I asked. "I *know* it still works… Has it been hurting them?"

245

"It doesn't appear to have," said Wade, studying the screen again. "But we should run more tests."

My face flushed as my mind went fuzzy, my brain a scrambled pile of goo. I'd never *really* thought I *could* get pregnant. Dammit, I hadn't ever gotten that Plan B pill, now that I thought about it, but I'd *had* my powers most of the time since. It hadn't seemed likely that even if an egg— or two—had taken that day that it'd hold on through everything, through *everything* that had happened since.

"I need to think," I said, swallowing.

Nash massaged my shoulder. "It could be... *they* could be anyone's," he said, looking at Jayden.

So he didn't think it was that first time, that time I was supposed to get the Plan B?

Jayden cleared his throat. "They'd be *ours*. All of ours. That is, if Aurora wants..." His voice went quiet.

"I do," I said, my voice choking. I hadn't even known it myself, really, hadn't bothered thinking about it. "Nash, Jayden..." I looked up at each of them, squeezing both their hands. "I do."

And now to have a mind-blowing conversation with my other two lovers as soon as their business took them back home to me.

"You're fucking what?*"* shouted Zander over our bond.

Oh, yeah. There was that way of telling them. I thought hard about Zander—felt his anxiety, his excitement—as he imparted a conversation he was having with Alarik.

"He says he can't wait to meet his little Nelian prince or princess," relayed Zander. *"I told him he was taking* our *baby to Nelia over my dead body. That child has four fathers."*

Yeah, about that, I thought. *There are two.*

"Two fathers?"

Two babies. I sent an image of the biggest smile I possibly could straight into Zander's mind.

Succubus Heart, a standalone sequel to *Succubus Lips*

Her aura takes powers away. Ally or foe, no Natch or Nelian elf can rely on their supernatural strengths in the proximity of the Nelian princess. Superpowered battles devolve into pandemonium when she enters the fray.

The only elf in her planet's history to have nullification powers, Alanna felt an outcast in her own village, but she knew she could always rely on her brother, the king of Nelia, and Xerxes, his best friend, to make her smile. Certain she would wed Xerxes one day, her heart was shattered when Xerxes led a coup against her brother, determined to take over the strange human-populated planet called Earth in his own way.

With her brother back in power, Alanna exiles herself to Earth, alone—until she finds herself the target of a band of underground Natch rebels wary about her brother's hold over the planet. Now she has four Natch men lusting after her, despite the fact that they lose all hope of winning in their crusade whenever she's near. And though her lust has only ever led her to heartbreak, Alanna can't stop herself from falling for each and every hot-blooded member of the maverick team.

THE SUCCUBUS SIRENS SERIES

Read more sexy reverse harem stories set in the Succubus Sirens world of superpowered heroes, villains, and elves:

Succubus Lips – Succubus Heart – Mutiny's Rebellion – Succubus Soul: Veras Academy

These standalone, interconnected novels can be picked up in any order, but if you want to avoid spoilers, it's best to read *Lips*, *Heart*, *Rebellion*, then *Soul*.

Praise for *Succubus Lips*:

"This is probably one of the most bizarre yet satisfyingly creative books I've ever read... If you're into kickass hero- ines and book boyfriends that make you swoon, this one is for you!" -The Lovely Books

"*Succubus Lips* is well-written and subversively funny, willing to toy with the reader's expectations and do the opposite... sexy without being tedious." -The Romance Reviews

Praise for *Succubus Heart*:

"This book kept my interest from the very beginning, and I enjoyed every scene. Absolutely recommended." ~The Romance Reviews

Praise for *Succubus Soul: Veras Academy*:

"With a great storyline, a bunch of brilliant characters (both main and supporting), plus some very steamy bits, this was a great book to read to while away the hours." ~The Romance Reviews

ABOUT THE AUTHOR

Lina Jubilee loves reading, writing, drinking tea, and rooting for her favorite fictional romances. When not lost in a book, she cooks dinner at lunchtime, plans errands in fewer trips, and does everything she can to get back to romping through fictional worlds ASAP.

Ravenous readers, if you liked this book, please consider joining my Facebook street team! Connect with me:

https://authorlinajubilee.wixsite.com/books/

amazon.com/author/linajubilee
bookbub.com/profile/lina-jubilee
instagram.com/linajubilee
facebook.com/authorlinajubilee

MY RACY REVERSE HAREM BOOK CLUB
STANDALONE CONTEMPORARY REVERSE HAREM

Nothing can keep Rose away from Romance Book Club at the library—not even the snowstorm of the century. Catching a ride home through the storm with Lance, the stunningly attractive librarian who happens to be her neighbor, and Vaughn, his chiseled, alluring housemate, Rose takes them up on their invitation to drop by sometime and join them for their own book club. Rose gets more than she bargained for when she's introduced to Rafael, their magnetically charming third roommate, and the surprising genre of books they love to read and discuss. As the blizzard rages, Rose joins the Racy Reverse Harem Book Club, whose members are open to trying just about everything together to get warm.

A standalone novelette by Lina Jubilee, author of the reverse harem urban fantasy series Succubus Sirens.

REVERE ME: FLEEING FROM
THE FAE KING
STANDALONE FANTASY ROMANCE

Brecc

I've waited an eon to find you. You, my bride, the other half to my soul. But I noticed you too late, the annual fete that was supposed to bring us together not your time to shine. My need for you threatens us all... Nonetheless, I will have you. The world is meaningless without you. Love me. Bow to me. Revere me.

Edony

I was supposed to be safe. My years as an eligible maiden were behind me, so no fae should have sought my hand at the Fae King's Fete. Yet you caught me breaking the rules, and my fate rested in your hands. Instead of banishing me to the labyrinth of madness surrounding your castle, you vowed to let the world crumble to have me at your side. But I won't let you sacrifice everyone I care for—everyone in your kingdom—for me. To escape you, I'll go willingly into the maze. I'll keep running so you never find me. You will never break me. I will never yield to your desires.

Even though I crave you. Even though when I close my eyes, all I see is your face.

Revere Me is a steamy fantasy romance recommended for ages 17+ for mature themes and scorching romantic tension. First serialized on Kindle Vella, this episodic novel reads as a dark fairy tale in the vein of *Beauty and the Beast*.

MY MINI LIBRARY ROMANCE
STANDALONE CONTEMPORARY
ROMANCE

Wallflower bookworm Quinn curates her neighborhood's Mini Donation Libraries, paying special attention to the Ooh-La-La Box filled with romance reads. When a series of steamy donated books wrecks her life for a few days, she's left wondering if the author is local. Before she can get her sleuth on for long, a friend introduces her to Allen, a man with deep pockets who wants Quinn to set up a Mini Library on his street—and can take her wildest fantasies from the page to under his sheets.

First serialized on Kindle Vella, *My Mini Library Romance* is a contemporary romance with plenty of sizzle and a dash of humor. Perfect for every booklover who's ever dreamed of becoming a romance novel heroine.

READ MORE HOT ROMANCES
FROM CRIMSON FOX
PUBLISHING

Crimson Fox
PUBLISHING

A BEAUTIFUL RISK: LOVE AT LINCOLNFIELD BOOK 1

One stolen kiss. One wild fantasy. One big risk.

When a gorgeous Viking-like stranger plants a smoldering kiss on Passi in the thermal baths, she goes home with more than relaxation on her mind. The stranger sparks a fantasy hot enough to overcome the climax-killing side effects of her very necessary anti-depressants. When she walks into work to find the same devastatingly handsome man as the hospital's new risk manager, she frantically emails her best friend, detailing the fantasy starring her hot, new coworker. Only, instead of emailing her friend, she accidentally sends the X-rated message directly to *him*.

Insert leg in mouth. Quit job immediately. Or not...

Single dad Magnus is intrigued by the lovely woman he kissed at the baths who got away before he could learn her name. Even more so when he opens his email and discovers he was responsible for her breakthrough orgasm. But she's now his new HR director, and the reason she needs the medication means she won't date guys like him.

Exchanging risqué letters at work may be good, nail-biting fun, but the only way he can have her outside the realm of fantasy is to convince her to bend her rules and risk her heart on all that he has to offer.

A single dad, second chance, office romance, *A Beautiful Risk* is the first book in the Love at Lincolnfield series, heart-warming, hot page turners about the love lives of men and women who work at a Chicago hospital.

ALL IT TAKES

Megan Green has her whole life figured out. She's six months away from graduating uni, then she plans on backpacking around Europe for a year, before following her dream of becoming an interior designer. What she doesn't account for is meeting local MMA fighter Kian Murphy. With his athletic body and Irish charm, Kian has no trouble scoring with the ladies, and one night is all he's after. But one night is all it takes to change the rest of their lives.

After a chance meeting and passionate encounter, Megan finds herself pregnant with Kian's child. But with a womanizing reputation, and a temper that often leads him into trouble, Kian is hardly boyfriend material, let alone father material.

Now Megan and Kian must work out if they have all it takes to turn their one-night-stand into a relationship that will connect them for a lifetime.